A

Judy Astley was born in Blackburn, Lancashire and educated at Twickenham County School for girls. After taking a degree in English, she worked at the BBC for a while and then became a dressmaker and designer for Liberty's followed by several years as a painter and illustrator.

Just For The Summer is Judy Astley's first novel. Her other novels, *Pleasant Vices*, *Seven For A Secret*, *Muddy Waters*, *Every Good Girl*, *The Right Thing* and *Excess Baggage*, are also published by Black Swan. She lives in Twickenham and Cornwall with her husband and two daughters.

www.booksattransworld.co.uk

Also by Judy Astley

PLEASANT VICES
SEVEN FOR A SECRET
MUDDY WATERS
EVERY GOOD GIRL
THE RIGHT THING
EXCESS BAGGAGE

and published by Black Swan

Just For The Summer

Judy Astley

BLACK SWAN

JUST FOR THE SUMMER
A BLACK SWAN BOOK : 0 552 99564 9

First publication in Great Britain

PRINTING HISTORY
Black Swan edition published 1994

10

Set in 11/12pt Linotype Melior
by County Typesetters, Margate, Kent.

Corgi/Black Swan Books are published by Transworld Publishers,
61–63 Uxbridge Road, London W5 5SA,
a division of The Random House Group Ltd,
in Australia by Random House Australia (Pty) Ltd,
20 Alfred Street, Milsons Point, Sydney, NSW 2061, Australia,
in New Zealand by Random House New Zealand Ltd,
18 Poland Road, Glenfield, Auckland 10, New Zealand
and in South Africa by Random House (Pty) Ltd,
Endulini, 5a Jubilee Road, Parktown 2193, South Africa.

Printed and bound in Great Britain by
Cox & Wyman Ltd, Reading, Berkshire.

With much love to the
Townshend, Nicholls, Chilvers and Vyvyan families,
none of whom, I promise, are in this book.

And to Jon, Zelda and Layla,
who are in everything I do.

One

Miranda, age sixteen and never been more than kissed, was getting pregnant on the beach. It was what her step-father, an art lecturer, would have called a cross-cultural encounter. Her partner was a nineteen-year-old fisherman, son of her mother's cleaning lady, whereas Miranda was the middle-class daughter of affluent and liberal 1970's parents who enjoyed the guilt of owning two homes. If this couple on the beach had been completing application forms for a dating agency, all that could have been found that they had in common was their current and momentary lust.

Miranda was celebrating the end of her GCSEs. Somehow she felt she was adding to her list of life's qualifications; you didn't, at her school, go into the sixth form with your virginity. She had certificates for a wide range of achievements already, in common with others of her class, grade 5 piano, Senior Grade ballet, gymkhana rosettes. She'd been collecting these tokens of tribal membership since the age of three, when joining the Penguin Club at Putney pool she had been given a badge for ducking her head under the water. Of course you didn't get a certificate for having sex, but Miranda felt she would be quite certain whether she'd passed or failed.

Doing it with Steve had been quite irresistible. A secretive person, Miranda was glad she hadn't chosen someone from the party circuit at home, someone who might discuss it with their friends, or worse still, expect her to do it again some time. She quite liked it, but then she quite liked maths. She certainly didn't expect to have to repeat her maths exam. This time next year, she thought, as she lay in the sand shielding her eyes from the sun, she would probably be taking her driving test.

While Miranda was crossing off another item on life's shopping list, Steve, a less calculating soul, was simply celebrating having an afternoon off on a hot day. Later, the two of them would sail away out beyond the harbour to collect his lobster pots and that night Miranda would confide to the diary she kept under the mattress and thought nobody read, that it had been the most romantic experience anyone, anywhere could have ever had, although not one to be devalued by repetition.

In a few weeks time when Miranda had learned that familiarity bre ds babies, and that yes, all those talks at school on co traception, AIDS and abortion did actually apply to her as well, she would think of both fishing trips and sex as messy, smelly pastimes best left to the grown-ups.

Miranda's mother Clare was also celebrating. In her tiny garden beside the creek in one of the most photographed villages in England, she dozed on a sun lounger beneath the pear tree, drinking her way through a jug of Pimms, the Wimbledon commentary murmuring on her radio. Although concerned at the depletion of the ozone layer, Clare remained unconvinced that milk-white thighs would ever be a hot fashion item in any summer and pulled off her dress, flinging it down in a careless heap on the grass. She pulled the straps of her swimsuit down as far as was decent and wished the cottage was not so overlooked, both from the opposite bank of the creek and from the nearby wooden footbridge.

Clare was celebrating all the things she didn't have to do: collect children from school; cook dinner; wear tights; listen to Jack complaining about another day of in-fighting among the polytechnic staff or telling her she was drinking too much. This three day break was supposed to enable Miranda to wind down after her exams. Clare needed to wind down too. She felt she'd just taken all nine subjects herself, and in a sense she had. When Miranda had gone palely to school on exam days, Clare had willed her own brain along into the school hall with her. She had spent the days padding nervously round the house, doing routine, thought-freeing things like ironing and floor-washing so she could keep an eye on the clock and think, 'Now she'll be just starting French/now she'll be halfway through/just going into lunch.' Clare had lurked in the hallway when Miranda was due home, ready with something to eat, available to hear how dreadfully or brilliantly she felt she had done, accommodating herself to whatever mood Miranda had brought home with her.

'Why don't you just let her get on with it herself?' Jack had asked petulantly as Clare had made laborious notes about the role of the nurse in *Romeo and Juliet*, and had sat up half the night trying to recall the technique for dealing with quadratic equations.

'But I'm her mother!' Clare had retorted. 'That's what I'm here for!' Jack had no reply to that one, for he was not Miranda's father. Clare-and-Miranda had come as a matched pair when he had met them, take one, take both. He had taken both, and loved both as far as he was allowed to. For Clare had, by the time Jack came along, already grown too accustomed to gazing down fondly at her sleeping toddler and thinking, 'I'm all she's got.' Several years later, when Amy and Harriet were little, Clare would say to Jack, 'Aren't they lucky? They've got each other,' which to Jack's relief and probably that of the little girls, excused Clare from the intense intimacy she had invested in Miranda's upbringing and left them more free to muddle through in peace.

Clare, dozing in her garden, thought she was

probably feeling very happy. She would quite have liked, as she had planned, to have taken Miranda to Newlyn to look at an exhibition, or have had her around to share the repainting of the kitchen, so they'd have time to talk to each other without the rest of the family scrabbling for attention.

But Miranda had taken to wandering off by herself and Clare tried hard to come to the conclusion that this small sign of Miranda's independence was a good thing. A nagging little witch at the back of her mind told her that she should get in the car and go by herself to the gallery, and that it didn't take two to choose a paint colour. Instead she tried to pretend that it didn't matter at all, was too hot to go anywhere, it was wonderful to have time to herself and that she wasn't really just sitting around waiting to be needed.

Clare closed her eyes and thought of Eliot. In a few weeks, when the school terms ended, he too would be here with his beautiful, vacant wife, his two sets of children and his dreadful dog. Clare would make sure that by then she would be tanned, fit from her twice-weekly exercise class, and ready for him. She left Jack and her own children conveniently out of her fantasy. In daydreams no-one gets caught and no-one gets hurt. In Clare's fantasy there was opportunity, best knickers, clean teeth and less fat around her thighs. Clare hadn't just taken up this daydream as an escapist hobby: there had been the necessary spark to kindle the fire. On one of the breezy Easter walks out on the headland, Clare and Eliot had taken a different path from the others, searching for his foul and wayward dog. They'd crashed through the ferns and trees back towards the path and quite without any signal of intent, Eliot had pushed her roughly against an oak tree and kissed her. The excitement of the unexpected. He'd tasted of whisky and Gauloises. Jack only kissed her when he tasted of toothpaste, never out in the open air, never in the car or in the street. Clare felt ravished and she loved it. And she was spending her spare fantasy-time waiting for it to happen again.

Down in the village Steve's mother Jeannie was cleaning a tidemark from someone else's bath. She went into the rented cottages on the tenants' changeover days to clear up and prepare for the next batch of clients. She had long since stopped being amazed by the mess they left. They seemed to think it was included in the rent, to leave the house as they'd never dream of leaving their own. In the kitchen, she briskly scoured away with a piece of steel wool, removing dried-on muesli from a dish, wondering to herself at the cack-handedness of those who, used to leaving a dishwasher to handle such stuff, had stubbornly refused to become adept with a sink and a dishcloth. You'd imagine, she thought crossly, that all those who went on and on about how much more hygienic a dishwasher was, would take the trouble to chip out the bits of dried-on egg from between the fork prongs. They never dried their dishes either, but left towering piles of crockery which had to be gently disentangled like a large-scale breakable game of pick-up-sticks.

No-one left anything extraordinary behind either, a constant disappointment to Jeannie, who no longer expected to find interestingly feathered condoms under the beds, or exotic leather underwear along with abandoned laddered tights. Jeannie would come in and idly open the kitchen cupboards, taking out the half-empty packets of breakfast cereal, the jars of instant coffee and put them, the perks of the job, in her shopping trolley. Then she'd go out to the back yard (described as 'sun-trap patio' in the brochure) and pluck a forgotten swimsuit from the washing line, to put with all the others for the autumn jumble. She never went short of washing-up liquid or tea bags during the summer. Jeannie's working tour of the cottages was often more fruitful and certainly cheaper than a trip to Tesco's.

Rented cottages were much easier to clean than those of Jeannie's other clients – second-homers such as Clare, and Eliot's wife Liz, because they were only stocked with essentials, no personal or decorative extras. Those who rented out their homes soon learned that one swish of a labrador's tail could knock a pretty basket of dried flowers to a heap of powdered fragments. Tapestry cushions could have their stitches unpicked by little fingers in less time than it takes to watch *Blue Peter*, and such items joined all the owner's personal stuff in the inevitable locked cupboard, from which, maddeningly, an inaccessible telephone would occasionally ring. The rented houses may be a bit spartan, Jeannie thought, but people would rent anything in this village, give them a bed and a view and a smell of the sea.

Jeannie didn't mind the trippers, they came for a week or two, spent a lot of money and were virtually the only real source of income to the village, now fishing was all a tangle of EEC regulations. Those she really loathed were the ones whose second homes were in the village, who thought it delightful as a place to visit, but so inconvenient and out of the way as a place to live, like some seaside leisure park. On these people, like Eliot and Liz, and like Clare and Jack, Jeannie placed the full responsibility for the closing of the school, the dreary emptiness of the village in winter and the outrageously high price of property, so far beyond the reach of the locals.

Jeannie folded her apron and her big yellow duster and packed them away among the booty in her shopping trolley. She pulled the front door of the cottage shut behind her and put the key under the flower pot ready for the next clients, due to arrive some time after 3.30 p.m. that afternoon. Out across the harbour she could see Steve's little boat scudding across the water to the lobster pots, Miranda's lemon hair streaming out in the wind like blonde seaweed. Jeannie didn't approve. It'll all end in tears, she thought pessimistically, and I don't suppose for one minute they'll be little Miss Miranda's either.

The village had already prepared for the summer, but Clare, used to school holiday bustle, thought she'd arrived out of season.

'There's nobody here,' she had complained to Jack on the phone, the night she and Miranda had arrived. But the next morning, strolling round the village she could see that it had, like a fete, already been opened and everything was set out and waiting for customers. The hanging baskets were up outside the post office and bakery, the sailing club had a freshly-painted tariff of (increased) mooring fees, and there were barrels of budding geraniums getting in the way of the cars outside the Mariners pub. Old people, young couples and families with small babies had been coming and going for their low-season breaks, avoiding the school holidays. Only the houses of the second-homers were still empty, and as Clare's friends were all among those people she noted only their absence, not the presence of anyone else.

While Miranda spent her few days drifting off into the village, Clare tidied her garden. She weeded out the casualties of neglect, the arum lilies that had given up the struggle to survive without help, the magnolia stellata that had been smothered by an enthusiastic hebe. Shamed by the perfection of Archie and Celia's garden next-door, Clare rushed to the local nursery and filled her car boot with instant garden: nicotianas on the point of flowering; large and expensive clumps of dianthus; a pair of huge daisy bushes for each side of the door. She rushed back and arranged her garden like a stage set, an artfully casual mix of flowers, all of which she hoped would last long enough for the extravagance to be justified. It was very satisfying to have found the plants she needed at the village nursery. She like to take part, show willing and fit in with village life. She supported the village shop, in spite of the expense and went to all available bazaars and coffee mornings to do her bit towards the church roof. All the second-homers were tolerated by the locals for their cash input and were allowed to win occasional prizes for crafts and flower arranging at the village fete, though not of course for their cakes or runner beans. They took part in the regatta in exchange for the exorbitant mooring fees they were charged down at the boatyard. They even, like Eliot Lynch, had been allowed to attend a few Parish Council meetings, just to make sure that the place was being kept up to standard. The locals were rightly sceptical of this fervour for village participation. It went straight back to London at the start of each school term. Their own part in this was to service this up market holiday camp until the summer ended. Then the local population held its own celebrations, their own thanksgiving rituals with a proper garden produce show, a harvest festival, and of course the counting of the money.

Two

Clare and Miranda, their break over, returned to London to wait for the end of term. There were just a few weeks left before the annual family exodus to Cornwall, and Clare used this time wisely.

She inspected her hair for signs of grey, and, to be on the safe side, coloured it a gentle auburn. She inspected the flab on her upper arms and told herself it looked better now the sun had softened its lardy pallor. She toured the sales and bought softly blowsy frocks in rich jewel colours, and long loose skirts generously gathered so she could feel her body moving comfortably beneath the folds. Excited by the anticipation of seeing Eliot again, Clare behaved fondly with her family, attending speech days and sports days without her usual reluctance. Jack was relieved: he still had weeks of work ahead and Clare wasn't usually so eager to take on the packing, sorting and preparing that this annual pilgrimage entailed. It gave him a small glimmer of hope for a plan that had recently been forming quietly in his head, that one day, soon he hoped, the packing, sorting and preparing would be for a permanent move out of London.

The school holidays started and the journeys were beginning. The suburbs emptied, milk was cancelled. Neighbours were feeding each other's pets and forgetting already to water the plants. Videos had been disconnected so that burglars would not be invited in by the little green light (winking in the night like the green light at the end of Daisy's dock in *The Great*

Gatsby). Dishwashers had been propped open to discourage smells, only to be shut firmly by cleaning ladies who took a professional pride in achieving a symmetrical line of kitchen units, never mind the pong by September. Agas were turned off, and by the end of August heating engineers would be earning overtime fitting in extra calls to those of the helpless middle-classes who had trouble with the annual relighting ceremony. In many a car, halfway to Exeter, people would be questioning 'Did you remember to lock the conservatory door?' Clare, Miranda, and the two smaller children, Amy and Harriet, sped past the fields of poppies and ox-eye daisies. Clare felt a tiny pang of regret that she would be missing the best of her lilies. By September only a few straggly nicotianas, irritatingly pink when they were supposed to have come up a tasteful if invisible lime green, and persistent geraniums, would be left. But she smiled quietly at the thought of her creekside bower, waiting with its heady fragrance to enhance whatever scene of summer romance was in store for her.

'What are you grinning at?' Miranda interrupted Clare's thoughts abruptly.

'Nothing much,' Clare replied, smiling more broadly at such an inappropriate description of the substantial bulk of Eliot.

'You look like you've got a secret,' Miranda said, turning in her seat to inspect her mother's pinkening face. Clare did some concentrated fiddling with the Volvo's dashboard controls and tried to control her blatant exhilaration. There were some things you couldn't discuss with your daughter, which seemed rather an unfair bargain, when Clare had spent so many careful years making sure that Miranda never felt there was anything she couldn't discuss with her mother. And it wasn't that she didn't love Jack, it was just that it was difficult to feel a constant sexual thrill for someone whose idea of foreplay, lately, had been to

16

switch off the TV. Thankfully, Clare became distracted by manoeuvreing the car into the crowded car park of a Little Chef.

'Time for a break,' she announced to her daughters. In the car parks of Little Chefs all down the A303, estate car tailgates were raised and left open to allow a breath of air to the drugged and basketed family cats. Dogs were walked briskly up and down the grass verges, while their owners looked round guiltily, hoping that this counted enough as open country not to have to scoop the poop. Clare herded her children into the café and waited in line for a table to become available.

'Smoking or non-smoking?' a harrassed waitress said.

'Non-smoking please,' Clare told her, watching Miranda's face as it turned an ominous grey-green.

'Can't stand the smell, sorry.' Miranda bolted for the exit and through the window Clare could see her leaning against the doorpost taking great gulps of fume-laden air in the car park.

Amy tugged at Clare's sleeve. 'Is Miranda going to be sick?' she asked loudly.

'Probably,' Harriet two years older and therefore at nine the voice of authority, said. 'Probably all over the step and then no-one else will want to come in.' Clare dithered, wondering if she should go to Miranda, but afraid of losing her place in the queue. It wasn't like Miranda to get car-sick. In fact it hadn't happened since the time Clare had let her eat oysters when she was three.

'I expect she'll come back in when she feels better,' Clare said vaguely, making her way, at last to a vacant table.

All around her, families ate cholesterol-filled fry-ups. Clare could hear them ordering 'an American-style breakfast please' in too-loud, clipped voices as if speaking in a foreign language, and then braying to their embarrassed children, 'Isn't this a treat, darling?' to show how rare it was for them to be in such a place eating such a thing. It was part of the celebration of getting away from things at home, especially all that careful muesli. Clare looked through the menu and listened to the din around her, reminded that Jack had once commented in similar circumstances, 'No wonder so many people die on holiday.'

Clare's Cornwall neighbours, Archie and Celia Osbourne were also on the A303, along with their son Andrew. They were proud that they never had to resort to renting out their cottage, so much would have been spoilt. There were two bedrooms, thatch, an immaculate creekside garden and an inadequate bathroom. Celia had filled the little house with embroidered cushions, pressed-flower pictures and family photos in silver frames. She and Archie visited often, towing their sailing dinghy behind the Rover like some faithful old hound on a lead. They spent most of the summer sailing sedately up the river and back, visiting favourite little quays and coves where they could tie up the boat and sit in the sun reading detective novels.

Celia used to tell the villagers, 'Of course we'd live here all the time if it wasn't for the boy.' But that wasn't really true, for the boy had been at boarding school for several years and it didn't really matter at all where they lived. Surrey was so much more convenient. Celia could travel up to town on a train later than the ones used by commuters and quite cheaply too with an off-peak Saver. She could tour Liberty's and the National Gallery and still be home in plenty of time to arrange supper. Quite soon she could look forward to qualifying for a senior citizen's railcard.

If everyone has an age to which they feel they are more suited than to any other, Celia's had to be the graceful latter end of life. From too young, she felt, she had been a person who liked bridge, golf and gardens and occasions which needed rather formal hats. She felt she would make an excellent Old Lady. She only wished the Goverment provided a senior citizens' Lunch-at-Harvey-Nichols card to perfect her days out.

In Cornwall Celia did not like to be considered 'just a weekender'. She thought that sounded rather vulgar. She felt that she and Archie, with their membership of both golf and sailing clubs, qualified for slightly higher status than say, their neighbours Jack and Clare who only visited the village in school holiday time.

Celia was sure that Andrew was more than happy on his own while his parents went off sailing. He had been an unexpected child of their late middle age, having been born long after they'd become accustomed to filling their lives with shared interests. It was a relief now not to have to find ways of entertaining him, as they had dutifully done when he was small, with all those games of Junior Scrabble, and helping him glue together model aircraft, taking him to museums and on holiday finding him suitable companions on the beach. They thought boarding school only sensible for an only child, and besides Celia had felt dreadfully out of place waiting at the local infant school gate with all the glossy young mothers. People kept asking her if she was Andrew's granny.

In the back of the Rover Andrew was thinking about the possibility of a sexual encounter in the village this summer. He knew he looked better than last year, the braces were off his teeth and he'd got contact lenses, though they still hurt a bit sometimes especially when the wind blew the dust in. He'd grown too, and not just in height, he was broader, less scraggy. When he looked in the bathroom mirror and practised what to do with his hair, he thought he didn't look too bad, a bit school-boyish perhaps, but then some women were supposed to like that, particularly older ones, he'd heard.

Andrew's summer fantasy woman was equipped

with page three breasts and legs that went right up to here and she would do all those unspeakable things to him that he read about secretly in the *Penthouse* letters page, which he kept under his mattress at school. Andrew posted some Mozart into his Walkman and dreamed away the hours on the comfortable back seat of the Rover. Perhaps this year Jessica Lynch would have turned into a creature of sensual allure, pouting lips and rose-pink nipples to which clung a damp translucent tee-shirt. A golden-hearted whore at sixteen. Andrew's fantasies whiled away the time and as the car pulled up at the cottage, he had to fight down his usual enemy, an ever-rising penis, which he knew would have to be dealt with before he could do any serious unpacking.

Andrew hauled a couple of cases up to his room and set about the urgent unpacking of his essential equipment. He cleared his desk surface and thought about what could be left lying around and what would be best locked away in his special box in the wardrobe. He had a notebook, personal stereo and a stop-watch and of course a ruler. The tape in the Walkman was blank to record personal reactions and in addition he had a small collection of magazines. These had been scientifically chosen, each one representing a different form of stimulation. There was *Playboy*, *Whiplash*, *Thrust*, *Spanking* (monthly) and a very old copy of *Forum*, *Leather Boys* and *Fetish* as well as a particularly disgraceful copy of *Hustler* smuggled in by a friend at school. He thought these were obviously best kept out of sight, along with the gloves, one each of silk, leather and string together with a pair of Marks and Spencers 100% cotton knickers with a blue floral pattern which he had stolen from the Lynchs' laundry room last Easter. He hoped they were Jessica's and he hoped the slight element of doubt would not cause any problems: he felt quite different and depressingly unexcited when he imagined that they might belong to

20

Liz. Perhaps a bra would have been better, but he wasn't sure Jessica bothered to wear one. He would have a jolly good look to find out.

Ideally, as he was conducting a form of scientific experiment, he should be doing this at the same time each day, with no incidental interference to the essential equipment in between. He could think about that later. Right now he was eager to fill in the chart on page one of his virginal notebook. He wrote above the ruled columns some neat headings: time of day; which hand; (a boy at school had said that doing it with your left hand was almost as good as having someone else doing it to you. Andrew wished he had the experience enough to compare, and frequently wondered if he ever would).

He also wrote another column for which glove (if any). Andrew's chemistry teacher would have been delighted at the thoroughness with which he prepared everything, if not quite so impressed with the experiment itself. While Andrew's mother, downstairs, fussed with the things in the kitchen and his father unloaded boxes of Surrey-grown vegetables from the car, Andrew locked himself into the little bathroom. Thankful that it didn't really make you blind, Andrew opened yesterday's *Sun* to page three and put on a rubber glove. Must buy baby oil, he thought, as he placed his stop-watch on the window ledge.

It was amazing, Clare thought, just how musty and damp a house could get after just a few weeks' non-use. She bustled round, opening all the windows (wasn't Jeannie supposed to have come in this morning and done that?) and propping open the back door with a stone hedgehog. 'Come on Miranda, join in a bit,' she called breezily towards the sitting room, where Miranda had flopped lazily on to the ancient floral wreck of a sofa. Miranda hadn't been sick, but had moodily evaded all Clare's attempts at solicitous enquiries: 'Was it something you ate? Bad period?' Clare was, she thought, a mother who could be told things, so why wasn't Miranda telling?

'You won't throw up in the car will you Randa?' Amy had kept saying anxiously, worried about having to travel uncomfortably with a Smell.

'I bet she does before Okehampton,' Harriet said cheerfully, 'I bet you 20p Amy.'

'Nah, I think Bodmin,' Amy had answered, and then added worriedly, 'But let's find a bag for it to go in.' Clare didn't want Miranda's grumpiness with her in the cottage. She wanted to regain her mood of secret anticipation, and most of all she wanted to know whether Eliot had arrived yet. Bringing in boxes of Sainsbury's food from the car, she wondered how soon she could decently stroll up the road, drop in at the converted coach house and wish Eliot, Liz and the family a happy summer. She'd send Miranda instead, she decided, it would give the girl something to do and an opportunity to cheer up a bit.

'Why don't you go and get some fresh air, Miranda,' Clare asked her casually. 'You could wander up to the Lynchs' house and see if Jessica and Milo are here yet.'

'No point,' Miranda growled, heading for the door. 'They're not coming till tomorrow. I rang Jess last night to ask.' It was quite a relief really, Clare thought later as she unrolled fresh honeysuckle drawer liners into the old pine chest in her bedroom. It gave her an evening for slopping around and arranging herself for his arrival. It also gave her a chance to see she was being rather silly. I've got everything I want, she thought, looking through the window at her three daughters, sitting in a row on the creek wall at the end of the garden. When the phone rang, and Jack was asking her about the journey, Clare was able to say, with some honesty, 'Yes, I wish you were here as well.'

*   *   *

At 6.45 a.m. the next morning Eliot Lynch drove his new Range Rover off the train at Penzance. How, he wondered, could a journey so expensive be so uncomfortable? He felt unrested, unshaven, jet-lagged and hungry. Liz and the twins shivered in the pale chill air, somehow looking pitifully out of place in their Knightsbridge clothes among the cars and the crowd, the Cornish mail sacks and the stacked newspapers. They all crushed into the car, Eliot opening the window to disperse Liz's cloud of Poison perfume. The twins squashed in the back seats along with the luggage, the golf clubs, fishing gear and new bits of sailing equipment, Eliot's new toys from Harrods, bought to tempt his son Milo into being his playmate for one more summer. Milo was now eighteen, and the time he spent with Eliot was now governed by his own choice and not by the long ago custody arrangements made with Wife no. 1. The deal had been that Eliot got Milo and Jessica for the summer, and the Cornwall house was where Eliot would continue to be each year while Jess and Milo still wanted to stay with him. The problem was that now Milo was old enough to match Eliot's skill at sports, he wanted to spend more and more time with his friends. Milo could be bribed by the new equipment only until its novelty wore off. This year Eliot was even more pessimistic. How could he look forward to spending time with Milo and Jessica when he hadn't got further than chapter six and had an October deadline?

All this pressure, all these children, for he had a total of four, and these wives (two) to support. They all brought Eliot many moments of panic and sometimes he felt close to abandoning ship. Often he ran away to foreign places with his passport in his pocket and an overnight bag, phoning home on the way to the airport and calling it work.

Liz, clipping their six-year-old twins firmly into their seat belts, was thinking about the practicalities.

Someone had to. Milo and Jessica would be arriving by plane from Heathrow that afternoon, so someone would have to drive over to St Mawgan. She couldn't trust them to get a taxi, they'd probably rush off to Newquay and not come home till 3 a.m., wanting £200 to pay the driver who they would keep waiting for hours. There was the steak for the barbecue to be organized for the next evening, and had she ordered enough food? Miranda Miller might have friends staying, Andrew Osbourne probably hadn't.

Perhaps she could ask Clare to make a salad. Liz hoped Archie wouldn't be pedantic about the wine this time, a barbecue was a casual thing after all. Vast bottles of plonk would do, surely, or something fizzy. Although, she thought as she looked sideways at Eliot, some of us seemed to need an awful lot of Scotch these days. Then there were the beds. Liz wondered how Jeannie always managed to put the wrong duvet covers on. Surely she could tell which colours had been chosen to go with which rooms? Did she do it on purpose? The garden lights needed checking too and the swimming pool. The gardener could never believe that anyone would want to go to the expense of heating a pool to over 80 degrees. Too much like getting into a hot bath, might as well take the soap in there with you. Eliot complained too that it was tepid, but Liz didn't want him to have a heart attack diving into cold water and his many over-indulgences made it fairly likely. Liz was too young to be a widow, even a rich one, and besides, she thought callously, nobody invites lone women to dinner parties.

Liz watched the hedgerows reaching out their scratchy branches to attack Eliot's precious new car. He was silent and preoccupied just now, but she knew how furious he'd be when he saw the damage later on. Then she would remind him yet again that there were lots of nice wide roads in the South of France, they didn't have to come here. She wished she could still rely on him to do what she used to think were 'men's things' around the house, but he was usually too irritable to be asked and she had promised to leave him alone to work on his new book. It was, after all, how the money, such a comforting lot of it, was earned.

Three

The temporary residents brought with them to Cornwall more than their luggage. Along with all the expensive sports equipment, boating paraphernalia and such they packed their little snobberies, the means by which to reassure each other that they may be roughing it in a village, but they certainly knew what was what.

'At the shop today,' Liz was saying, 'I asked for walnut oil and they actually had it, isn't that marvellous? A few years ago you couldn't even get a decent extra-virgin olive, now there's all sorts. Just like home.'

'Well I suppose the foodie culture had to get here eventually,' Clare said. 'I brought some beers, I thought the boys might like some.'

The village was now full. The summer residents were re-establishing their flimsy part-time friendships with people they lived only a few miles from in London but only socialized with on holiday.

Clare had spent a long time getting ready for Liz and Eliot's annual start-the-holiday barbecue, and Miranda had been banging on the bathroom door, impatient to get at her make-up. Clare, looking in the mirror had caught Miranda staring at her in astonishment.

'Mum, you don't need to dress up, you never usually do here.'

'Makes a nice change,' Clare had mumbled, caught without an excuse. Miranda squeezed past her, reaching across to the window ledge for her make-up bag.

'It's not your colour you know,' she had said to her mother, inspecting Clare's green-painted eyes in the mirror. Clare had picked up a black and gold scarf, wondering if it would be going just too far over the top to tie it round her hair. It would look good against the black linen dress. Or at least it would if she was going to a formal dinner party.

'What, the green? I always wear it, it matches my eyes,' she said to Miranda, still deciding about the scarf.

'Too stark, now you're getting a tan. You should be wearing grey or bronze.' Well, Miranda thought, she couldn't let the poor old thing go out like that.

'This is all the wrong way round,' Clare said. 'How come my daughter knows more how I should look than I do?'

'Anyway,' Miranda continued, 'Why are you all dressed up?'

Clare closed her eyes to wipe off the green goo, 'Well I'm just looking forward to seeing Liz again, it's been so long.'

Miranda's eyes were wide and incredulous: 'But you always said she was a dumb broad, with a fish for a brain.'

'Rubbish,' Clare lied briskly, avoiding Miranda's exquisitely made-up eye in the mirror. 'And anyway I don't get much adult conversation, surrounded by you infants all day and Jack still in London. I'm looking forward to a party.'

'Party! Fish-brain Liz, drunken Eliot and boring old Celia and Archie! You're wasting your lovely frock!' She was probably right, Clare thought, scrabbling in the crumbed depths of her handbag for a lipstick. It would probably be another of those well-behaved parties where there are just enough people so the conversation did not run out, but not so many that anyone could slope off without the others noticing. The opportunity to behave uncharacteristically dreadfully only arose at a vast gathering where only one's own partner kept an eye on what one was up to and

27

could easily be lied to later. Not that Clare had any practice at this, but she did read a lot.

Clare blotted her inexpert lipstick and glared at herself in the mirror. Why am I thinking in this appalling way? she asked her reflection. It's immoral, it's unsisterly, it's despicable. It was also fun. She put her hands each side of her face and pulled gently on the soft skin, flattening out the lines and taking away a good ten years. It's my age, she concluded.

Now they were on the Lynchs' terrace, by the pool. Clare had brought a tomato salad and a very large bottle of Beaujolais along with the beer. The Lynchs' pool was splashy and noisy with small children. The older ones sprawled on deckchairs, renewing their holiday friendships, going over their recent exams and showing off as to who had done worst.

Clare envied the Lynchs their domestic arrangements. Bringing plates (no cracks, everything matching) from the kitchen, she had had a quick look round at all the stuff, the dishwasher, the microwave, icecream maker, food processor. Clare had a kitchen just like this back home in Barnes and she wondered as she stood amongst Liz's paraphernalia why on earth she left it each year to rush to a cottage which was hardly better equipped than a campsite. If this was their summer place, what must the Lynch Hampstead homestead be like? Liz was so good at these things, she could give lessons. She had towels the right colours in the bathrooms, matching sets of bedlinen, complete canteens of cutlery, proper napkins, just like a new bride. She had lampshades that looked like they'd been chosen for the rooms they lit, not just moved from place to place haphazardly as and when they were needed like Clare's. There were rugs that toned with the pale sofas, which had frilled and tasselled cushions all in quiet earthy co-ordinated colours. Liz's interior was designed, Clare's cottage was left-over bits and pieces from London, items evicted from the Barnes house on their way to becoming jumble. Both houses were cleaned by Jeannie, though on a quick glance round, Clare suspected that Liz must be paying her more than she was. Clare would be willing to bet folding money that Jeannie had been round for a last-minute flick with the duster just before Liz and Eliot arrived. And opened all the windows, no trace of mustiness here, no hint of damp. Clare, strolling down the lawn towards the pool terrace, could see Liz rearranging the salad. Liz was in Barbecue Outfit, too-short gingham dungarees, hair in plaits with outsize girly pink bows, white baseball cap and trainers. She looks like bloody Pollyanna, Clare thought, feeling uncomfortably over-smart in her simple cap-sleeved black linen shift. When she'd bought it the dress had seemed deliciously understated. Clare didn't like clothes you had to live up to. Even the sales assistant had said, doubtfully, as if it was what she'd been trained to say, that she supposed it was the sort of thing that could be Dressed Up for Evenings. Now Clare simply felt sedate and matronly compared with the youthful, boylike figure of Liz, and she wondered if the dress was, after all, a bit tight across her stomach. She put the pile of plates down on the table next to Liz's salad.

'Is Jack coming down?' Liz asked Clare, careful in case she was treading on marital stress.

'Probably next week,' Clare told her. 'He's got to do some last minute interviews for next year's course. They'd rejected so many of the original applicants they had to advertise the extra places. Jack says they were all as thick as bricks.'

'Milo says it's getting harder to pass A-levels,' Liz said, turning the steaks in their glossy marinade. 'But I think he's paving the way with excuses in case he fails.'

'I still remember that awful waiting for exam

results,' Clare told her, 'And that feeling that your entire future depends on it.'

Liz giggled. 'Heavens, I didn't do A-levels. I was finished in Paris and then launched, such fun!'

Clare had a sudden vision of Liz being shot from the top of the Eiffel tower, long limbs flailing round and round like a Catherine Wheel, literally a social whirl.

'And then I met Eliot. Wasn't I lucky?' Clare looked at Liz, but Liz hadn't stopped smiling.

Clare sipped at a glass of wine, looking around for Eliot and feeling tight little apprehensive knots in her stomach. Too much fantasizing leads inevitably to disappointment, she tried to tell herself, sensibly. She couldn't, in all honesty, do much with Eliot, they were both married after all, and besides, you never knew where he had been. Also, she thought ruefully, if she took off all her clothes he'd see her cellulite and stretch marks. No-one goes through three pregnancies unblemished. Possibly one of the reasons he had traded in his first wife for Liz had been that an ageing life-scarred body was no longer what he wanted to live with. Still, it was exhilarating to feel again like a schoolgirl fancying a rock star. It would do.

Eliot came out on to the terrace at last and Clare gulped down more of her wine too quickly and nearly choked. He gave her a chaste kiss on the cheek and she noticed the aroma of whisky and the growing paunch. That wouldn't be too pleasant unclothed either, she thought. Why were romance and fantasy so much better than sex and reality? Eliot gave Clare no hint that he remembered the Easter incident, no sideways smirk or conspiratorial wink. Probably does it all the time, Clare thought, disappointed.

'I've lit the barbecue,' Eliot told Liz. 'And I saw Archie and Celia coming up the drive. They didn't seem to have Andrew with them.'

Celia, formal in Jaeger and Archie trying his best to

be casual in cords and Argyle cashmere, arrived with champagne.

'Hello all,' Archie greeted heartily, 'I've brought champers to celebrate our fifth barbecue here. Five years is a nice round number to celebrate, I think.'

'Oh goody Archie, how lovely,' Liz said, coy and giggly with the older man. Clare watched Eliot's lip curl with scorn as he turned away to the barbecue, and she felt both interested and embarrassed to be witnessing private tensions. Briskly, expertly, Archie began to open the first bottle. It would be well chilled, the cork would come out quietly, with no undisciplined and extravagant spray of froth. Archie was known to be good with wine.

'Where's Andrew?' Milo shouted from his deckchair.

'He's on his way,' Celia said. 'He's just finishing writing up some experiment for his holiday project.' To Liz and Clare she added, 'He does seem to be working awfully hard. They really pushed him to retake last year's exams, but this time he should do all right so it's probably a good thing.'

'Milo's mother thought he might have to go to a crammer for his A-levels,' Liz said. 'But Eliot said he couldn't, because he'd forked out enough school fees already and he had to stay where he was. Apparently Milo is very bright, just terribly lazy.' Liz sounded, Clare thought, as if she was quoting from her stepson's school report.

'New garden furniture, Liz?' Clare asked, feeling that they had, after all, six weeks in which to discuss the children's education, to show off politely and with pretended exasperation. It was also the second most popular dinner party subject in Barnes, one of those things Clare was glad, each summer, to get away from.

Liz had bought some teak steamer chairs, fatly cushioned and with matching low tables. For tonight there were little arrangements of roses, and pink linen

31

napkins. Anyone else would have made do with paper ones, especially in the garden, Clare thought rather nastily.

'We had to hire a truck to get them here,' Liz was saying, 'General Trading don't deliver this far.'

'Cost a fucking fortune,' Eliot growled, grabbing a padded glove and attacking the barbecue coals. The glove was fish-shaped, and Clare thought again about Liz's brain. She wasn't that dim, she'd managed to hang on to Eliot for nearly eight years, which was more than anyone else had.

Archie cut in, changing the subject. 'Seen the hippy out in the harbour? He or she is living on some kind of raft. Looks dreadfully unsafe to me. I suppose they're on the dole.'

'So are a lot of people,' said Liz. 'Poor thing, it must be dreadful when it rains.'

'What, on the dole?' said Celia, confused.

'No, the raft,' Liz said, giggling into her champagne.

'It looks like a leaky old wigwam,' Eliot said.

'Lucky sod, when he gets fed up he can just paddle away. Wish I could.'

'I don't imagine he's being made too welcome here,' Celia said, sounding rather unwelcoming herself. 'I don't mind,' she continued, 'if there's just the one, but if hundreds turn up to join it will be frightful.'

Clare laughed. 'It isn't very likely is it? There's not going to be a peace convoy of raft-dwellers just waiting to moor up in our harbour is there? I was a hippy once,' she added, 'though really only at weekends. I still care about personal freedom of course.' What an idiotic thing to say, she suddenly thought, after all who would ever admit to not caring?

Liz had organized different tables for the three different age groups. She fed the small ones first, indulging their preferences with a large tray of oven-chips and beans to go with their steak. The children squabbled over which drinks to have, all wanting

32

different ones and then changing their minds. Clare knew that Harriet as usual would hardly eat anything and that Amy would eat enough for two, still munching long after the others had finished. It seemed incredible to Clare that there wasn't an enormous difference in their sizes. Also, she wondered to Celia, what was it that made children from nouvelle-cuisine homes absolutely mad about fish fingers, sausages, and ketchup on everything? But this was holiday. Clare poured more champagne and decided not to care. Let them eat oven chips.

The older ones could not long endure another of their parents' ritual barbecues. As soon as Andrew arrived they grabbed pieces of raw meat, slippery from the marinade, poured some of the carefully arranged salad into a Tupperware box, and ran off to the beach.

'You don't mind, do you Mum?' Miranda shouted, too far away to hear the reply.

'Jessica has become a vegetarian,' said Liz. 'I think most of her friends are. I can't tell whether it's all the food scares, peer group pressure or a concern for animal welfare. She doesn't show much interest in the dog, so it's probably not animals.'

'I tried it once, in my teens,' Clare said. 'My parents thought it was absolute nonsense, some kind of affectation and refused to take any notice. I suppose when you've had rationing it's unthinkable to turn your nose up at good food. Each meal I was given the usual meat and two veg. I tried for about a week, just leaving the meat, but in the end of course I gave in. I remember my mother looking enormously pleased with herself, it was so humiliating. She loved to be proved right, that I was just being "faddy".'

'We try to respect Jessica's views,' Liz said, 'and I'm quite prepared to go along with it, but she makes such a big morality thing out of it. I can't bear the looks she gives me every time I carve a chicken or chew a chop bone. I've told her that if she wants me to put up with

33

her views she's got to tolerate mine. She can't imagine how tedious it is never to cook a meal that everyone will eat.'

Archie said to Clare, 'Miranda is looking paler and more fragile than ever. She's not got that anorexia thing has she? You read about it.'

'I don't think that's very likely,' Clare said, 'Any mention of diets bores her rigid, and that's how it usually starts, isn't it? I think it's just a bit of post-exam stress, all that work.' Clare continued, 'I brought her down here for a long weekend a few weeks ago. I thought she might be bored without anyone here, but she managed to have some fun I think, Steve was around.'

'Is that Jeannie's boy?' Celia asked.

'That's right,' Liz said, then giggled, 'Lucky old Miranda, have you *seen* Steve lately, he's turned out to be rather gorgeous!'

'Oh I don't think it was anything like that,' Clare said quickly, thinking two steps ahead of Liz, although, she thought, why on earth shouldn't it be 'anything like that'? 'After all they've known each other for years, just as friends . . .'

'Don't take any notice of Liz,' Eliot said, kindly, for he saw the beginnings of concern in Clare's eyes. 'She'll never grow out of looking at the boys, will you darling?' he said, giving his wife a cold look.

'Only when you grow out of looking at the girls, my love. More drinks anyone?'

Along the edge of the river, round beyond the headland from the sailing club and boatyard, the trees grew thick and heavy, deep moist and velvety, right down to the water. Sailing in the early evenings was an unnerving experience, for at that time the water, the birds and the dark green bankside forest were all at their most eery stillness. At high tide there was no land to be seen between the water and the foliage, at night it

34

was all a valley of blackness. But at low tide there were rocks, slimy and pooled, and tiny beaches with fallen washed-white branches and boulders, gulls searching among the tourist picnic debris, children in the rock pools. At nights, such as this one, Milo, Andrew, Miranda and Jessica would climb round the rocks from the boatyard to the little hidden beach which they had claimed as their own five years ago, when they had first gone there as gangly pre-adolescents. Each of them had been secretly afraid of being cut off by the tide, but even more fearful of saying so. At high tide the beach was almost under water, and they each had a favourite rock on which to perch under the overhanging branches. It was, they thought, their own beach, they had never seen a casual intrusive tourist picnicing there, too much of a climb for the average wind-break and beach-bag carrier.

On this night, escaping their parents' barbecue, they clambered over the rocks, lit a driftwood fire on the shingle and wandered about, skimming stones, picking up shells and checking over the beach for tripper-invasion signs. A new sign had been put up, instructing visitors to clear up after their dogs.

Still town-smart, they looked an incongruous bunch perched like exotic gulls on the damp rocks and seaweed. Jessica wore an assortment of vests in shades of grey, and several belts. Her short hair was in stages of blonde with tinges of pink left over from experimental dyeing. Miranda had piled her long hair under an old straw hat of her mother's. She'd recently discovered Clare's bin-liners filled with clothes from her antiques era and was wearing some fairly priceless 1920's pieces, carelessly tied together and about to be ruined, for one has little regard for the fragility of silk chiffon at sixteen.

Andrew felt conscious that his clothes were still bought by his mother, usually in his absence, and his jeans and trainers felt somehow that they had probably come from the wrong shop. His sweatshirt was very clean, and had creases down the sleeves from determined ironing. He still wasn't brave enough to arrange his hair as he had for the bathroom mirror, it felt unfashionably long and insistently curly. When he had had the brace taken off his teeth ('fixed appliance' the dentist had called it, as if it was a washing machine), he had thought that he would be instantly not shy, would have no spots, have manageable hair and be totally confident. All that had happened was that he felt exactly the same, but had good teeth. Well, that was something he supposed, but wondered what it took to turn into the man he thought he was going to be from the boy he actually was.

Milo had never been gauche. He looked elegant even in his stained old cricket sweater and no shoes. He didn't dress for effect or for women, only for the weather and for sport and comfort. He sat on a rock and lit a cigarette, holding it delicately in his long pale fingers. Miranda and his sister were really the only females he liked and as he'd known Miranda for five summers, you couldn't call them years, she was almost an extra sister. He was also uninterested in girls for sex, but at school there was a small boy called Oliver who for £1 would allow Milo to fondle his pale and naked body after games on Thursdays. Oliver was as smooth as a baby, blond and acquiescent and Milo loved him. Oliver had a lot of money too for Milo, who did not know this, was not his only customer.

'God, those barbecues,' Milo was saying as they all skewered steak and bits of potato salad on to twigs, trying to roast them on the fire, before the whole lot caught alight. 'They're always the same, and they're always dying for us to leave so they can get drunk and show off about us to each other.'

'More likely complain about us,' Miranda said.

'Yes, but in a showy-off way, you know, "I'm so sick

of Jessica, she won't do any homework, she gets into so much trouble at school, I don't know how she passed all those exams,"' Jessica mocked Liz, accurately.

'If you get them,' Milo interrupted.

'I don't care either way. Anyway this isn't the place to drag over school to each other, let THEM do that.'

'They drink a lot more when we're not there too,' Miranda said. 'Mum will have a hangover tomorrow and be horrible to Amy and Harriet for making too much noise, and she'll tell me her headache is because of the heat.'

'Why is it,' asked Andrew pensively, 'that men always cook the meat when it's a barbecue? I've never seen a man go near a cooker in a kitchen wearing an oven glove and an apron.'

'You should live in our house,' said Miranda, 'My father always cooks when it's an occasion, dinner parties and things and gets all the credit. Poor old Mum does all the everyday stuff and gets all the complaints from us. He just likes to show off how liberated he is, goes with the art teacher image.'

Jessica remembered being a vegetarian and swopped her meat for more salad.

'Men barbecue,' she said, 'because it's so macho. They feel like cavemen, wrestling with live coals and a dead animal. Have you noticed, they're always turning the meat over and prodding at it, they can't just leave it to cook. I sometimes think Dad would like to have to make a fire with a piece of flint and two boy scouts instead of those cute little barbecue fire lighters with their own special dayglo matchbox.'

Milo said, 'I remember when we were little and he had that very basic barbecue and he used to pour gallons of meths on it, blowing on it till he felt he'd achieved a fire, not just lit one. Now Liz has got him one of those gas things, she's emasculated him. She'd rather have a poolside microwave, clingfilm and everything clean.'

'I sometimes think she'd like to wrap Dad in cling-film to keep him more hygenic too,' Jessica giggled.

'You should see the cooking at home when we're with Mum,' Jess told the others. 'She just flings stuff in the Aga and hopes one of us will remember when to take it out. It's never dull, but you never really know if you'll get food.'

'Probably one of the reasons Dad left,' Milo commented, 'Liz's cordon bleu diploma.'

At the end of the evening the others left Miranda at her gate and she went into her garden, her feet feeling for the steps in the darkness. She was tired but didn't want to go into the cottage, the air in the night was still warm and in the house she felt she would be choked by dry air. Sitting on the low branch of the pear tree she heard Clare open the door.

'Is that you Miranda?'

'Of course it's me,' she replied rudely. 'I'll be in soon,' she shouted, which would have to make do as a gesture of apology, but the door had been shut smartly and with obvious hurt.

Inside the cottage Clare went upstairs, a little drunk and rather depressed from the champagne. She missed Jack, the little ones were asleep and now Miranda was leaving her out. When she was a teenager herself she and her friends squirmed away from the idea that one could be friends with one's parents, they'd been horrified at the very idea, recoiling from the false matiness that some of their contemporaries had to put up with from their mothers. Parents had been old then. But Clare wasn't ready to be old, she still felt it was other people, people like Archie and Celia who were grown-ups. She and Miranda had always been so close.

Clare sat on the window seat in her room, not wanting to spy on Miranda, but not wanting to close the curtains against the warm night. Miranda was talking to someone in a rowing boat down by the creek. Clare, at her window, heard her laugh softly, and she could see the dim pale outline of a figure in the boat – undoubtedly a male figure but otherwise unidentifiable. Clare wondered if this was indeed Steve, for who else could it be? Which made Liz, irritatingly, right. Clare, the ardent feminist, believer in self-determination, couldn't go out to the garden and demand that Miranda come into the house and retire to bed in celibacy. Nor could she demand that Miranda come and confide to her, woman to woman, all the secret things she did. Whatever she's doing, Clare thought enviously, she might as well make the most of it this young. It goes all too soon.

Steve sat in the boat, holding it steady by a rope threaded through a mooring ring on the creek wall. Right now he'd like to have pulled the rope, tightly, round the pale throat of Miranda, from which came such mocking, uninhibited laughter. It was no good her protesting, as she was, that she was not laughing at him, just at the idea. So far removed from the conventional boys of south-west London, she had thought she could rely on Steve to be beyond wanting the tedious boyfriend-girlfriend arrangement. Yet here he was, prowling the creek in his dinghy, one step away from serenading under her window.

'But that was weeks ago, this is now,' she protested, mid-giggle, at the point when he thought he was playing the unbeatable trump card, reminding her of what they had done, and wasn't the first one at least supposed to be something special for a girl, to mean something? Her rejection angered him. He wanted to tell her, to impress upon her that there were girls by the dozen hanging around the harbour every day waiting for him to finish work, just about begging for it. The fact that Miranda was not to be impressed like that was what most attracted him. She just didn't care. It was both appalling and compelling: both of them knew quite well that she was simply out of his class.

Four

Clare found it frustratingly impossible to sleep late when she was in the village. It was either the sun blazing through the flimsy, unlined curtains (useless in winter), rain on the pear tree leaves, or the wind blowing its branches against the windows. At home in Barnes she used to think that on holiday one of the great pleasures would be staying in bed late in the mornings, but here she realized that it was only the term-time compulsion to get up that she hated so much back in London. She resented that frantic early (often still dark) time of racing round the house pushing everyone else to be ready for their various schools, getting lunch boxes prepared for the little ones, the finding of gym kits and recorders, remembering appointments, who was going where after school and with whom. There was the collecting and taking, the ballet classes, riding lessons, birthday teas, skating, swimming and tennis and none of it was her own. Clare just had to programme the organization of it all, even for Miranda who was too lazy and forgetful to remember boring things like lunch money and dentists. Everyone in Barnes and thereabouts did things so competitively too. Even the school run was done most efficiently by the affluent mothers in vast Space Wagons. It wasn't enough, either to learn tennis at seven: you had to be in the right kit, in the right club, and win tournaments. And your tears had to be mopped if you didn't win. Clare had never heard anyone say to their distraught, failed child, 'It doesn't matter, darling, it's only a game,' because it *did* matter.

There are no good losers in London, only losers. Jack had started hinting lately that they could all drop out of the ratlet race if they lived in Cornwall, but Clare didn't believe him: her children had already trotted many miles on the middle-class running track, so in the end it would simply mean doing the same things, but with much further to drive to get to them.

Now in the moist morning air, Clare sat on a damp garden bench enjoying the early stillness, watching the tide flow into the creek and letting the others sleep as late as they wanted.

If she chose, she could find small worries to play with, like wondering what Jack was up to in London, all alone. Was he having the same mid-life doubts that she was having? Did he lust after a slender young thing who sat giggling with her friends on the other side of the polytechnic canteen? Some eager young student with a body that was free of life's battle-scars, someone in whom the habit of chewing on their split ends was still endearing, rather than horrendously irritating?

Clare leaned forward to pick up her coffee cup and as she did so she felt the soft warm flesh of her stomach under her cotton kimono nestle on to the top of her legs. Surely, she thought, it hadn't done that this time last year? She prodded her waist and gathered up a handful of loose flab: perhaps the day was fast approaching when she would be buying her under-wear from the Firm Control rack in Marks and Spencer and Jack would be trading her in for a sleeker model. The thought brought her back to Eliot; wasn't that exactly what he had done when he'd abandoned his first wife (a successful psychotherapist, slightly older than Eliot), and met the juvenile Liz? Clare leaned back on the bench and her stomach flattened out comfort-ingly. It was her own fault, she thought, for having chosen such a sedentary occupation. Clare's gesture at remaining in the world of paid employment was to design and make knitwear for a shop where a £400 sweater could be cheerfully added to a customer's credit card bill along with rather outrageous underwear and intimidating hats. Clare had lately thought she would like to expand into a wider range of designs, one can only do so much handknitting without getting wrist problems. Investment in machinery would be needed, perhaps a course at a college. It could easily become a Proper Job and might jolt Jack into being impressed.

For now, Clare knitted her way through summer afternoons and winter evenings, and on her conscience was the knowledge that the clicking of the needles drove Jack absolutely crazy. The more she told him how complicated the patterns were, sneakily over-emphasizing her skill, the more he was certain she couldn't possibly be taking in a word he said while she was doing it. While he told her in detail and at length exactly what sort of day he'd had at the Poly, intending her to pick up the undercurrent of miserable dissatisfaction with his job, and therefore show sympathy, she'd knit-one, pearl-one away with an expression of cheerful but absent absorption. If she had more equipment, outworkers, more structure to her life, Clare thought, perhaps he'd take her more seriously.

For now, though, Clare's fingers were involved in nothing more demanding than pulling a few dead flower heads from those plants which were within reach and watching the ritual unrolling of the awnings on the bungalows up on the hill, rather like the daily raising of colonial flags in the farthest reaches of the empire. Back home under the Heathrow flight path, with early commuter cars racing for parking space on the common near the station, and the lorries heading for London deliveries on the South circular, there was no such luxurious calm.

Just along the creek, Clare could hear Celia briskly hoeing her garden, getting it done sensibly while the day was still cool and the dew-damp earth still pliable. Archie's secateurs could be heard snip-snipping brightly at the fading rose blooms, ruthlessly cut off the moment they opened past neat perfection. Clare liked them to unfold as far as they could, their stamens exposed for the bees. She was not the kind of woman who rushed to sweep up the fallen, velvety petals.

Through the superficial toying with shallow little worries, there was, at the bottom of Clare's emotional pond, a murky and menacing reflection that kept catching her attention. It was a wavering image of Miranda with Steve: an invented picture, constructed from Liz's idle remarks and the shadowy figure in the rowing boat. For all Clare really knew, it could have been Andrew or Milo in the rowing boat, but that wouldn't match with Miranda's soft laughter, laughter so much older and more knowing than Miranda herself. It was lovers' laughter, not the sort that is shared with casual friends.

Miranda didn't seem very interested in boys at home. When Clare asked her about them, about the parties they all went to, Miranda usually just groaned and said they were all pathetic, stupid. Clare wondered if Miranda was organized enough to take the pill, and if she was doing anything that would even require it. Did she like sex? Or perhaps no-one did it any more. Invented in the 60s and discarded, for being too dangerous, in the 90s? Clare found it deeply painful that there might be something about Miranda's personal life that she wasn't being told. To displace the pain, she got up stiffly from the damp bench and went up to her bedroom to get dressed. As she pulled on her leggings she tried to remember back to her early twenties: when was it that she had last felt the thrill of a stranger exploring her body? Would it never happen again? Given the chance (perhaps the last chance) would she really do all that with Eliot? How many women out there of her age were leaping into beds other than their own just for the reassurance that they were still attractive, and then feeling bad because they knew, intellectually, that they shouldn't need the brief sexual attention of a man to make them feel good about themselves?

Perhaps, the night before when Liz had commented about Eliot looking at the girls, she had been reading Clare's thoughts and been quietly warning her off. Jack would say that Liz would have trouble reading a cereal packet let alone thoughts, but women are never that dense when it comes to reading their husbands, whose wayward imaginings are as easy to read as those large-print books in the library.

Below Clare, noises in the kitchen told her that the house was waking. Without looking, she could tell who was getting out the cereal packets, she could hear the milk being taken from the fridge and not being put back again, a drawer was opened and not shut. She sighed and went downstairs, to remind the children, incorrectly, that it was as easy to clear up a mess as it was to make one.

Up at the Lynchs' house on most mornings there was bad temper. Liz had given up employing live-in au-pairs because Eliot used to frighten them off, either leering at them drunkenly or being extremely rude about their cooking; which he did depended on the size of their tits. Liz was always having to ring up the agencies and explain that it was nothing personal but the girls would probably be happier with a different sort of family, less artistic perhaps. So here in Cornwall there was just Jeannie to clean the house and Liz thought that everyone should be up by nine so that Jeannie could get to their rooms. Milo lazed down under his duvet saying she could surely start with the twins' room and why not do downstairs first if it came to that. Liz had been brought up to consider the servants and argued with Milo. Eliot had a hangover, as he had most mornings, and was slopping coffee clumsily into a mug. He paced the kitchen looking for sugar and took his cup outside on to the terrace, complaining that no-one in this place delivered a newspaper.

Liz had wanted it all perfect and was disappointed. She liked the house, and was proud of the way she had blended the colours, organized the furniture from London, dealt with builders and designers. She sometimes caught herself wishing that one or other of the family would leave the room, when they did not match the decor, or Jessica's hair colour clashed with the sofa as she lay stretched out watching TV, scuffing her dirty feet on the cushions and leaving coffee cups on the carpet to be tripped over. Liz had to remind herself that it was a place in which they were to live, (even if only for a few weeks per year), not to sit around posing for World of Interiors (a secret ambition of Liz's). Relationships within the family were less harmonious than her colour schemes. Eliot's moods were increasingly unpredictable, with gashes of anger slicing through the days without warning.

Also, these annual six-week exposures to the clever children of Eliot's first wife rather unnerved her. Milo and Jessica had so many private jokes between them they might as well be speaking another language. The night before they had been telling her about a film they'd seen, and Milo had said 'But of course it's allegorical.' Liz had wanted to go and look up the word in a dictionary, but the only one in the house was hidden away in the depths of Eliot's unfathomable computer. If she wanted to know what it meant she would have to write to her mother, secretly.

Liz watched her little sons calmly eating their breakfast, wrapped up in their remote twin-world. Even they don't need me for anything more than basic housekeeping services, she thought sulkily. And soon, in a year or so, they'd be going away to prep school and no-one would need her at all.

Liz indulged in some panic and loneliness as she took her tea out on to the terrace. She sat next to Eliot who ignored her. They sat in silence surrounded by tubs of lilies and agapanthus and the scent of honeysuckle. Together they watched Jessica swim, counting with her the lengths of the pool and wondering, but not to each other, how long she would keep up this passion for fitness.

Liz gazed out beyond the garden towards the village, where she could see Clare walking up towards the shop. I wouldn't want to have her hips, her house or her husband, Liz thought, but apart from that I bet it's a lot more fun being her at the moment than it is being me.

Celia and Archie, in their fifties and very content, never wondered what Andrew listened to on his Walkman. In the little kitchen, clean, efficient and a place for everything, tuna salad sandwiches were being prepared. They assumed Andrew would not want to come sailing with them. They had bought him a boat of his own, but occasionally they made the gesture of asking him, quite safely, knowing that he would rather stay with his friends. The daily picnic went into the pink cool-box, always including a good dry white wine, and equipment for making Darjeeling tea. In matching Guernseys and very old sailing boots, the Osbournes would pack up their selection of novels and their picnic and set off early in the scarlet dinghy, needing no extra excitements, and with the enviable knowledge of how to achieve perfect relaxation.

As they left the house, Andrew climbed out of bed and unlocked the box in his wardrobe. He always woke with a monumental erection and it seemed a shame to waste it. He could see that this was going to be the best time of the day for the experiment and this time it was going to be under control conditions, no props, just the fleeting thought of Jessica's breasts, her nipples showing in outline under her yellow swimsuit, perhaps also the thought of a stray pubic hair coiled against her tanned thigh . . .

It was still quite early when Clare walked through the village to the shop to collect the papers and see if there was any post. She didn't recognize anyone: it was a place where the population was almost entirely different each time she visited and those she did know seemed to be keeping town-hours still, venturing out only after the sun was well up.

Down below in the low-tide mud of the creek, her small daughters were picking their way over pebbles, barefoot with sticks, nets and buckets and slices of breakfast toast and marmalade. There were other assorted small children and even Miranda was out, helping the little ones to search for scuttling crabs, shells and mussels discarded by seagulls. The treasures would soon make up decomposing collections on terraces throughout the village.

From the lane above, Jeannie, on her way to clean the Lynchs' house, could see them all. Only ignorant tourists, she thought, would wallow about in that mud. What did they think happened when they flushed the loos at those creekside cottages? Where did they think a soakaway soaked away to? You couldn't get an appointment with the local doctor in summer, not in under three days, for tourists needing something for an upset tummy and thinking that they'd over-done the sun. And for Miranda, she fervently wished a dose of dysentery at the very least, after the state in which her Steve had come home last night.

Clare watched Miranda giggling with the young children, admiring their shells. She marvelled at the ease with which Miranda, her skirt tucked up in her knickers, could now be out in the creek being a child

47

again, when just last night she had been definitely a woman. Clare took her shoes off and padded down the steps into the creek.

'Show me what you've caught!' she called cheerily to Harriet and Amy as she picked her way across the mud and stones.

'Hermit crabs,' Amy said, shoving a bucket at her that seemed to contain nothing but sticky stones. 'You can't see them though, because they hide under things and don't want to be seen.'

'Like real hermits,' Clare said.

'What *is* a hermit?' Amy asked, puzzled.

'A person who likes to hide away from the world and live all alone, very privately,' Clare explained, pushing aside the stones in the bucket with her finger to try and see the crabs.

'Don't prod them then,' Amy said suddenly. 'Not if they won't like you looking at them.'

Miranda looked up suddenly and grinned at Clare.

'Yeah, Mum, don't invade their space,' she said, and Clare was left wondering if she had imagined the hint of a challenge in Miranda's voice.

In the post office Clare collected milk, eggs, a packet of Special K for the diet and a WI cake in case someone called in for tea. She pretended she herself wouldn't eat it. In the shop there were sunburnt families choosing postcards, small children clutching their mothers' skirts and wailing for ice-creams. A rental family were trying to order *The Guardian*. 'It just doesn't seem to get this far, it isn't worth us ordering it. We can get you *The Times*, *Telegraph* or *Independent*. Usually.' The customer, with two children and a spaniel all clamouring to get to the beach, said yes all right, *The Times*, but his wife wouldn't like it. Clare smiled at him in apparent sympathy, but inside she thought, who needs news in summer? Why not take a holiday from all the little routines, all the world's problems. But perhaps they were addicted to the crossword. Perhaps it was the only time they got to do it.

As Clare walked she watched the bright umbrellas going up over the terrace tables outside the bungalows. Clare had not, yet, at the summer drinks parties, met any of the retired couples who lived on the hill, but she assumed they were the ones who drank late at the sailing club in the afternoons, and who kept the golf club and the village shop just about functioning in winter. Celia had told her once that she had visited in November. 'The place was closed,' she had said, as if she was talking about Harrods on a Sunday.

Clare walked further on through to the edge of the village, quickly passing through the little streets and heading out towards the cliff. Out at the harbour entrance Clare could see the makeshift raft that Eliot had been talking about. It wasn't at all pretty, or idyllic or romantic as she had imagined, more like something from *Huckleberry Finn*, precarious, rickety and incongruous in the elegant harbour. A squatter among the clean smart sailing boats and business-like fishing boats. It looked like a giant duck's nest that had gone adrift. The raft seemed to be planks, poles and oil cans held together with frayed ropes and with a grubby teepee perched on top making the whole structure look terrifyingly top-heavy. Clare wondered what would happen in bad weather, where it had come from (and how) and who lived on it. They didn't seem to have a dinghy, unless someone was already out in it, so how did they shop?

'The man across the creek from us has lost his cat,' Archie, *Daily Telegraph* in hand, stopped next to Clare, on his way to the pontoon.

Clare followed Archie's gaze out towards the raft.

'You have to butter a cat's paws,' Clare told him, 'then they don't leave home.'

'Bloke out there has probably buttered its paws, and its legs and its body,' Archie said, still looking suspiciously at the raft. 'Cut off its head, could easily taste like rabbit. Bit of garlic, and some thyme . . .'

Clare turned and stared at him. 'Archie, you don't think it's been eaten, do you, not seriously?'

Is this what growing older really means, she thought, lining up with the old guard and acquiring ludicrous prejudices?

'Well you hear such stories, you never really know, do you?' he said, grinning at her.

'Archie, you're sending me up!' Clare said, laughing, 'You are, aren't you?' she suddenly added, just to check.

Archie gave her a cheerful wave, and went off to join Celia in their boat. Clare continued her walk, down past the Mariners pub and towards the boatyard.

She could see the boys down there, hanging around the pontoon and pretending they were working. They showed off to a couple of holiday-making girls with loud Midlands accents, heading for a hire-boat and dressed in identical turquoise shorts, cut high to show as much leg as possible. They giggled and wobbled their chubby thighs along the walkway, tripping on their too-high heels and staggering, shrieking, into the boat.

They looked back at the boys and grinned, posing, but the boys had lost interest and were looking for more entertainment, someone else to show off to. It was Steve who steered the hire boat out of the little marina.

He saw Clare and waved. Clare waved back, relieved that she would not have to talk to him. She saw too, the girls in the boat, whispering together and looking speculatively at Steve. Anyone would, really, Clare thought.

It must be the hot weather, and missing Jack that was making her feel like this. The boys on the pontoon weren't going to look twice at her: Clare couldn't remember the last time someone had even whistled at her. Probably when they did she'd been angry, wishing she had a piece of politically-charged wit ready for a stinging reply, seeing it all as part of Women's Oppression. But feelings like that were for London, where the sweet seductive scent of mown grass has the suspicion of dog shit about it, and only the most determined insomniac is awake at the time when the pure glory of birdsong is untainted by traffic noise.

Here in the fresh, rich air, Clare felt as if she'd been turned inside out, all her senses on the outside, exposed and alert, too easily responsive and too easily bruised.

Five

Jack was a teacher of art and he was tired. He felt that
art, more perhaps than any other subject, represented
the old saying, 'Those who can't, teach.' Students
applying for his course, coming to interviews, had
become less cowed by the grandeur of the building,
the once-famous names of their interviewers and had
started asking why they couldn't see examples of
Jack's work so that they could understand the view-
point from which he was inspecting theirs. He hadn't
got any creative work left to show them, hadn't for
years, for his job was to channel their creativity and in
doing so had contrived to frustrate his own. It was
possible he thought, relaxing with his feet on the seat
on the earliest possible train out of Paddington, that
the only reason he would ever pick up a paintbrush
again was to slap another coat of Dulux on the sitting
room ceiling. Hardly the Sistine chapel. Jack had
listened wearily as one after another the tedious
candidates, eager and hopelessly unoriginal had talked
about the implications of one-sided judgement, the
politics of landscape and such, straight from the sixth-
form common-room culture magazines. Jack was
greying, into his mid-years, an ageing hippy who now
worried that his contributions might not add up to a
decent pension. He had got old enough to be content in
a secure and proper job, which his late mother-in-law
would have loved, but deep inside there was a growing
urge to get back to what he had always thought he
wanted to be: a fine artist.
Summers in Cornwall were like a relic of a freer

past when he had hitch-hiked with most of suburban youth to be thrown out of St Ives and sleep in the fields. Then he had pretended to be an artist, now he pretended he had been one. Inheriting money and a second house had been a blow to his politics, but the increasingly comfortable life-style had eased him from angry young communist to a casual liberal, surprising himself with occasional intolerant leanings towards the right. He had credit cards, practically a full set, a Volvo, he thought about private education with a growing amount of approval.

After each frustrating year of trying to organize the chaotic creativity of his students, each batch of which turned out to be as tediously conventional in their gestures of rebellion as he had been in his time, Jack was ready for nothing more energetic than to sleep in a deckchair, an emotionless snooze with only the rhythms of the home, the tides, opening hours and the weather to disturb him. He didn't want to think any more about whether or not he should be dissuading the students from spending an entire term on an art installation project that involved taking radiators off the corridor walls and lying them in a straight line. He was unfashionably unconvinced by that kind of art, but had quirks of conscience that he might be wrong, depriving the world of a great thinker. Problem was, he knew and they didn't, that every year some kid straight off a foundation course had exactly the same idea.

Jack was looking forward to doing nothing in the sun, he liked watching Clare and Miranda changing colour, bronzing in the sun like cakes through a glass oven door. He watched his little daughters growing, playing and fighting. He liked to watch Liz Lynch with her tight slim body and he wondered why she bothered to keep it all so well organized for the drunken and unappreciative Eliot. She was like a meticulous herbaceous border for him to crash

53

through. Women in shorts, swimsuits, the heat, all gave Jack a comfortable summer randiness that he could normally use to advantage, keeping Clare happy, and if Clare was happy the family was happy. Summers were so easy.

Travelling from Paddington however, earlier in the day than was bearable, this year Jack was a dissatisfied man. This year he had to find the moment to tell Clare that he wanted to change all their lives, give up teaching, take his last chance at doing what he should be doing: painting. He had spent an uncomfortable week alone at home, with only his brooding thoughts for company. There had been no secretive dinners in unfamiliar restaurants with a willing and attractive colleague, no adulterous deeds in the sacred marital bed, and no guilt to nurture and feel smug about. There had only been the usual staff-room bickering, the unexceptional interviews and lonely pizza suppers watching depressing TV repeats of twenty-year-old comedy shows. None of his colleagues was particularly attractive, and they were very unlikely to be willing, but Jack was a man whose capacity for fantasy was still as intact as a fourteen-year-old's, and he had felt like an excited teenager wanting to issue whispered invitations to a secret party: parents away, house empty.

But it hadn't even felt like his own home. Clare's preparations for going away had taken no account of his being left behind. Miranda had turned off the Aga on her way out, leaving behind only an electric kettle, plugless microwave and the rusting barbecue. Someone had let themselves into the house as Jack was dressing one morning, to feed the fish. It was as if he wasn't expected to function as a human being in his own home. On the phone, Clare hadn't said, 'Dying to see you tomorrow.' Instead she had said, 'Don't forget to put the cleaning stuff down the loo.'

In such disgruntled and unsettled mood did Jack arrive at Truro in the drizzle to find Clare enthusiastic, (did she really call him 'darling'?), Miranda petulant and the younger ones bored and squabbling.

Clare drove fast, talking about nothing, to Falmouth for a late Sunday lunch which she had booked to please Jack.

'A proper Sunday lunch, we don't get many of those in summer do we?' she said, smiling round the car as if, Jack thought, they were all five years old.

Jack wasn't very hungry. He was full of British Rail's cheese and ham toasted special. The thought of roast anything made him feel rather queasy, especially at the speed the Volvo was weaving along the narrow lanes.

Clare waited patiently for Jack to relax, to be pleased to see her. She'd made this special effort for him. She felt responsible, holding the family together with her arrangements for them. She waited like a dog to be patted and praised and appreciated. It would, after all, have been much easier to have had a sandwich and Sunday papers lunch back at the cottage. This lunch, traditional Sunday symbol of family harmony, was important to her: she could, she thought, use the occasion to re-establish Miranda as her friend and confidante, Jack as the object of her affections, re-balance the family. She would be motherly at the table, passing round potatoes, celebrating the Family Unit.

The hotel matched Jack's mood more than Clare's. It was dismal, typically 1930's seaside architecture painted in faded ice-cream colours, with some tacky plate-glass additions from the mid-fifties to accommodate games areas and a pool. It was crowded with bored and wandering residents who wondered what they were supposed to do in the rain. Everyone seemed to be waiting for something which gave the place an atmosphere as appealing as a chiropodist's waiting room. The staff looked fraught, expecting their guests to go out, not hang about and get in the way.

In every public space and lounge children sat wriggling, old people shifted their walking sticks and their arthritic feet, clutching handbags and macks, victims of the weather. They kept looking out of the window at the drizzle, the shades of grey of the sea, sky and cliffs. It didn't look like the postcards.

Clare couldn't wait any longer:

'Well, aren't you pleased to see us?' she said to Jack as she marched her uneasy family through to the empty restaurant.

Jack, wishing he could only doze on the squishy old sofa in front of a log fire, said, 'Yes of course I am, but you didn't need to go to all this trouble.'

'It's not trouble, it's a pleasure, isn't it everyone?' Clare said brightly, refusing to take up the hint of apathy in Jack's voice. 'After all, it's less effort than having to cook isn't it? I think we all forget sometimes that this is supposed to be a holiday.' Clare bit her lip and regretted her words. Both she and Jack knew from years of experience that there was no way 'this is supposed to be a holiday' could be said without it's being an accusation, whoever said it just had to be having a subtle whinge. Still, better that Jack should think she was lusting after a different kind of holiday than lusting after a different man.

Clare settled herself in a seat by the window, overlooking the sodden crazy golf and the children's playground.

'Where is everyone?' she said, looking round the empty room. 'The hotel is full of people and hardly anyone is having lunch.'

'Perhaps they know something about the food here that we have yet to find out,' said Jack pessimistically, looking round for a waiter and needing a drink. At a table near them sat a family of four neat holiday-makers. Jack looked at them and then at his own family, noting the contrast.

Amy had not brushed her hair, probably for several days and its fairness had a greeny tinge to it and a look of brittleness, like doll's hair, presumably from the chemicals in the Lynchs' pool. She was wearing green dungarees, rainbow wellington boots and had spilled something down her front that wasn't breakfast. At least Jack couldn't think of anything red that she ate for breakfast, unless she'd taken to adding tomato ketchup to Shreddies. Miranda was in a tangle of old silk and ribbons, shivering in the unnecessary air conditioning. She looked beautiful but remote. Jack wondered what she was thinking about, probably, like him, about being absolutely anywhere but here.

The other family had neat, well brushed children and soberly dressed parents. Jack felt suddenly self-conscious, in his ancient jeans and a sweater that was a colourful and large version of the ones Clare had made for the children. He looked, he suspected, rather like a *Playschool* presenter. The little girl on the next table had shining plaits and silver hair-slides. How on earth, Jack thought, do people produce children who can find matching hair-slides in time for Sunday lunch when they're on holiday? They must bring a special pre-bagged selection of stuff labelled 'clothes for special occasions, plus matching accessories'. The girl's little brother, only about nine-years-old, wore a proper suit and tie, a little version of his father, all pressed and polished.

Jack felt sudden affection at the contrast with his own children. He softened towards them, appreciating the signs of them taking their own chances, choosing their own personalities. He wished sometimes they were a little less noisy and a little more considerate. Harriet was touring the many empty tables with Amy following her, rooting among the decorative china vases of flowers for a carnation with a stalk long enough to thread through her hair. Clare was watching them, defiantly withholding discipline under the disapproving gaze of the other family. When she had been their age she had gone into hotels only for weddings and special anniversaries, where she had sat quietly in her best frock among unfamiliar cousins, trying to Remember her Manners, as her mother had told her. She was proud now of her children's lack of reverence, that they didn't know what it was to feel intimidated. Only Miranda frowned at them, wondering how they were allowed to get away with making such a mess, she was sure she wouldn't have at their age. Disgruntled, she fiddled with her cutlery and kicked off her shoes under the table.

'What are we doing here?' she said loudly in the direction of either parent. 'We never go to places like this. If you wanted to go out we could've had lunch at the sailing club.'

'We can have lunch there any time,' Clare muttered. 'I thought this would make a change.'

'It's a change all right.' Miranda scowled, glaring across at the neat family, who stared back, interested. 'And not one for the better.'

'I expect you're hungry Miranda, you'll feel better when you've eaten.'

'Not hungry,' Miranda mumbled crossly.

Across the restaurant another family was settling. There were two sets of parents, each with a small baby and an assortment of young children. It took several minutes just to seat them all, and the children fidgeted as soon as they were on their chairs, impatient for the end of this ritual meal when parents would be too mellow to notice how noisy they were all getting. The children eyed Amy and Harriet enviously, while the parents fussed over the babies, sorting their collections of equipment: buggies; bags; bottles; clip-on baby seats that fitted to the edge of the table suspending the baby in uncertain insecurity. So much paraphernalia for such small animals. One baby cried and the mother leaned across, concerned.

'No you stay there, Jane,' said the relevant father. 'You're on holiday.'

Clare and Jack, listening, smiled at each other.

'Guaranteed to make the poor woman feel thoroughly guilty,' Clare said, pouring wine.

'Just a quick reminder that he gets three weeks off a year and he's giving up his time to help her out,' Jack said laughing.

It was bad enough that she hadn't been allowed to go off windsurfing with Jessica, without listening to all this, Miranda thought and said,

'God, you're so patronizing. How do you know what it's like for them. Maybe she works as well, maybe he gets up every night for the baby, maybe he's just nice and wants her to enjoy herself. You always think you know what everyone's life is like.'

Clare didn't want a fight in the restaurant, she was not yet that uninhibited. Miranda's outburst had left her out of control of everyone's lunch and she wanted to put it all back together again. She tried to be bright, to talk about what they would all do this summer, who they would sail with, picnics, coast walks, remote beaches. But no-one was joining in, she could feel Miranda's flashy tension, Jack looked tired and the little ones had run off somewhere. The service was slow. It wasn't much fun playing happy families. At the other table the babies had goo from jars spooned into them. They leaned forward eagerly, sucking the mess from the spoons, spitting and dribbling contentedly. The baby food Clare had taken out when hers were little had been home-prepared with elaborate care, ahead of her time with concern about salt and additives, all those ground-up carrots, cheese, yoghourty things. They had spat it out, crying and squirming out of reach of the spoon. Clare had longed for jars from Boots, but thought she should do it right.

The soup arrived and Clare enthused unconvincingly. It was beige, Miranda said it was inedible and went off to round up her little sisters.

'What's wrong with Miranda?' Jack asked, as Clare

hoped he would. He thought Miranda had been right about the soup, but didn't dare say so, any comment could so easily sound like criticism that Clare would take personally. The vast window overlooking Falmouth Harbour trickled with grey rain, making him feel he was inside a great fish tank. He glanced at the next table, in time to see the little girl with the hairslides trying surreptitiously to pick her teeth with her finger nail, and getting her hand slapped for it. He rephrased his question, 'Has something upset Miranda?'

Clare waited, so unused to having problems concerning Miranda that she didn't know how much she wanted to say.

'I don't know,' she said. 'I thought she would be happy to come out on a day like this. There's not much else to do. I think she'd probably rather be with the others, or at least, with Steve.'

She'd said it. She put down her spoon and looked at Jack, trying to convey that here was a dramatic point being made. She gestured meaninglessly and rather lamely said,

'I think they're having a, well, a thing.'

'A thing?' Jack looked puzzled for a moment. He caught the eye of the woman on the next table, obviously listening intently. He looked at the neat silver-hair-slided daughter and thought smugly, 'You've got all this to come.'

'A romantic involvement, do you mean?' he said to Clare.

'Oh Jack, stop talking like a social worker. Yes of course that's what I mean, though a "thing" is probably more accurate.'

Jack smiled cheerfully, 'Oh well, I suppose that will give her something to think about this summer, though I expect we'll get tears and tantrums when it's all over. You're surely not worried about her are you?'

He raised his voice for the benefit of the woman on the next table.

'Do you think she's sleeping with him?' he asked.

'Sleeping with.' Clare considered the phrase, the euphemism. It suggested a calm sophistication that Miranda was too young for. Miranda laughing in the garden in the dark had been like a young, spontaneous animal, knowing by instinct things that her mother hadn't taught her, like a creature gone back to the wild.

'Do you mean do I think she's getting laid, are they screwing?' she said loudly, protesting jealously at the unwelcome thoughts Jack had put in her head.

'Calm down Clare,' Jack hissed, looking round for reactions, thankful that the occupants of the other tables appeared now to be too engrossed in the pudding menu to be paying attention to his domestic dramas. The one exception was the mother of the Neat Family, who had the grace to look away guiltily as Jack's eyes challenged hers for judgement. She fussed with her daughter's hair-slides, as if constant attention to presentation would ward off the traumas of the teenage years to come.

'You're over-reacting,' Jack feebly attempted to pacify Clare. 'I didn't think you'd mind that sort of thing so much, you told me you were doing it by that age.' Jack wanted to ask Clare if her period was due, but didn't dare.

Clare started crying as the waiter took away the soup plates. A lot of soup had been left, but a lot of bread, he noticed had been crumbled on the table.

'That was different, times were different, it was safer. I don't want her exploited, she's not like I was, she's somehow much younger. And,' Clare wailed, 'and she hasn't talked to me about it.'

This, Jack realized, was clearly the point, but it was more comfortable to ignore it for now.

'Well if she's doing it, I think we can take it that it's because she wants to, not because she's being used. Miranda likes herself, she doesn't care what anyone else thinks. And anyway, as long as she's careful, surely . . .' he finished limply.

Jack didn't know what he was supposed to say. He didn't know what Clare wanted from him. He only knew, depressingly, that it wasn't the moment to tell her that he never wanted to see another art student in his life.

Miranda, returning in time for the rather grey roast lamb, was surprised and scornful of Clare's tears. Clare was eating steadily and sulkily like a child who had to eat up all her meat before she was allowed pudding. Her make-up was smudged and her hair wild. Tears from an adult, tears especially in public, seemed to Miranda an appalling weakness. They should keep them private, except perhaps just a small glistening round the eyes for funerals, smiling through tears at weddings, that kind of thing. They should have it all under control. Tears were the protests of a child. Miranda was hard on her mother, but unused to her emotion. Clare had always hidden her tears away in the bathroom, where she could be locked in to cry in peace, convinced from the start that Miranda had enough disadvantages being born to a teenage student (unmarried – in the days when these things mattered) without the burden of Clare's occasional bouts of misery as well. Silently enduring the pudding, Clare wished she was up on the headland lying in the damp ferns, the reassuring bulk of Eliot next to her. If she'd been pathetic and cried with him he'd probably have spanked her. Instead, later she'd probably have to have sex with Jack and would then, irritatingly, find that it had been just what she needed.

While Clare loaded everyone into the Volvo and Jack waited for his receipt, the lady who had so shamelessly eavesdropped approached him. He smiled tentatively and she gathered up her handbag in front of her as if for protection.

'If you don't mind me saying,' she began, in a way

that made Jack feel he was about to mind a lot, 'I think you were most unsympathetic to your wife. If a daughter of mine had been behaving like a little tramp I'd expect my husband to give her a good hiding, not make a lot of excuses. If the head of a household can't make a stand what hope is there for Future Generations?' She stared at Jack smugly as if daring him to disagree.

'Quite right,' came the voice of one of the listening legion of hotel residents, still cluttering up the hallway. Jack looked round, where was Clare when he needed her? Surely this would restore her sense of humour?

'Lady,' he said, 'I am sure no-one would dare offer a daughter of yours the opportunity to behave like a tramp.' The woman looked as if this might do by way of an apology, till he added, 'which is unfortunate for her.'

'Disgraceful,' came another voice from the sofas.

I'm going, thought Jack, before it gets any worse. As he leapt for the door his too-hasty foot sent a pot full of geraniums crashing from its pedestal. It was quite satisfying to see just how much carpet could be covered by one medium-sized pot of earth.

Well that was a good start to the holiday, Jack thought as he climbed into the driving seat of the Volvo. He wanted to tell Clare about the woman, but thought perhaps it would keep till bedtime, put her in a good mood. Humour was the only novel form of foreplay he had left after so many years.

The afternoon shone with fresh sunlight and in the back of the car the children were full and happy peering into the broken clouds for signs of rainbows.

Clare looked calmer now as the car delved into the deep maze of hedgerows, the rich greenness renewed by the rain. Miranda sat quietly in the corner of the back seat, her head resting against the window, not, as her mother imagined, thinking about Steve, for she rarely gave him a thought. For her, with a hard-heartedness that would have shocked Clare, he was an experience and an incident, no longer a person at all.

Back at the house, Jack, solicitous, irritated Clare further by treating her like an invalid, tucking her into a deckchair with tea and the Sunday papers, the frivolous ones with all the scandals, the ones she would never let anyone in Barnes see her reading. She looked at the moist steamy earth in the beds of pinks and nasturtiums and read idly, gradually losing the suspicion that she had made rather a fool of herself. She just wished Miranda's bursts of growing up would coincide with her own readiness for them.

Clare looked up at the window above from where she could hear Jack asking the smaller children to be quieter, please, Mummy's resting. Just let him say, just once, 'It's probably your age.' Just let him dare, that's all, Clare fumed quietly.

Upstairs, Jack piled socks and teeshirts into the chest of drawers. He fished a lily of the valley scented sachet out from the back and dropped it among Clare's underwear, not knowing that it would clash with a honeysuckle one that already nestled there. He looked out of the window at the busy creek, the gulls, the children, the overhanging thatch and felt that at last, he was home, something he felt nowhere else. All he had to do now was find a way of telling Clare.

Six

It took only a few hot days for it to become one of those summers where people keep telling each other how lucky they are with the weather.

Eliot, with typical hangover pessimism, complained to Jack that next year you wouldn't be able to move in the village for all the blasted trippers, all those Costa Plenty tourists who were being told on their return, 'I don't know why you bother to go abroad, there's nothing like England in a good year.' They'd realize that a good tan wasn't something you had to qualify for by spending eighteen hours being delayed at Gatwick. Jack and Clare, in their tiny cottage, stuffed their duvet into a dusty cupboard and stretched, hot, under sheets instead. The heat made them feel sexy, but their sweaty bodies glued together and made slapping noises like seals clapping. Worried that the children might hear, they pulled apart thankfully, rolling to cool islands on the far sides of the old brass bed. It was, Clare felt, weather for outdoor sex, which she knew, resignedly, that she was unlikely to get. On the one evening she had managed to lure Jack out alone for a walk in the bracken on the headland, he had complained that ferns were possibly carcinogenic and paid more attention to his sketchbook than to her. The only excitement he had expressed had been at the purity of the light.

In London, in the tubs and patios and the smart Versailles planters of the absent two-home families, petunias, lilies and fuschias wilted and died in the dust-dry heat, neglected by cleaning ladies or careless schoolgirls who had promised they wouldn't forget.

Only garish brazen geraniums flaunted themselves and blazed salmon pink and lobster red against the dust.

Down in Cornwall, Clare, Liz and Archie worried in the pub about a possible water shortage and the banning of hose pipes. On their terraces the tubs and pots and borders were full and thriving. Liz watered her lilies in the evenings when she could savour their delicious scent, but left the rest of the garden to the man whose job it was. Clare nurtured her cottage garden of lavender, larkspur and snapdragons. She watered them virtuously with water from the washing-up bowl, so the plants tended to be draped with limp spaghetti and bits of potato peel. She let the children plant their calendulas round the corner where they wouldn't clash, and where they flourished wonderfully, watered by the potent, stinking liquid from the old rainwater butt.

The good weather meant that time spent crammed damply into the cottage was minimal. In search of some cool air, Jack and Clare wandered up to the local craft centre to look at the things real tourists looked at, but the second-homers usually avoided.

'I've heard some of the stuff in here is really quite good,' Jack said to Clare as they paid their 50p entrance fee. Clare was looking doubtful. She and Jack went to quite a lot of exhibitions in London, mostly private views of friends of Jack's who were still bravely trying to make it in the art world. One of them, she recalled, was an advertising executive whose spare time was spent painting turgid seascapes (from memory – his house overlooked nothing more watery than a fish-pond) and another was a children's book illustrator with a passion for constructing vast papier-maché nudes. Clare didn't know any artists who sold anything – but their private view invitations made a pretty display among the mismatched arty pots on her kitchen dresser in Barnes, and added to the feeling that she had a culturally acceptable social life.

The exhibition was what could only be described as 'mixed', both in standard and content. Jack tried to steer Clare towards the paintings, which he thought good, and which carried price tags high enough to help him win his 'I-could-do-that' argument. But Clare was not to be steered. She wandered around, an incredulous look on her face, occasionally turning over a jug to look at its price, or fingering a tapestry wall-hanging.

'How can people turn out such ugly things, when they've clearly got so much skill?' she said to Jack in a loud whisper. 'Look at this,' she demanded, pulling him away from a row of landscapes. 'Just look at all the work in this.' Clare indicated a huge patchwork quilt, exquisitely sewn and delicately quilted, but made up of pieces of dull greens and yellow ochres. 'All that work for such an ugly result! Who'd want that in their bedroom? Whose decor will that match?' Jack sighed, unable to do anything but agree silently. She didn't seem in a mood for water colours, so he tried another tack.

'Come and look at the knitwear,' he said, pulling gently on her arm. 'Some of it is rather good.' Clare looked at the range of heathery-coloured sweaters and admired a couple of colour combinations which she resolved to use herself in London. 'You could sell your stuff here, Clare.' Jack said, persuasively. 'It's better than this.'

'Not for the prices I get back home,' Clare said. She picked up a khaki knitted bikini and giggled. 'I wonder how many of these they've sold,' she said. 'It looks like it was made by someone who hasn't been on a beach since 1926.'

Clare wandered out into the sunlight and Jack trailed behind, feeling the sad loss of an opportunity. He should have been more insistent, drawn Clare's attention to all the red 'sold' dots fixed to the paintings.

They might not do a roaring trade in baggy bikinis or gloomy patchwork, but the craft centre seemed to be a good outlet for pictures. He wondered why, and who was buying them. Presumably holiday makers, wanting an up-market reminder of a good time. They might not want to risk travelling hundreds of miles home with a delicate, newspaper-wrapped piece of pottery or glass, but could find a safe, flat stowing space behind a Passat's passenger seat for a local painting. He'd have to show Clare what could be done, he resolved. Next time they visited the gallery it would have to be to look at his own work hanging there, and if the paintings didn't have a convincing enough number of red stickers, he'd just have to buy a pack of them and apply them himself. He thought about telling Clare he intended to start painting seriously again, but at that moment she caught sight of Amy, Harriet and Miranda leaning over the sailing club balcony across the creek. Jack looked closely at Clare's face, finding in it a mixture of expressions: a concern that the younger ones might fall over the edge, a delight at seeing Miranda and an indefinable something else which might just be an anticipation of lunch.

The second-home families separated themselves from the holiday makers for the day's important rituals: lunch; pre-dinner drinks; their late-night corner of the pub. Liz liked to have lunch at the sailing club. If she had to spend summer out in the sticks, she certainly didn't intend to use her time housekeeping for everyone, surely someone should be hired to do that?

'You can't honestly expect me to do cooking,' she said. 'You either all get your own lunch or we go out.' Eliot was just as happy to drink in the club bar as he was at home, and there he could watch the summer women, talk comfortably to Clare and envy Jack his earth-mother wife, safe that she wasn't his to live with and could therefore never bore him.

Eliot didn't like anyone very much, not unreservedly, except his son Milo, who seemed to be growing up to be an all-round perfect man, with no spots, no awkwardness, totally at ease in the world. Eliot wished he was like that, aware that conversely, most men want their sons to be like themselves. Eliot particularly didn't like Liz, whom he had married because she was so beautiful and efficient and because he thought she would be able to organize Jessica and Milo better than their own work-distracted mother did. Instead she had produced the twins as soon as she and Eliot were married and too late Eliot realized that family life is not to be run like boarding school; his own wife had not been incapable of efficiency, it was just that caring for small children is simply difficult by nature and ruinous to domestic bliss.

Now he didn't really like Liz much. He never really had now he came to think about it. He thought back occasionally to their first sexual encounter, when after a languorous lunch they had wondered where to go to consummate their deliciously illicit affair. Eliot, waving impressive credit cards, had suggested the Ritz, but Liz, with what had seemed at the time sweet girlish daring, had insisted on Eliot's own home, the sacred marital bed. After a bout of rather nervous (on Eliot's part) sex, Liz had shamelessly made use of his wife's bathrobe, played with her cosmetics and had a critical look-see through her wardrobe. What kind of a girl behaves like that, Eliot, years later, now thought. Eliot did not bother to consider what kind of man actually marries that kind of girl.

Eliot was now becoming a fat man, a drinker with a red face, and stringy, too long sandy hair. His responsibilities overwhelmed him and his vast earnings were no longer the comfort they had once been.

At lunchtime Eliot sloped up the hill, slightly more out of breath than the day before, wearing badly-fitting old jeans that gripped uncomfortably somewhere in the region of his hips, and a cigar-burnt Guernsey. He watched Liz's long muscled legs striding in front of him. Detached, he was unimpressed, seeing her body all day long from its first cat-like stretch to its evening workout on the bathroom carpet. He'd watched her cosmetic routine with disgust, so much stuff for taking the goo off her face and another lot for putting something else back on again, all of it costing a mint. She had the most pampered body Eliot's money could buy, London perfection. Her idea of self-catering, Eliot thought cattily, was manicuring her own nails.

Liz would have preferred Corsica to Cornwall. She didn't like sand, it got everywhere, even in bed. It stuck to her Clarins Huile de Soleil, factor 7. She preferred a sunbed tan. She liked the feeling of the sun on her body though, but she liked the sun's presence to be dependable. Stretched out on a deckchair on the sailing club balcony, there was usually some cloud or other up there ready to get between the sun and her. And there was the nagging little breeze. The sun in England was a half-hearted lover, reluctant to caress and stroke. Liz prepared, exposed and surrendered herself and it crept impotently away, or it blazed briefly, gone too soon and leaving her wanting. Rather like Eliot, she thought.

Eliot saved his passion for the women he was not supposed to have. As a child he had eaten little at meal times, preferring to raid the cupboards secretly at midnight. He still liked the furtive selection of life's forbidden goodies, though not, these grown-up days, in terms of food. On his many foreign 'research' trips, the possibility of catching a disease transmittable to Liz or fatal to himself was a risk he undertook with the thrilling terror of a gambler putting someone else's money on an outsider. The thrill was almost better than the sex, however exotic. He sometimes imagined, perhaps sitting in the bath or on a lazy two-continent flight, what he would do if he caught AIDS, or herpes, or just good old-fashioned gonorrhea. The thought of breaking open capsules of antibiotics over Liz's paté maison or lacing her martinis with the latest state of the art medical cure-all made him smile quietly to himself and then more sensibly avoid her for a while, inspecting himself for symptoms and biting his nails.

At the sailing club Liz settled herself with a crab sandwich and a dry sherry and looked around at the holiday women.

'I do wish women wouldn't wear high heels with shorts,' she murmured to Clare. 'It looks just too frightful.'

Clare nodded non-committally. Liz looked down at Clare's battered old tennis shoes and wished she hadn't said anything. Clare looked at Liz's Gucci pumps and wished the same.

Clare sat close to the balcony where she could keep an eye on Amy and Harriet. Somehow it was assumed that Liz didn't have to do the same for her twins, as if she knew that it wasn't really her job. Clare felt like an all-purpose mother, automatically taking over and checking now and then that the little Lynches hadn't wandered off the beach and into the waves, that a giant seagull hadn't plucked them from the shore and carried them, stork like, to a cliff-top nest, all those things that proper mothers worry about. Mothering Liz's children, Clare felt she was mothering Liz and minded. It defined their roles: she, mature and responsible, Liz young, free and enviably frivolous. It was Eliot who took the sausage rolls down to his children on the beach, and Clare's heart warmed menacingly, fired by that gentle gesture of a caring father. She looked down tenderly on Eliot sitting in the sand with his children and with her brain befuddled by love did not wonder once about the duality of her own standards: that her own husband should nurture his own children at a level equal to her own would never be a matter for congratulation in her family.

71

Jack was in the bar buying drinks. It was cool inside, sparsely furnished with dark wood and rather gloomy, the walls glinting with trophies and the gilt-engraved lists of past commodores and presidents. They mostly had letters after their names, a pompous inclusion Jack thought. It could hardly be relevant to their sailing ability or competence with the treasurer's records if they were MA (Cantab) as opposed to O-level (failed).

'Don't forget your change, sir,' shouted the big Australian barmaid as Jack wandered absent-mindedly back out towards the balcony.

'Cracking Sheila behind the bar,' Eliot leered, coming up the beach steps to help Jack with the drinks. 'Wouldn't mind having her down under.'

Jack smiled, the way he thought men were supposed to.

'Hardly competition for Liz, I'd have thought,' he said, watching Liz unfold for the sun. Pitying her for her lecherous husband, Jack went to sit next to her, sidling past Clare and hoping that she wouldn't notice he had chosen not to sit with her.

'Thank you so much, Jack,' Liz purred, opening her blue eyes briefly to acknowledge her second sherry. Jack grinned, puppy-like, and wished he had thought to sit next to Clare after all, opposite Liz, where he could get a better view of her smooth body, as inviting to stroke as a rolled-out cat. Jack looked at her naked painted toes, inhaled her Poison and breathed in the good life at the same time.

'Paid your subs, have you?' A shadow fell across the table. Jack looked up and there stood the sailing club commodore, clipboard in hand. For a dreadful second Jack had imagined that his thoughts were being read and here was the moment of disclosure, along with judgement and punishment.

'Of course I've paid,' he said, more crossly than he knew he should. 'Standing order, every May. It must be on your list. Miller.'

'Sorry Mr Miller, mistook you for a Temporary.' The Commodore strode away, staring at his clipboard and caught sight of Eliot in the bar. He didn't like Eliot, not the kind they wanted at the club, no respecter of tradition. It wasn't right that scruffy, unkempt, mutinous individuals should chain-smoke their way round the estuary, winning races and wearing too-expensive docksiders. But Eliot was a life member, untouchable, contributing so much to the bar takings that it would be foolhardy to blackball him for dressing to lower the tone.

Down below the clubhouse the tide was high. Jessica and Milo were preparing their dinghy for sailing. All their equipment lay piled in an expensive heap of neon-coloured wetsuits, life jackets, centre-boards and sailbags. Andrew and Miranda were skimming stones into the creek. Miranda tried to find the moment at which the tide would turn, doing ritual magic: if she got it right, she wouldn't be pregnant. That couldn't happen to her, surely? There were always girls at school, the ones who came in looking pale and worried, telling just their best friend, and then anyone else who'd listen that they thought they were pregnant. For a few days they enjoyed the brief glamour and the speculation, and then would come in, all smiles and saying it was OK after all, this time. Miranda had no time for them – they were, in her opinion, just showing off that they were getting sex. As Miranda threw her pebbles, she could see her mother up on the balcony, watching her fondly. Always watching her and waiting to be told things. Could Clare guess what Miranda was doing? All that freedom to talk about absolutely everything, so that feelings could be brought out and discussed and nothing hidden or glossed over in their household – Miranda felt great surges of anger that in all Clare's tales of Lone Motherhood, she had never mentioned this awful am I/aren't I dread and terror that must have been there

73

at the beginning of Clare's own pregnancy.

Miranda hadn't told Clare anything of real personal importance since the day she'd had her first period and Clare had celebrated this rite of passage with a special family dinner – lasagne, Miranda's favourite, though at the time the tomatoey sauce had only reminded her of the blood.

There had been roses in her bedroom, and Clare had slapped Miranda's face gently – telling her it was an old French tradition and was to bring her luck in sexual matters (doesn't work, thought Miranda now). Miranda had almost expected an announcement in *The Independent* personal column: Congratulations to Miranda Miller of Barnes, who Became a Woman Today!

Clare was also watching an excursion boat full of sun-scorched holiday makers, the ones who didn't qualify for lunch at the sailing club. They were the people on days out from caravan sites, bed and breakfasters, campers.

They brought with them their dogs and grannies, towels with palm trees on them, inflatable crocodiles, lilos, frisbees, radios and windbreaks. There were buckets, spades, babies in sun-shaded buggies all crammed into the boat. People were fretful and hungry, there would be a long wait for pasty-in-a-basket at the pub and Beryl the barmaid would be pink with overwork and the strain of being pleased to see everyone. How hard it can be to enjoy the ritual of being British on a seaside holiday. It was harder than work, and you had to be happy, you'd saved all year, you sent cheery postcards home.

'How lucky we are,' Clare said, watching the awkward unloading of the boat. 'Our own houses, own boats.'

'Well at least they've all got cars,' said Jack, politically uncomfortable at being reminded of his own

74

good fortune. 'Years ago you went to the resort by train and that was where you stayed for the duration, unless you caught a bus.'

'I've never seen a bus round here,' Liz commented, eyes still closed, face up to the sun. She sounded, Clare thought, as if she'd never seen a bus *anywhere,* but to do so once in a while might be rather amusing.

'I remember those holidays when I was little,' Clare reminisced, ignoring Liz. 'My father used to carry these two huge suitcases, wobbling from side to side like giant scales. My mother used to carry this little vanity case, like a big sugar cube with a handle. We went to Swanage every year.'

Liz hoped Eliot wouldn't start on his, 'We were so poor that . . .' memories from his rural Ireland days. She'd had all that from his mother at their wedding and had refused to see the woman since.

She said to Clare, 'My parents used to drive down to Avignon in the Bentley every August to see my aunt. My sister and I used to be sent on later by train, like parcels, because we got so horribly car-sick. A Universal Aunt used to take us as far as the Gare de Lyon and put us on the train, and then we were on our own. It was such fun, the best part of the holidays.'

'Weren't you sick on trains too?' Jack asked.

'Of course not darling,' Liz drawled, smiled at Jack. Rich bitch, Eliot the self-made man thought with bad-tempered scorn. He paced about restlessly on the balcony. Clare noticed that he never seemed to finish his drink, but then realized that he kept wandering back into the bar for a refill. He smiled a lot at the Australian girl, discovered she was a Sandra not a Sheila and cheered up when she offered him a windsurfing lesson. She and the Scotch would keep him warm in the water. He trailed after her as she collected glasses from the balcony tables.

'He's such an old tart,' Liz said suddenly, watching Clare watching Eliot. 'If it moves, he's going for it.'

Down on the shingle Andrew wanted to get Jessica alone to invite her to his cottage. Celia had told him that morning that she and Archie had booked a four-day trip to the Scilly Isles and that he could stay, trusted, by himself at home with Clare to keep an eye on him. Getting Jessica was now his greatest ambition, his only ambition and this was the perfect, probably the only, opportunity.

Jessica was so warm and friendly, she wouldn't be so hurtful as to refuse his invitation. He couldn't have asked Miranda, for he loved her in a pure and abstract way. He could hardly bear it when she wore her tiny bikini, he didn't like to think of her as mortal with a prosaically ordinary body that functioned like anyone else's. Under the thin drifty silks that she liked to wear he could imagine that her body was all of a piece, joined up all the way round underneath like a doll's. But with Jessica he felt just plain randy, raunchy, for he had inherited some double-standards from his father and his school. Skimming stones next to Miranda, he kept looking at Jessica, close to ecstacy as he watched her glide her warm brown body into her blue and orange wetsuit. She chatted and giggled with Milo. The two of them never seemed to be apart, thought Andrew. Perhaps if he'd had a sister he'd know how to deal with girls. Milo never seemed to have any trouble, he just treated them like normal people and said just any old thing to them. There ought to be a GCSE course in it, Andrew decided.

Eliot couldn't relax. Life was passing and he was ageing and he was now drunk enough to be thinking about the work he should have done that morning. At five in the morning he had woken up with the birds and realized that in chapter two he had introduced a couple of shady characters that were crucial to the novel's outcome. Driven downstairs by curiosity as to what he'd done with them, he checked with his computer and found that they hadn't been mentioned since and here he was in the depths of chapter ten.

He looked down at the beach and wished that he too was a teenager, lithe and fit like his son. Then, full of paté and Scotch, belching, overweight and staggering slightly, he tottered down the steps and yelled to Jessica in the boat, 'Wait for me! I'm coming with you!'

Liz sat up and looked out, disbelieving. Jack looked up from *The Independent* and gazed over the balcony. Eliot was lolloping down the shingle to the edge of the water, pulling off his Guernsey and revealing a faded grubby tee-shirt from a long-ago rock concert. He climbed heavily into the little dinghy and collapsed, exhausted from the effort.

'He should at least have a life jacket if he's going out with those two,' Liz commented coolly. 'They always fall in.'

'Perhaps they'll sail extra gently for him,' Clare said.

'When he's in that state,' Liz commented, 'I honestly don't care if they take him out and drown him.'

She gave herself back to the sun as the overloaded dinghy sailed precariously out towards the estuary.

What an encumbrance he must be to her, Clare thought. Liz was so perfectly put together, he was like a clashing accessory, a bright pink plastic hand-bag, overfilled against an elegant Armani suit. But then what would Liz be like if it wasn't for Eliot's money? But then Clare thought, accurately, if it wasn't Eliot's money, it would be someone else's. Liz wasn't the type to go around being poor.

A lot later that afternoon, as tired children whined for ice-cream, Miranda read Colette and Clare read Fay Weldon on their terrace, and Andrew sat in his cherry tree with binoculars watching for Jessica's return, all these people witnessed a wet fat man being led gently home by his children. They took an arm each and hauled him out of the dinghy. Still in wetsuits and life jackets they pulled him carefully up the hill through the village like two young ponies pulling an over-loaded cart. They handed him over to Liz like one of the smelly treasures the twins kept bringing in from the creek. Her reaction to Eliot was exactly the same:

'Leave him on the terrace to dry,' she said crisply, 'I'll deal with him later.'

Seven

'Sorry,' said Eliot the next day.

'You always are when your head hurts,' Liz snapped.

Eliot spent a long time in the shower, resolving to be kinder to Liz, less embarrassing to his family and more tolerant to humanity in general. The world couldn't help being composed entirely of fools after all. He decided to be less brutal to his body too, for it felt as if it needed some attention. He could feel it stewing in alcohol, full of air and cholesterol, full of the good things in life but in much too large a quantity. He ran the shower long and hard, wishing the hot water would melt away the excess flesh and restore him to the vigour of his youth. Eliot drank weak tea that morning, instead of strong coffee, and tried to like it. He sat with Liz on the terrace, still apologizing for his constant drunkenness.

Unmoved, she said, 'It's nothing to do with me. It's Milo and Jessica you should be apologizing to.'

'I don't suppose they mind too much,' he said, unwisely.

'Well no-one could say they aren't used to it by now,' she retorted tartly.

Eliot felt forlorn, already in need of another drink, and deprived of sympathy. Perhaps it was all her fault, he thought, looking sideways at Liz and her angular, unforgiving body. What he really needed was someone warmer, more compassionate, a mother-figure. Someone like Clare.

Clare at that moment was feeling like Everymother.

Celia was in her kitchen leaning against Clare's Aga and giving last-minute instructions about the care of Andrew in much the same way that people do to a neighbour who is to feed a lonely cat. Clare wondered if she was imagining it, or was Celia really sniffing the air like a labrador, as if to discover whether Clare's bunches of hanging herbs were covering up some sinister aroma of bad housekeeping?

'I've left plenty of prepared meals in the freezer, he won't run short of shepherd's pie,' Celia said. 'But I feel he needs to be reminded of the small things, like if you should happen to notice whether his hair looks brushed, perhaps you could have a quiet word?' Celia looked a bit doubtful, as well she might, Clare thought, seeing as Amy and Harriet both had hair tangled like birds' nests by this stage in August.

Clare didn't at all mind taking on the care of Andrew, but her mind was on things other than his welfare. Miranda seemed to be spending an awful lot of time in the loo, and although Clare made herself carefully alone and available to be confided in, she was now completely certain that Miranda had things going on in her life that she was keeping to herself. All that sex, Clare thought enviously, imagining that when Miranda wandered off alone in the day, saying she was going to sail or swim with Jessica, she was actually going to meet Steve secretly. The problem with the frequent visits to the loo she put down to cystitis, which Clare had once had during her early days with Jack, when sex had been delightfully, but damagingly frequent and she had had to take her resulting bladder problem to an unsympathetic doctor. Clare wrote 'potassium citrate' on her shopping list, along with French beans and Coco Pops and planned to announce loudly and cheerily over supper that it was she who had a nasty attack of cystitis and that the bottle in the bathroom cabinet was for her, the children were not to drink it. Miranda could then help herself to a few doses without having to pay-by-confession first.

Archie and Celia were going to 'do' the gardens on Tresco. Gardening was their great passion. At home in Surrey their herbaceous borders would have rivalled those of Gertrude Jekyll (whose name they always pronounced correctly to rhyme with treacle), and after reading Christopher Lloyd there was an area of meadow, full of carefully naturalized wild flowers. A visit to Sissinghurst had also resulted in their front garden being given over entirely to white flowers, all neatly bordered with box hedges that had to be trimmed arduously with dressmaking shears. The postman, feeling their garden lacked colour, frequently brought round his left-over home-grown marigold seedlings, which Celia gave to her cleaning lady. In Cornwall each year, she and Archie made visits to gardens at Glen Durgan, Trelissick, Trengwainton and Trebar, all with the same enthusiasm as if it were their first visit. Their shrubs were tagged with permanently legible labels, they knew Latin names. They were life members of the National Trust and bought each other hardback gardening manuals for birthdays.

'Now you'll be all right won't you Andrew?' Celia fussed. 'There's plenty of food and Clare will be checking up on you to make sure you're surviving. She says to go round for supper and for anything you might need.'

Celia had doubts about the supper, as she had about Clare's supervision of Andrew's hair brushing. Clare and Jack seemed to barbecue everything, and Celia had a deep distrust of burned food.

'Don't worry,' Andrew said impatiently, longing for privacy, making plans of his own. 'I'll be all right, send me a postcard.'

Andrew watched them drive away in the Rover and then wandered round the house looking for something that he could not normally do. He didn't count his experiment, he just had to do that whether anyone was around or not. In fact it was more exciting with someone on the other side of the bathroom wall. Making love to himself was unsatisfying though, even with the string glove and Andrew was longing for the real thing, for Jessica's warm body, soft and thrilling against his. He had started having to make excuses not to swim in the Lynchs' pool, terrified that his lust for Jessica would show, that his uncontrollable penis would swell to overwhelming size, bursting out and taking over the garden. He imagined them all talking, laughing, then the rising feeling, and all of them gradually stopping to stare, horrified. It would writhe out towards Jessica, a pinky-purple serpent and everyone would see.

In truth Andrew had few illusions that Jessica would be overcome with passion for him, and the offending item had yet to be measured at larger than five inches, but it rose with shameful ease, encouraged by Andrew's habit of idly fingering it from inside the pocket of his shorts. Milo never gave any indication that he had the same problem, in fact Milo never seemed to be interested in anybody in that way, just water skiing and wind surfing. A wetsuit, Andrew thought, now surely that would keep the beast in place.

Andrew wandered aimlessly round his parents' bedroom, picking things up, putting them down. He looked through the pile of books beside the bed, nothing rude enough for him among the collection of detective stories and classic novels. He opened and closed drawers at random, not prying, but looking for clues to his parents. The contents of the drawers were ordinary clean sensible clothes, with which to deal with the weather, with walking, sailing and the sun. His parents had no secrets. Did they still do it? Andrew wondered. He thought probably not, not at their age.

As Celia and Archie drove towards Penzance,

changes were taking place in the village. It was Friday, which the residents liked for this was changeover day. By 6.30 a.m. sleepy children were being fastened into backs of cars, dogs were being walked to their last tree this side of the Tamar. Overflowing rubbish sacks were already splitting open next to overloaded dustbins. The children of the second-homers had done their goodbye crying the night before, bereft of their new friends, sure they would never, at least till the next afternoon when the new lot came, meet anyone like Alex or Emily ever again.

Clare tended her garden, watching the renters struggle to be out of the cottages and flats by 10 a.m. Some were gone much earlier – there was the Tamar bridge to be queued for, or roadworks at Okehampton and a lot of motorway to be covered before the midday heat set in. Or there was simply the urge to get home in time to watch *Neighbours* or catch the supermarket before it shut. New clients weren't allowed in till after 3 p.m. and those who arrived too early hung around the village trying to get a restorative drink at the Mariners, or shopping for toilet rolls (there were never any in the cottages, Jeannie and her friends had any spares stuffed into their shopping trolleys). Cars were still full of luggage and babies, bikes and surfboards on the roofracks.

But between 10 a.m. and 3 p.m. the residents mostly had the place to themselves. This was the tranquillity for which they had bought their cottages. There was a suburban Sunday atmosphere as they strolled smugly round the village, congratulating each other on how quiet it was, doing things to their boats. Some even washed their cars, mowed the lawns. Their children ran round the village collecting up abandoned buckets and spades and fishing nets. Later they hung round throwing stones into the creek, slyly appraising the children of the new arrivals, who stared back at them, pale and shy. By 4 p.m. the shop would be full of

83

customers, for the brigade of cleaning ladies would have done their fruitful tour of larder and kitchen cupboard, to make up for having their busiest day of the week while everyone else seemed to be resting. Jeannie would have cleaned out at least three of the properties, somehow finding time in each to have a quiet smoke, (someone always left a cigarette or two in packets under the beds), while watching a bit of daytime TV.

That evening Clare and Jack did their duty by having Andrew round to supper.

'You'll stay in for it, won't you Miranda?' Clare had hardly dared ask, 'And if there's anyone else you want to invite . . .' she had then ventured.

'Milo and Jess?' Miranda had answered promptly.

'Sure, and I'll ask the Lynch twins as well for Amy and Harriet,' Clare had said, planning an al fresco supper, a noisy, relaxed barbecue for all the children.

'Can't we have some more adults too?' Jack had asked nervously, fearing an evening of over-excited children all too close to the creek at high tide, and with no alternative fathers to help take charge.

'Don't be silly. What can go wrong?' Clare said. 'And if you want someone to talk to, you can talk to me can't you?' she added sweetly, kissing him fondly on the cheek as she walked past on her way to the kitchen.

'If you'd only keep still long enough, I would . . .' Jack called after her, but his words faded at the doorway and Clare did not turn back.

For the few months of the year that Miranda spent living in the cottage she tried hard to make her surroundings compatible with her current choice of personality. Miranda believed that you were what you read. Depending on her mood she spent a lot of her Cornwall time drifting about in a fantasy. She was Claudine, Juliet, Tess. Inside her head was a nonsensical porridge of daydreams, dramas in which she played the starring role. It was easier, more private living in her head like this and it was the only way in which to co-exist with Clare who tried too hard to get close. Clare's insistence that Miranda was so special for Clare had always made it difficult for Miranda to think of Jack as a father. The moment had long passed when she could have pointed this out, now it would be too hurtful. Miranda and Clare were no longer a lonely and crusading unit battling through Clare's degree, sleeping in the same narrow bed, sharing tins of beans. When Clare still told people about how Miranda used to play with Lego during lectures, or talked about hitching to rock festivals, Miranda felt embarrassed, and alienated from Jack, who Clare at that time had not yet met. Miranda had been Clare's biggest drama in life, and it was now too far in the past.

Miranda escaped into the contradictions of her bedroom which was full of what she thought of as false starts. There was all the stuff from her riding phase, not that long ago, when she had galloped a local fat pony along the beach, pretending to be Rebecca. She piled up the old Ruby Ferguson books with the too-small riding boots ready to pass on to Harriet. There was a pile of opera CDs from her infatuation with Puccini. The CDs were hardly played arriving on a birthday too near the end of the phase as she turned from Mimi to Madonna, filling the house with loud tarty music and wearing loud tarty clothes. Right now, prowling round the unusually tidy room she found it impossible to escape being simply Miranda. Hardy's heroines had never had to deal with the instructions on how to use a pregnancy test kit. Miranda wandered back to the bath-room and sat on the edge of the bath, watching the sol-ution of urine and chemicals. She wrapped her jumble sale robe round her thin self and stared at the tiny test tube. If she kept watching it perhaps it wouldn't change colour, she wouldn't be pregnant. She ran water into the bath, watching it creep up over the stains on the old enamel, which got worse every year.

She pulled back the curtain, the fabric so old it was almost fashionable again, and looked out through the honeysuckle to the river. Steve would be out there putting petrol into the hire boats, bringing them to the pontoon now that the tide was high, ready for the day's customers. Already the holiday-makers were out, swarming round the village, diligently entertaining their children, taking them fishing.

Miranda looked back at the test-tube. The girl in the magazine advert for the kit had been photographed sitting on the edge of her bath, in a warm-looking room lush with thick carpet and cosmetics, ornaments, plants, pretty things. She looked like the career type, young, married, plenty of money. She was only an adman's fantasy. Miranda was the real customer. A girl with bitten nails, unable to wait the extra days for hospital bureaucracy, the family doctor with his kind but disappointed concern, or worst of all her mother knowing before she did. This was a sordid way to find out if you were growing a human. Collecting early-morning pee and shaving your legs in the bath, perfecting the skin care while you kept watch on a phial of liquid, daring it to change colour. But when Miranda got out of the bath, the liquid was pink. It must run in the family, Miranda thought, so this must have been how Clare felt when she realized I was on the way.

Clare was in the kitchen, envying Jack. He'd taken on the cooking of the barbecue that evening and therefore had earned himself an afternoon off in which to gather his strength. Clare, therefore was left with whatever domestic duties had to be done that day, and resented it.

'I'm supposed to be having a holiday,' she fumed to the washing machine. Other people on holiday get room service: I AM room service.

At home in Barnes at least she could fling the

laundry in and out of its gadgets as and when she thought of it. Here, in time-bomb mood, she had to stand over an ancient twin-tub washing machine that must have been the last word of luxury in its day. Now it seemed to plead to go away and be left to retire in the recycling plant. Water slopped on to the kitchen floor, all over Clare's espadrilles, the soles of which were soaking up the dampness like blotting paper. The machine could do nothing without intervention. It was helpless and unwilling, slow and stubborn. Like an old lady crossing a busy road, it could not be rushed but had to be encouraged gently along in case of disaster. Clare cursed and pushed her collapsing hair out of her face as she dragged hot and heavy sheets from one half of the machine to the other. The spinner made the whole thing dance madly across the floor, skittering sideways trying to pull the hoses from the taps at the same time. Clare kicked it back towards the sink. She might as well, she thought, take the sheets down to the creek, bash them with stones and gossip with the villagers. But the real villagers all had state-of-the-art automatics. One day, she thought, one day I'll persuade Jack to sell this bloody inefficient house and we'll take real holidays like everyone else, in real family hotels where real chambermaids take away the used bedlinen and I never have to see it again.

In the garden Jack, who was supposed to be shopping for chicken wings and lamb for the kebabs, was trying to remember what artistic inspiration felt like as he sharpened his pencil and opened a new pad of cartridge paper. He hardly wanted to defile the clean white pages, afraid that he wouldn't be able to capture an impression of the hydrangea and make it acceptably recognizable. Flower paintings seemed to do well at the craft centre, along with local river views and boats at sunset. Jack had taught his pupils to look first at the overall shape of their subject, and at the shapes made between the parts of the subject. He tried doing the same. The hydrangea had so many petals, such delicately shaded colouring, through pinks and lilacs to blue. It was a plant for watercolour, oil was too heavy, a human hand with a pencil was too heavy. Jack made some sketching gestures over the paper, not quite touching it. He looked out towards the hippy raft across the creek and closed the pad. Another time. He couldn't concentrate. The noises of Clare in the kitchen fighting with the washing made him feel guilty that he wasn't in there helping. But if he went in now he would be cursed for being too late. When they moved down here properly, Clare would have all her usual gadgets with her then, that should help. He went towards the kitchen, if he didn't go there at all there'd be a resentful silence to live through later.

'Shall I make you some coffee?' he asked Clare.

'You can't fill the kettle, I'm using the taps,' she snapped at him.

He tried harder: 'Next time I'll take it all to the launderette in Helston for you. You shouldn't have to do all this.'

'I know that. You could do it, or Miranda could. Even Amy could. It isn't brain surgery, it's easy. But no-one else wants to because it's so bloody tedious.'

'Helston then,' he said.

'No not Helston. Not to the launderette anyway, if we go there at all we collect an automatic washing machine and a dryer too. This is not my idea of a holiday.'

It was on the tip of Jack's tongue to say that they wouldn't be needing any more gadgets, they would be able to move the ones they'd got when they sold the house in London, but yet again this wasn't the moment. When did all this become just my job? Clare wondered. Jeannie at least got paid for doing the ironing.

Later, Clare was at last relaxed on a sunbed under lines of drying sheets, with coffee and a novel. Jack was having his turn at being cross in the kitchen, marinading lamb in sticky yoghourty mixtures that the smaller children probably wouldn't like and wishing he'd thought of buying frozen hamburgers instead. He could see Clare having her time off under the billowing laundry and both of them saw Miranda walking slowly up the path to the Post Office across the creek. Jack went back to the marinade but Clare watched Miranda go into a phone box, and she wondered why. What could Miranda have to say to anyone that couldn't be said on the cottage phone? Someone in London, she thought, serious boyfriend gossip with a friend, secrets. Clare went back to her book and pushed from her mind a suddenly vivid memory of herself in her sixth-form uniform, running furtively from her house to the phone box round the corner with just enough money for a three-minute call to Cambridge. He had been out, and in a moment of resentment and panic Clare had said to his room-mate, 'Just tell him I called, and you can also tell him I'm pregnant.'

Clare's attempt to entertain Andrew that evening was not as successful as she had hoped. Clare had, after the struggles with the laundry, looked forward to an evening of teenage liveliness, relaxed and casual. She liked to feel she was the kind of parent that didn't inhibit a good time for her children. Miranda had always brought her friends round to the house and she had always enjoyed their careless and irreverent chat. She had never wondered if it was unwise of her to join in. With Miranda now so slippery and reclusive, she was missing out and hoped to restore the balance a bit over supper.

But when the Lynch twins arrived they wanted to play on the creek wall, a dangerous balancing game with the tide high beneath them. They would need, Clare realized, constant watching.

'Just make them wear their life jackets,' Liz had instructed as she tottered off in high heels and a minimal slinky yard or two of clinging black jersey for a grown-up dinner with Eliot. Clare had felt instantly frumpish in her bunchy purple Monsoon frock and dirty pink espadrilles still soggy from the leaking washing machine. The twins ignored her and Clare chased after them to the wall.

'You must keep your life jackets on if you want to play by the water,' Clare insisted as kindly as she could manage. How could she join in with the evening if she had to run up and down the garden grabbing hold of the twins all the time? 'If you fall in, you will drown. And that means you won't be around for any fun tomorrow, or the next day, or any other days after that.'

She was kneeling on the grass, at their six-year-old level. Their blank blue eyes looked back at her and the twins said nothing. Clare wasn't used to children like this — Barnes children listened and learned and understood when things were explained patiently to them. These two should be saying 'yes Clare' and going off obediently to play on the swing. Instead they looked at each other and restarted the unzipping of the life jackets. Clare felt a strong urge to tie them firmly to a tree, the wrong reaction for a liberal parent.

'Jess, keep an eye on your brothers please, while I help Jack,' she said, passing the buck.

'Are they really that stupid or is it just a cleverly calculated method of getting their own way, do you think?' she asked Jack as she helped turn over a few kebabs.

'Probably take after Eliot,' Jack said, watching the two little boys fighting to get away from Miranda and Jessica. 'He's an awkward bugger to deal with as well.'

'Oh I don't know,' Clare said, defensively, reaching in through the kitchen window for a bottle of wine on the draining board. 'He's the intelligent one. And Liz is the one who knows how to get what she wants.'

Conversation did not sparkle over supper. Clare, thinking about Miranda's dash for the phone box, kept having to stop herself asking if the bladder problem was getting any better today. Amy and Harriet bickered over the chicken wings, each claiming it wasn't fair, the other one had too many of them.

Andrew, Clare noticed with interest, pushed Milo quite roughly out of the way so that he could sit next to Jessica at the big round garden table. Taking plates into the kitchen later, Clare said to Jack: 'Did you notice the way Andrew was looking at Jess? Obviously has quite a crush.'

'I'm not surprised. If I was his age I probably would have too,' Jack said, opening a second bottle of Chardonnay.

'I wonder if he wants to talk about it?' Clare mused as she scraped plates. 'I don't suppose he would be able to confide in Celia.'

'Shouldn't think so, Clare. Don't forget, boys of that age are horribly embarrassable, I should leave him alone with his thoughts.'

Clare felt she'd been warned off and went to sulk on the terrace with a glass of wine. I should be drinking mineral water, she thought, in case I have to jump in the creek after one of those boys. She went and looked down into the murky water, but the tide was going safely down and she wouldn't have to swim

The teenagers disappeared in a rowing boat, leaving the younger children to play hide and seek in the garden. Clare peered with interest at the families she could see having a lateish supper in uncurtained rooms round the village. It was Friday night, visitors had settled in and the second wave was arriving – the weekend commuters who arrived in dusty suits, taxied from the airport at Newquay for two days of a different kind of executive stress. Wives who had slopped around their holiday homes all week with no make-up and cheese sandwiches in bed with the children, suddenly had to iron a skirt and find a proper pair of shoes to compete with the smart city women their husbands had been sharing their weekdays with.

'I'm glad we don't have to spend our summers like that,' Jack said, sliding on to the bench next to Clare and watching the lawyer across the creek pay off his taxi driver and haul his weekend case into his house. 'There'll be tears by Sunday,' he went on.

Clare giggled. 'That's because they have to fit a whole holiday into two days. Frantic rounds of beach picnics, French cricket with the kids, drinks with the neighbours, people round for supper. Poor sod probably wants to sleep and lie around reading the sort of book Eliot writes.'

'Just shows how lucky we are,' Jack ventured, wondering, perhaps correctly for once if this was the moment he should suggest moving away from London. He took a deep breath. 'You know Clare, I was thinking, what we could do is . . .'

It was really quite a dramatic splash. Jack was still halfway through his sentence as Clare stumbled down the creek steps in the twilight and jumped into the water. It wasn't deep, but the thrashing child had gone right under and was ploughing about helplessly in the mud.

'It's OK, I've got you,' Clare yelled, grabbing Amy by her dungarees.

'It's their fault, they dared me!' roared Amy, howling muddy tears of fright and pointing at the satisfied faces of the Lynch twins peering down over the wall. 'They said I had to walk along the wall with my eyes shut!'

'You should have cheated,' Harriet, older and wiser said scornfully.

Eliot, arriving at that moment from his cool, brief dinner (so brief, due to the lack of stimulating conversation between himself and Liz, that he calculated he had spent money at the rate of £2 per minute), at the Parrot restaurant, thought he had never seen Clare looking so delectable. Her eyes were blazing with relief and anger, her hair was wild and matted and her soaking dress was caught up under the clutched child, showing a tempting lot of squeezable thigh. Liz stood coldly shimmering next to him, still as unruffled as when she had, earlier that evening, finally completed her hour-long stint at the bathroom mirror. Eliot wanted to roll on Clare and get mucky. Clare, for once, didn't even register his presence at all.

'Is it one of mine?' Liz enquired without much interest, and being careful not to rush closely to get a look, because of the mud.

'No,' Clare said, 'It's Amy, apparently because of a silly dare made by your two.'

'Oh well, no harm done,' Liz said complacently, relieved that she would not be the one having to hose down the filthy child. Then she smiled benignly, 'But you know, Clare, I'm really surprised you don't insist they wear life jackets near the water, like mine. They soon get used to it, don't you boys?'

Eight

'I'm a terrible mother. The one thing I'm supposed to
be good at and I'm terrible. Even Liz, who couldn't
take proper care of a hamster, knows I'm useless.'
Clare, straight from a bad night's sleep, was immediately into picking at the evening before.

Jack sighed and rolled over into a vague wakefulness.

'No you're not,' he tried, on auto-pilot, to reassure
her. 'It was just one of those accidents.'

'There's no excuse Jack, she could have drowned.'

'No she couldn't, we were there weren't we?'

Jack hadn't even opened his eyes yet. Clare had
agonized all the same things the night before, going
over a range of safety options from barbed wire fences
to banning the children from the garden. But another
one she came up with was selling the house. Jack could
feel, through the sheet, the vibrations of her twitching
fingers, picking tensely at the frayed edge of the tatty
patchwork quilt. He wanted to wake up enough to get
out of bed and escape to make a reviving cup of tea
before Clare's morose thoughts moved on, inevitably,
to Miranda.

Clare was wide awake, staring critically round the
bedroom for more signs of failure to blame on herself.
Her big calico work-bag was on the window ledge,
over-flowing with neglected knitting yarns, reproaching her for weeks of non-creativity. Threads were
trailing, tangling on the moth-eaten rug. The brass on
the bed was getting tarnished, and the soft butter-
cream paint on the walls was flaking and had an age-
acquired greeny-grey tinge to it.

I don't take care of this house properly, Clare lamented. Not like the other one. In Barnes she would have lovingly mended the rug, polished and sealed the brass, and rag-rolled the walls with a carefully thought-out mix of unexpected colours. At home she had paint in her bedroom that had been expensively distressed – a similar effect here in Cornwall, worn by time and not by decorators, was merely paint that looked bloody miserable.

'I think we should repaint this room,' Clare said to Jack as he tried to sneak out of bed.

'Oh, yes, good idea. What colour do you fancy?' Jack asked, encouragingly. The more of herself Clare put into a house, the more reluctant she would be to part with it. Clare, who unknown to Jack was starting to think of attracting potential purchasers, said, 'Oh, something fairly inoffensive. Cream again, possibly, or pale green.' At home, she and everyone else she knew chose their paints from the limited sludgy range issued by the National Trust, or the Georgian Society, or from Coles. Expensive experts were hired to apply translucent layers of flat oil paint. Many a south west London front door was peeling because of householders' refusal to compromise their good taste and overcome a horror of hard-wearing gloss paint. Clare reached across to the calico bag and started pulling out skeins of silky yarn.

'And the kitchen. I just hate the kitchen, all that grubby stained wood,' she said, rummaging through the wools and silks. 'I'm going to paint those louvred doors. What do you think of these pinks, all together? I can do the louvre bits this pale shade, and the bits round the edge darker, and pick out the drawers in a third shade?' Clare shuffled the dusty pink shades on the bed. Jack was impressed, he made plans to take her out that night, take advantage of her enthusiasm and put his master-plan to her.

'You can get the paints mixed at that place in Truro,'

he said. 'Or do you want to order it from London?'

'No, Truro will do,' Clare said, smiling at the view of the creek, 'I don't want any of that arty farty precious stuff, just plain old easy-peasy vinyl matt.'

In a much-improved mood, she climbed out of bed and wandered downstairs to be a good mother, prepare a nourishing breakfast for her children and ban them from the creek wall.

Andrew was lying in his small bed, thinking about Jessica. In fantasy his hand slowly stroked her thigh, pushing her dress up past the magical line where her tan met pale creamy skin. Andrew watched her pleasured smile, her small teeth biting her bottom lip . . . then he sat up and looked around the room. Where were they going to do all this? It couldn't possibly be here, it was a small boy's room. He still had curtains with aeroplane patterns on them. There was a collection of old teddies and pandas, balsa wood planes hung on dusty string from the ceiling. There was nothing to indicate the personality of a Playboy Man, not even a token poster of Kim Basinger. On the wall instead there was a collection of souvenir youth hostel badges, framed by himself, inexpertly, from a kit, photos of himself fishing with his father, sailing trophies. It was a room full of hobbies. Also it was too light, for Celia believed in putting the highest possible wattage of light bulb into any lamp, in case of eye strain.

Andrew wondered about the chances of buying an orange light bulb in the village store. There was not much hope. And anyway he hadn't even asked her yet. He got out of bed and opened the window, suspecting that the room had the aroma of old sock and airfix glue. Not exactly seductive. And then there were the sheets, he'd have to change them and then Celia would wonder why. It was so complicated. And the bed was so small, so narrow. How could he and Jessica roll around in ecstasy when they were in danger of crashing to the floor? If only he had a huge sheepskin rug.

What about his parents' bed? Andrew rushed into their room to look. It was so . . . parental. He might get instant impotence because of the sheer sacrilege. Jessica would know what to do, Andrew decided. Lost in his fantasy he thought he would let her seduce him on the sofa. She must have done it hundreds of times.

But now it was 8.30 in the morning and he hadn't even asked her. He slopped down to the kitchen in his wool checked dressing gown, which was getting too short. He wished he was on a tropical terrace eating muesli, wearing one of those bright towelling robes advertised in special offers in colour supplements. He wondered if Celia would buy him one. Men wearing them looked virile and exercised, photographed with rowing machines and blonde clean wives.

Andrew was munching cornflakes outside the back door when the phone rang. It was Milo.

'Can I come out with you later for a sail on your Laser?' Milo asked.

Andrew said he could, and knowing that the Gods in charge of teenage boys send opportunities like this only very rarely, he asked Milo if Jessica was there, could he speak to her.

He'd done it. He couldn't believe it. She said she'd love to come. Andrew could not finish the cornflakes. He did excited little dances in the kitchen, chewed his fingers, giggled like a small child. He rushed upstairs and checked he'd got plenty of shampoo, aftershave, deodorant, mouthwash to disinfect away any smell of the human about himself, rushed back downstairs to clear up the kitchen and then raced back upstairs, too aroused to wait thirty-six hours for Jessica. Locking himself in the bathroom, (well you never knew) he

97

very quickly and cheerfully ruined one of his mother's best silk Hermes scarves.

'Why did he ask to speak to me?' Jessica wondered to Milo. 'He could just as easily have asked you, then I wouldn't have had to trail up from the pool.'

'Why? What did he want?'

'He asked me to go round to his cottage tonight. Don't forget his parents are away, he must be planning a party and probably wants me to invite the others. He's a bit shy.'

'Good,' said Milo, 'I'll get some drinks from the Mariners. What time does he want us?'

'He said about eight. He probably thought you'd forget if he asked you. His sort of family usually do expect women to do the organizing. How many shall we invite?'

'Oh everyone we can think of, there's plenty of room and we can overflow into the garden.'

'Do you think Celia and Archie know about it? It doesn't seem very likely somehow,' Jessica said.

'He must be breaking the parental bonds at last. We must make sure he has a good time.'

Milo strolled idly into the village towards the boatyard to invite everyone he could find to the party that Andrew didn't know he was having. He ambled along slowly, calculating in his head how much beer he would need to order from the Mariners and wondering how many bar staff there were as Jessica had told him to invite them all. She had said, 'There's nothing worse than a party with not enough people, it's even more embarrassing than not enough drink.'

Milo found Steve sitting on the harbour steps waiting for hire-boat customers and sketching the gulls as they dive-bombed the beach, scavenging after crisps and bits of mouldy sandwich. The summer boatyard workers had lost their city pallor and Milo noticed a tanned boy with white-blond hair pulling a dinghy into its place on the pontoon, reminding him of Oliver at school. Milo was staring absent-mindedly, reminiscing fondly, and the boy noticed, smiling at him and coming towards him up the steps.

Milo started gabbling nervously to Steve about boats, anxious that the boy had read his thoughts, but instead as he approached he just said, 'Hello, I met your sister on the beach just now and she invited me to a party.' The boy was grinning cheerfully. 'Couldn't believe my luck, sort of thing you dream about! Is she with anyone?'

'Well she's with us, with the family,' Milo said, not understanding.

'No, I mean is she going out with anyone around here, you know?'

'Er, no, I don't think so,' Milo said, rather disappointed that a potential object of his own affection should be interested only in his little sister.

'Well maybe I'll get lucky then,' the boy said, with a conspiratorial smile.

'Yes, who knows?' Milo said, making an effort, joining in but thinking, God, is this Men's Talk? About his sister? He thought briefly of all those things he didn't want to do to girls, the things that other boys did want to do. Girls were sticky, with damp, hidden unknown places. He didn't want to be in them. He didn't want to think of anyone being in Jessica's either.

Andrew searched through the dusty cupboard under the stairs, peering into the dark for his father's special occasion wine rack, full of investment bottles, collectors' items. He groped past the sailing equipment, the boots and life jackets and started pulling out bottles, looking for one with an impressive label. He thought he'd better take two, just to be certain to get Jessica and himself nicely relaxed. One bottle might seem rather mean, and he didn't want the embarrassment of having to rootle around in this cupboard with Jessica watching from the sofa. He put a couple of the priceless bottles into the fridge to chill and wondered how he would ever be able to afford to replace them. He knew how much they were worth because his father was always reading Hugh Johnson's wine guide out loud over dinner, and Andrew, from his fourteenth birthday had to sample the wines with due respect and reverence. Stealing wine, Andrew thought, was probably the greatest sin he could commit in this family, probably worse than fornicating in the parental bed.

Clare, walking in through the open kitchen door, caught sight of the bottles before Andrew got the fridge door shut and grinned at him:

'Having a party?' she said in a matey sort of way, pointing to the fridge.

Andrew leaned on the fridge door, protectively and felt a blush seeping through his body. He shifted his feet about nervously.

'Er, just someone might be sort of coming round later.'

'Oh good,' Clare said breezily. 'I was going to invite you round to supper again, but if you've got other plans...'

She waited, smiled and leaned comfortably against one of Celia's polished oak dining chairs, ready to be told what Andrew was up to. But Andrew didn't know this game, because he hadn't played it before. What was supposed to happen was that he should make Clare a cup of coffee, and while occupied with cups and milk and sugar and spoons, he should be saying things like, 'Well the thing is, all I can make is mackerel paté and I think it might be a bit iffy for the breath, so what else can I do? And do you think she'll mind frozen pizza?' That had been the sort of thing Miranda and her friends, gathered cheerily round the kitchen table in London used to ask her. She felt a sudden nostalgia for Miranda's pre-recluse days. All that advice and reassurance she had been needed for, the confidence she had always tried to inspire that she would give fair comment without damning judgement. She'd always tried hard to be on their side. How carefully she'd dealt with Miranda and her friends and their anxious questions, like 'My mum thinks thigh boots are really tarty, but don't you think they look OK if you've got the legs?'

How tactfully she'd been able to point out that thigh boots severely and boringly limited the range of clothes you could wear with them, instead of telling the whole truth which was that anyone of 5' 2" with legs like a sparrow would look horribly as if they were trying on their dad's fishing waders.

'Oh well, I'll leave you to it,' Clare said to the uncommunicative Andrew. 'But if you need any help with food or anything, just pop round.'

Jack had been very lucky, getting tickets for the Minack theatre that night without having to go and queue for them.

He'd been in the post office that morning collecting his *Independent* when he'd heard one of the elderly bungalow-dwellers from up the hill whispering loudly to Jeannie that he couldn't face the thought of sitting through three hours of Shakespeare on cold stone, because of his Little Problem. Not as fascinated as Clare would have been to find out whether the Problem was piles or prostate, Jack had nevertheless butted in shamelessly and offered to buy the tickets.

The play was *The Tempest*. Clare, padding around her bedroom and looking for something suitable to wear, was still, that evening, touched at how hesitant Jack had been about telling her which play it was. It was almost as if, she thought, he imagined she wouldn't want to be reminded of that time, studying the play for A-level, when she had first been pregnant with Miranda.

101

'If I hadn't loved the play so much, I wouldn't have called her Miranda!' she said to him, laughing. 'Of course I don't mind seeing it. You rarely saw the plays back in those days, you just read them, it'll be lovely.'

It would soon be time. Andrew stood in front of the bathroom mirror looking for new spots and wondering whether to risk aftershave. His father had left some in the bathroom cupboard, but when Andrew sniffed at it he was reminded of golf clubs and Sunday lunch, rather than the necessary macho sport and passion.

That afternoon he had had a ritual disposing of the stolen pair of knickers. They no longer held any tantalizing aroma of what he imagined was musky woman, but smelt of musty dried semen and grubby-handed boy. Appalled almost to impotence at the idea of them being in the house at the same time as Jessica and therefore with the potential for being found, he had kissed them goodbye, wrapped them reverentially in a freezer bag and hidden them deep in the dustbin under the Sunday papers.

He went downstairs and got some candles out of the kitchen drawer. This, he had decided was the way to solve the lighting problem, and he had taken four empty wine bottles from the bins behind the Parrot restaurant that afternoon, praying that no-one would see him. The candles were not impressive, just the dumpy household type of white ones that everyone in the village kept for power cuts. There should have been slender pink ones in silver holders, scented if possible. Another problem was when to light them. Before Jessica arrived? It would still be light. Perhaps later as it grew dark he could lean casually across her and light them in mid-sentence as if he did it every night. A Dunhill lighter would be more suitably colour-supplement, but he'd have to make do with a box of Swan Vestas from the barbecue kit under the sink. Andrew was just forcing the last candle into its bottle when Milo arrived.

'I thought I'd come early,' he said, 'and deliver this lot for you.'

Milo was piling six-packs of beer and wine-boxes on to the kitchen table. 'Do you think there's enough?' he said. 'I asked everyone to bring a bottle too.'

'Enough?' said Andrew, perplexed for a moment, but then the tangled rope of confusion inside his brain began to straighten into a realization that, well, surely he couldn't have expected to be that lucky after all. He never was.

'For the party,' Milo was saying. 'Oh and I wouldn't light candles if I were you, they're bound to get knocked over. I don't suppose Celia would thank you for burning the house down.'

Taking over, Milo collected the candles and wine bottles and disposed of them in the kitchen. Andrew was still standing in the doorway slowly absorbing the fact that he was about to have a party that his parents would never forgive him for, that the house was to be taken over and probably destroyed by a large number of people that he didn't really know, and that he was, saddest of all, not to have Jessica to himself for even an hour, not even to talk to. Also he must move all evidence of his experimental activities before a curious and drunken guest opened the box in his wardrobe and said 'Hey everybody, look what I've found!'

Milo was rearranging furniture with the confidence of one who had done it many times before, saying, 'I didn't know how many people you'd invited, so we asked the boatyard lot and the people from the Mariners and Jessica saw most of the sailing club crowd this morning, so I suppose we've asked about sixty. What about you?'

Sixty! The house, the damage, his parents! But Andrew knew that he'd rather the house be burned to cinders than admit to Milo that there'd been a mistake.

103

He tried to anticipate the social kudos of having had a memorable party to see if the thought could begin to compensate for the disappointment of not having had Jessica. Or even the opportunity to have had Jessica.

'What about music?' Milo was asking.

Andrew had thought quite a lot about music for his evening of lust with Jessica, and had chosen a few tapes of Chopin and Debussy. He said that he thought he'd better leave it to Milo and added: 'I hope it will be warm enough for people to be in the garden. I mean, they will be careful, won't they?'

Miranda didn't feel like going to a party. She just felt sick. She never liked getting ready to go, or the anticipation, even when she'd been little and there'd been a going-home bag full of sweets and plastic toys to look forward to and sticky cake wrapped in a paper napkin. Her mother had always insisted, through tears and tantrums, saying 'You'll enjoy it when you get there, you'll have a lovely time.' If this hadn't worked, Clare would use her second weapon, guilt, saying 'You've said you'll go and you can't let people down, they'll be so disappointed.' So Miranda would go and would bring home her prizes for musical bumps and pass the parcel and Clare would always say, irritatingly, 'You see, I told you you'd enjoy it'. Now that Miranda was old enough to choose to stay at home, she always chose to go out, to escape Clare's anxious enquiries about why she didn't want to go, 'Don't you feel well? Is there someone you'd rather not see?' An invitation to confide. She too much wanted to be Miranda's friend.

Miranda put on a floral crepe dress that had seen its best days before the Second World War. An afternoon dress, her grandmother had called it, and Miranda had imagined it on a slim young married lady who liked to tend her roses and embroider duchesse sets for her dressing table from transfer patterns in *Woman's Weekly*.

Miranda smudged kohl pencil under her eyes and decided that Andrew's party couldn't possibly be as bad as the usual ones at home. This wasn't the kind of place, or was it?, where public-school boys talked about nothing but their driving lessons and how they'd persuaded their fathers to buy old convertible VWs at great expense because they couldn't bear to be seen out driving the family Mercedes Estate. Miranda recalled boys shoving their tongues inexpertly down her throat and losing their way in her clothes. Clare, who thought things must have changed since 1970's feminism, had no idea that although the boys her daughter saw knew that girls now studied engineering and technology, they still rated them one to ten for sexual favours and sniggered about the size of their breasts.

'So, what is Andrew having, a dinner party?' Clare said, meeting Miranda outside the bathroom door. She made immediate plans to go round to Andrew first thing in the morning, to help him clear up and find out what had happened.

'Dunno,' Miranda mumbled. 'I don't much want to go.'

'Well you can stay in and babysit for Harriet and Amy if you like,' Clare said. 'I hated having to ask Liz if she would have them.'

Miranda giggled. 'No thanks! Anything but that!'

'Anyway, it would be rude to cancel now,' Clare conceded, 'He's probably got the numbers worked out. Are you going by yourself?' she couldn't resist asking. There was always an outside chance that Miranda, in a good mood, might loosen up and mention Steve.

'Of course I am! It's only next door!' Miranda shouted mockingly as she ran down the stairs.

You know quite well that's not what I meant, Clare thought despairingly as she went to find her gold scarf to tie up her hair.

*   *   *

The first breakage was a small Staffordshire dog, one of a pair, swished to the floor by Beryl's sleeve as she waved a bottle of sweet sherry at Andrew and shouted 'This is all I could steal, hope it's all right.' Andrew smiled bravely and poured his third glass of the wine he had been hoping to share with Jessica. He couldn't blame Jessica, she'd obviously misunderstood his phone call. She probably wouldn't have come anyway, he thought mournfully, not for an evening alone with him. He was trying not to feel sorry for himself and was determined at least to get drunk on the good stuff, not the plonk-in-a-box. So he finished the first bottle and decided he had better drink his father's Chivas Regal before the uncivilized louts from the boatyard could get their unappreciative hands on it. He felt a numb kind of regret when Jessica arrived, tanned and vibrant in black and orange, so bright it hurt his eyes to look at her. She seemed to be all the time in front of him but beyond reach, chatting to him brightly like a cousin, someone too familiar for the pretence of flirtation.

She was talking to the boy from the boatyard, her head too close to his for Andrew's peace of mind. Her hair was swishing across Paul's face, clean hair, for touching. They laughed a lot, Andrew wished he could be that amusing, just once.

He had got drunk too quickly to have a good time. He cruised the rooms, unfamiliar as they were now full of strangers. He spoke occasionally to people, but mostly they had no idea who he was and he felt like a gatecrasher in his own home. He decided to go and sit quietly in his room to recover a little, but when he opened the door there was a scuffling from the direction of the bed and he was told rudely to go away and put the light out. So at least someone hadn't been put off by the narrowness of the bed. There seemed to be quite a lot of people in his parents' room too. They didn't have the same scruples that he did about the parental shrine, but then the bed didn't belong to their parents. It looked as if he was going to have to change the sheets after all. How long, he wondered, did the local laundry take, and how much did it cost?

Andrew wandered into the garden where the music seemed to be just as loud as in the house and where groups of people were abandoning drink cans among the carnations, discarding cigarette ends all over Archie's immaculate lawn and generally trampling about in an unconcerned way. Andrew wished they'd all go.

Someone, at the window above him shouted, 'Hey look at this!' and Andrew froze. Oh God, he thought, someone's unearthed the secret box. He lolled against the cherry tree, prepared to throw himself into the creek if a hand appeared at that window, encased in a string glove. Instead a balsa wood aeroplane whizzed down from the window and landed in splinters at the foot of the tree.

Andrew couldn't see too well by now, so full was he of Scotch and wine, but across the creek there were dark silhouettes against lighted windows, the village being kept awake, watching. People started to say to Andrew, 'Are you OK?' as he lurched round, still clutching the Chivas Regal bottle, but he didn't recall they'd said much else to him all evening. By this time tomorrow, he thought, it will all be normal again. He used to think that way about dentists. It can't last for ever, he'd think on the way to a filling, two hours from now I'll be on my way home again.

Jessica was coming over to him, too late to raise either hopes or excitement. She was very close, the orange and black shimmered in front of him, in and out of focus. Andrew lurched towards the rose bed and was suddenly and thoroughly sick over a fragrant floribunda called Pink Parfait. Last year it had won prizes for Archie.

Jessica fetched Milo and Miranda who guided Andrew carefully up the stairs, past the debris, past couples kissing, boys playing football with Celia's embroidered cushions, and placed him on his rumpled bed. Andrew accepted their kindness like an over-tired toddler who has had a hard day out with too much ice-cream.

As Milo put out the light Andrew was aware of the disgusting taste of his own mouth, and suddenly wished his mother was there, just to remind him to clean his teeth.

The play ended. The open-air theatre, carved in rock on the cliff edge and lit by stars, was in soft warm darkness. Clare, walking with the rest of the audience up the steps to the car park, could hear the sea gently washing the rocks far below.

'Look at that,' Jack said, pointing upwards. 'You can see the milky way, it's so clear.'

'Do you know,' Clare said, following his gaze, 'I don't think I've ever seen stars like that in London. Too much pollution I suppose.'

'Too little time, more likely. We just don't have chance to look, there. We have no real connection with nature,' Jack said, 'The closest we get is the odd fox on the common and making sure we keep the children away from all the flashers in the park. It's a better pace of life here.' Jack put his arm around Clare and led her through the crowd to the Volvo.

'We should do this sort of thing more often,' Clare said, climbing into the car. 'I did enjoy it so much.'

'What, in spite of Ariel looking just like Rod Stewart?' Jack asked, packing their blanket, cushion and flask into the back seat.

'Even in spite of Prospero looking exactly like a gay biker! All that studded leather!' Clare laughed.

As the trail of cars snaked slowly along the road towards Penzance, Clare thought about the last time she had seen *The Tempest*. The long coach trip with the sixth-form across London, when each mile had made her feel iller and she had pretended it was travel sickness. Only a few weeks pregnant, she had sat in the stuffy theatre, full of noisy uninterested school parties, quite sure already that her school skirt was tighter than the week before. She remembered having to give a girl called Elaine a bar of chocolate to swap places with her so that she could sit at the end of a row, for easy escape if she felt sick. It was while watching the play that she'd decided to call the baby Miranda if it was a girl, and therefore realized at the same time that she'd made, unconsciously, the decision not to choose either abortion or adoption.

The car sped through Penzance. In London, Clare was thinking, after a theatre visit, they would by now be either waving fruitlessly at packed taxis or pretending to ignore the beggars and junkies at Piccadilly Circus tube station. She would be tripping along in spike-heeled shoes and a too-thin dress and worrying about being late for the babysitter. How much cosier it was to go out to a play like this, dressed snugly in old jeans and thick socks and taking a blanket to wrap up in, a bag of sandwiches and a flask of tea.

'You know, nights like this remind me how dreadful it will be going back to the Poly. The contrast, I mean,' ventured Jack, bravely.

'Nobody likes going back to routines, not after all this freedom,' Clare sympathized. 'I'm just glad you aren't one of those poor men who only gets a couple of weeks a year for a break. Imagine, no time at all for the luxury of forgetting you actually *had* those routines.'

'Well actually, I've been thinking,' Jack said hesitantly. 'I've been thinking quite deeply in fact . . .' he added to show he was absolutely serious and needed to be listened to.

'I think, in fact I've decided, there isn't any real reason why I have to go back at all.'

Clare sat silently for a moment, trying to work out what he was really getting at.

'Isn't any reason? What about the thousands a year they pay you? Isn't that a reason?'

'We'll manage,' Jack said, rather limply.

'Are you trying to tell me that they haven't renewed your contract?' Clare challenged him. 'Have you been keeping it from me all this time like I was some feeble little woman who must be protected from reality?'

Jack increased his speed in an attempt to make himself feel more powerful.

'No, it's not that. They'll renew it if I want them to. I just don't want them to, that's all,' he said simply.

'That's all? What do you mean "that's all"? What will we live on?' Clare asked, incredulously. 'I do my best but I don't exactly earn a fortune knitting posh sweaters.'

'I'll paint,' Jack said, as if that would solve everything.

'Paint? You haven't painted in years. We even had a girl in to stencil the kitchen. All your oil paints dried out and went in the dustbin.'

'I'll get new ones. Anyway I rather fancy water colours.'

Clare felt bomb-shelled. She tried doing a few quick sums in her head: electricity bills; gas; water; two lots of council tax; the car and all its expenses. Jack earned some interest on inherited money, enough to be a comfortable supplement to their income, but not enough to replace it. The money from selling Clare's dead mother's flat a few years ago had gone on renovating the Barnes bathrooms and building a conservatory.

She supposed there must be self-employed artists ekeing out a living of some sort in south west London, but not, she thought, the kind of living she and Jack were used to.

Clare was just trying to work out how much they

were likely to get from selling the Cornish cottage (the only way to survival, she thought), when the car turned down the lane into the village, where there was an atmosphere of unusual midnight liveliness.

'What on earth is going on?' Jack said, parking the Volvo. People were on the street, waving bottles as if it was carnival time. Every house in the village was lit, people were in their gardens, staring across the creek towards Clare and Jack. Clare's insides sank with foreboding. The thud, thud of music could be felt inside the car even before she opened the door. Celia and Archie's house, when she dared to look, was alive at every window and their garden swarmed with shrieking strangers.

'Oh God,' Clare groaned, 'I just know that somehow this is all going to be my fault.'

Nine

'I'll have to go round and help Andrew clear up the mess.' Clare said, sliding out of bed. 'There's bound to BE a mess, I hardly dare look.'

She went over to the window and lifted a corner of the curtain carefully, unwilling to be confronted by Archie's bottle-strewn garden.

Across the river, on the hillside an elderly man was standing on his lawn, arms folded aggressively, staring across to Archie and Celia's house. He looked, Clare thought, as if he'd been there all night, waiting for someone to emerge so he could get his accusations about sleeplessness and mayhem in before anyone else did. Clare could also see Jeannie down below, crossing the footbridge on her way up to the Lynchs' house. As Clare watched, Jeannie stopped and turned to look at Archie's cottage. I bet she'd love to come and help clean it up, Clare thought, then she could tell all those in the village who don't already know, just what a disaster area it is. Clare pulled on last night's clothes and went along to Miranda's room to start the inquisition.

'Did you know he was having a party?' she demanded of Miranda's still sleeping body.

Miranda stirred lazily and made an attempt to open her eyes.

'Miranda, wake up.' Clare prodded her impatiently. 'You said he was having a few people in. I thought that meant a dinner party or something.'

'Oh Mum, it's only people your age who have dinner parties. We go out for pasta or a burger. Except here

112

you have to get someone to drive you a million miles for that.' Miranda stretched languidly and sighed. 'I didn't know there'd be that many people. I don't think Andrew did either.'

Clare went down to the kitchen and Miranda, wearing one of Jack's old tee-shirts as a nightdress, padded down the stairs after her.

'Are you going to help clear up?' Miranda asked, watching Clare delving under the sink for a bucket and a pack of J-cloths.

'Yes, and you can come and help too.'

'Er sorry, I promised to take her and Jessica into Truro this morning,' Jack said, arriving in the kitchen behind Miranda.

'And it was you who said you'd look after Andrew . . .' Miranda added, ducking round Jack before the packet of J-cloths that Clare threw could hit her.

Clare groaned quietly to herself and went back to searching under the sink. A pair of rubber gloves, she thought, because there might be all sorts of disgusting things to be handled. Used condoms, sick to be mopped up. If she went there expecting the worst, perhaps it wouldn't really be that bad.

Clare put all her cleaning equipment outside the door and then came back in to make some tea. I'll give him an hour or two to make a start on it himself, she thought. It was, after all, more Andrew's fault than hers. Why, she thought, shoving bread into the be-crumbed toaster, should I take this on entirely myself, just because I'm the nearest female of the right sort of age and I happen to be a parent?

That morning Andrew tasted bad, smelt bad and felt dreadful. He lay in bed flinching away from the bright sunlight and thought childishly, it's not my fault. At the same time he knew that this was no compensation, that of course he would get the blame, and that worst of all he would have to do the clearing up. Most of all

113

though he blamed Clare and Liz and Eliot. They were, after all, Parents. And even though they weren't his they should have been around to protect him from this sort of thing. The noise must have been tremendous, way beyond the level at which Archie and Celia would, in Surrey, have called the police. This was what happened when you got liberal parents in charge: no control, no sense of responsibility. Archie's old school had done a good job on Andrew. Certain moral standards were being maintained by him at any rate, if not in the rest of this slack world. Andrew would never have gone to the home of a total stranger and stubbed out cigarettes on the floor, spilled beer all over the sofa or got into an unfamiliar bed with a girl he'd just met. Well maybe he'd do that, oh God just give him the chance. And who was it, his conscience reminded him, who was sick on the rose bed, and who drank all that Chivas Regal? Andrew wished he had the amnesia of the practised drunk. He wished and wished the whole thing had never happened. He never wanted to see Jessica again. He felt dreadful, still nauseous and his throat was sore too, like when he was about to get the flu. Perhaps he could just stay in his sordid bed for a few days and then his mother would feel sorry for him. But she'd be home in twenty-four hours and he hadn't even inspected the damage in the cold revealing light of day. He bathed and tooth-brushed away the worst of the remaining taste of alcohol and went downstairs carefully, as if afraid he was about to see the remains of a massacre, not just the typical leftovers of a party. One brief glance round told him that there was not the slightest chance that he was going to get away with this. He would have to spend forever clearing up the mess. Thank goodness Celia didn't have a cleaning lady who would come and report the damage around the village. There were probably things missing and broken, it was hard to tell until some sort of order was restored. Celia knew every tiny ornament in the cottage. Although she seemed a briskly practical woman she was also a great sentimentalist and every item she collected reminded her of some happy time or other. The smell was the worst thing. Almost gagging in the stale fumes, Andrew cleared a way through the discarded cans and glasses to the kitchen. He pulled out a bin liner from under the sink and started randomly collecting cigarette ends, bottles and cans from the table and floor. Must have been the boatyard lot, thought Andrew snobbishly, decent people wouldn't make such a mess. And why was the fridge empty? And the bread bin? Even if he'd felt like breakfast they'd left him nothing to eat. He filled the plastic bag quickly and looked around. He'd made very little impact. Every surface he looked at seemed to have something sticky and spilled. And why was he having to do all this by himself? Couldn't some of the girls come and give him a hand? But given the hypothetical choice between clearing up everything himself and having Jessica turn up to help he decided he'd rather be alone, even if he hoovered way beyond midnight. How could he ever have been so stupid? How could he ever have imagined that she would have so eagerly accepted an invitation to do rude things on his sofa with him? It really was, after all, entirely his own fault.

Up the hill at the Lynch household, Liz was cowering in the kitchen from the sounds of Eliot swearing at his word processor. She didn't see why Eliot should bother to work at all. He certainly didn't need to, especially not to the point of getting up before daylight and crashing round the bedroom looking for something to wear. If he retired, she thought, they could stop going to Cornwall summer after summer, because there would be no need for Eliot to take a rural break from all those so-called research trips he was always taking to exotic places during the rest of the year.

Exotic places could then be for holidays. When Eliot got to Cornwall, all he did was go sailing, or get in the way, or get drunk, or complain that he couldn't work, they all made too much noise.

Over breakfast, Liz took out her frustrated rage on Jessica and Milo:

'I hope you're going round to help Andrew clear up after his party,' she said to the two of them. 'You must have been having a good time, you could be heard all over the village and probably right across the Lizard. It was just like being back in London.' Liz wanted to go to a party too, she wanted to dress up in a sleek little Dolce y Gabbana number without fear of it being attacked by river mud or beach sand.

'Wasn't bad, actually,' said Jessica, buttering toast. She smiled at Milo. 'I don't think Andrew had such a good time though.'

'You could say he wasn't too well when we left,' Milo explained to Liz, 'I don't think he's used to our kind of parties.'

'Do you think Celia and Archie knew?' Liz asked.

'Hardly. Even Andrew seemed a little unprepared to say the least. You could say he got a bit tired and emotional.'

They're talking to me, Liz thought, like a friend, a family member, not a wicked stepmother.

'Anyone nice there?' she asked Jessica, risking rebuff.

'Very nice,' Jessica grinned. 'Called Paul, he's working at the boatyard for the summer and he's doing Peace Studies at Bradford.'

'I don't think Andrew liked that either,' Milo said, teasing her. 'He was moping around all night after you Jess.'

'You can't be serious, that was just the baby-bird look men get when they're drunk. Not that he's yet what I'd call a man. God, I like him but he's a bit of a double-bagger. And he's too young. Milo, you've put me off my breakfast.' But she was laughing too.

'What on earth is a "double-bagger"?' Liz asked.

Jessica grinned at her. 'It's when you have to put a paper bag over your own head in case the one over his head breaks while you're, you know, doing it.'

They were all still laughing when Eliot came in, wanting breakfast. They were having fun and he wasn't. His mood deepened.

'So you are coming with me to clear up his house?' Milo said to Jessica.

'Not a chance,' she said, sliding out of the kitchen door, 'I'm off to Truro with Miranda and I'll have to go now or they'll have left without me. See you later, and Milo, please send Andrew my regards, but not, I'm afraid, my love.'

The weather was cloudy, threatening much-needed rain. A good day for a hangover, Milo thought, thinking not of himself but of Andrew as he sauntered down the lane carrying a roll of extra-large dustbin liners and a powerful vacuum cleaner.

'Well it could be a lot worse,' he said cheerfully to Andrew as he strolled into the cottage and surveyed the damage. Worse? thought Andrew. What kind of social life did they have back in Hampstead?

'Not much worse,' he said to Milo. 'The parents are home tomorrow and I'm in for a lot of trouble.'

Milo suspected that Archie would be more angry about Trust being Abused than about any amount of breakage and felt it would not pay to continue the conversation on this subject.

'It won't take long,' he said encouragingly, 'This thing will sweep up anything.'

Andrew was bound to be feeling morose, Milo thought, his head must hurt like hell. He looked droopy, wilting like Archie's poor roses.

'Why don't we just do the worst of it for now and then have some coffee? You should have some aspirins too.'

'Is Jessica coming too?' Andrew found the courage to ask.

'Er no,' Milo turned away to hide a smile. He couldn't help thinking of the term 'double-bagger'. He fiddled with the plug of the cleaner. 'She had to go to Truro with Miranda, long-standing arrangement or something.'

Well this is funny, two men cleaning a house, Andrew thought. He wasn't used to this kind of arrangement in Surrey. There were always the women. When Celia and Archie had a party ('people in for drinks') their Mrs Fletcher came in to do the handing round of sherry, and plates of canapes and she wore a neat frock and sparkly earrings for the occasion. In the morning she'd be back again in her familiar apron to do the cleaning up. Not that it was ever on this scale, just a little accidental ash, and the odd ring left by a careless glass, someone forgetting to use one of the little mats. Celia wouldn't call them coasters.

'Oh look,' Milo said, looking through the kitchen door as Clare walked up the path, 'the cavalry's arrived.'

''Bout time,' Andrew muttered, holding his head.

Clare, clanking her bucket of cleaning stuff, stopped dead in the doorway.

'What a dreadful smell!' she said, wrinkling her nose. 'The entire village must have come in here and smoked a pack of Silk Cut each! We'll have to take the curtains down and hang them outside on the washing line. And hope it doesn't rain. Fresh air will blow away the smell.'

Clare glared at Andrew who didn't appear to be able to move. He looked terrible, pasty and baggy-eyed. His shoulders drooped and his hair looked matted. Clare squashed a surge of sympathy and handed him a packet of Flash and the bucket.

'Go on,' she said, 'you can make a start upstairs on the bathroom. I don't have to go up and look, I can imagine what it's like.' Andrew slouched out of the room and trailed dejectedly up the stairs.

'I'll get the curtains down shall I?' Milo said softly. 'Don't be too hard on him,' he said, pushing his floppy blond hair out of his eyes and smiling at her. 'It wasn't entirely his fault. In fact it was probably entirely mine.' Milo told her the truth with disarming honesty. His lazy blue eyes looked deep into Clare's and she could see more than a trace of Eliot's wicked Irish charm. If I were twenty years younger, she caught herself thinking.

Soon, every curtain and rug in the house was hanging from the washing line and from branches of the cherry tree, like prayer mats for all the village to gaze at and comment on. Clare, scrubbing the kitchen and polishing tables, was past caring what anyone, except Celia and Archie, thought. Milo wielded his vacuum cleaner with casual power, whistling cheerfully as he played with its various attachments, seeming to find a scientific satisfaction in discovering the right tool for getting cigarette ends out from down the sides of the sofa.

Clare scrubbed, polished, wiped and scoured. Andrew, even paler after cleaning the bathroom, trailed round the house and garden filling bin liners with empties and wishing they wouldn't clang so loudly. In case of stains, Andrew didn't dare look at Clare as together they stripped the beds and shoved sheets into plastic bags.

Clare, feeling that she'd done more than her best, took the sheets with her and drove off to Helston to the launderette. I'm in for a tedious evening of ironing, she thought, but at least it would give her chance, at last, to think over what she and Jack would do with the rest of their lives.

Milo, feeling sorry for Andrew's hangover, volunteered to make the coffee while Andrew hosed down the garden. He'd hoped it would rain in the night, good and heavy rain to eradicate any sign of where he'd disgraced himself in the rosebed. It hadn't and Andrew avoided getting too near the area by hosing with his fingers over the end of the pipe to increase the pressure and drive away the disgusting evidence over the end of the lawn into the creek.

They sat on the bench with their coffee. Andrew's courage advanced as his headache receded. 'Is Jessica going out with anyone?' Andrew asked.

'Funny, you're the second person to ask me that. Paul from the boatyard asked me the same thing two days ago, or maybe it was yesterday. Recently anyway, why do you ask?'

'Just wondered. She always seems to be with you, or girls down from London, or Miranda. She looks like, you know, like she'd be quite sort of interested in men.'

'Do you mean she dresses like a slag?' Milo said, laughing at Andrew and watching him getting confused. Andrew blushed helplessly, because of course that was exactly what he had meant.

'No of course not,' he lied. 'Anyway, does she like Paul?'

'Don't know. We don't talk about that sort of thing much. We prefer windsurfing.' Milo didn't want another discussion about his best friend, his little sister. 'Paul's doing Peace Studies at university,' Milo said mischievously, knowing that would get old Andrew going. His politics were as predictable as his father's.

'Peace Studies! Is he a communist?'

'Is anyone these days? Anyway surely you don't have to be a communist to study peace? Does that mean that if you're right-wing you can only study war?'

'Suppose not. I've never really thought about it.'

Andrew's head wasn't yet straight enough for all this. There was an awful lot he'd never really thought about. Perhaps he should take up more sport. Apart from sailing, which everyone here could do as far as Andrew could see, there was really only swimming or windsurfing or water-skiing. All those had far too much potential for making a fool of oneself. What he needed was a few head-clearing hours out on his Laser, practising for the regatta, then he'd show them.

On the road halfway to Truro Miranda had to get out of the car to be sick.

Jack, driving, said 'You haven't been car-sick since you were about three and we had a bouncy old Ford Anglia.'

'Hangover I expect, or something I ate,' Miranda said.

'Ate when? You didn't have any breakfast.'

'Oh well that's it then, I should have.'

Well he wasn't going to win this one. Jack didn't care. He felt quite happy. For the past couple of days he'd been staring into the hydrangeas still trying to capture the point at which they changed colour from pink to blue, purple to lilac. If they needed water colours he'd just have to go to the art shop and buy some. It was years since he'd bought any, he remembered all the hours he used to spend hanging around in Cornelissens, savouring the smells of oils, the jars of pigments. He'd just read a popular philosophy book and had learnt rather late in life that saying 'I can' is as much a matter of choice and as easy to say as 'I can't'. 'I can't' was just a matter of laziness and fear of failing. Boy Scout stuff, Jack thought, but true nonetheless. He intended to find the book and give it to Clare before he rang up the estate agents and sent them round to value the house in London.

Meanwhile there were art supplies to buy. He loved that feel of new sable brushes, the soft powdery colours of the pastels, the virgin wood of the palettes. He often thought he could spend his days working in such a shop, what an indulgence. Customers would

121

wonder if he'd been just a little famous in his time. But it still was his time, he thought, he still had some painting to do. And there never would be any fame without any painting.

Jessica and Miranda wandered round the shops together. Jessica, for clothes, was missing Sloane Street and the Fulham Road. Miranda missed jumble sales.

'You can buy good beach stuff here, but not much else,' Jessica said. 'Let's get some shoes, or some tee-shirts at least.'

Miranda was feeling queasy again but let Jessica drag her into a loud shop full of lurid lime and lemon-coloured clothes. They chose a random pile and giggled in the communal changing room over the various permutations.

'Your tits have grown Miranda, are you on the pill?' Jessica said.

'No, it must be puberty at last or something,' Miranda said. 'Perhaps I'm going to be a big girl after all.'

'Not you, you're as slim as a reed. Kate Moss eat your heart out! I'm going to be huge, I wonder if Paul likes big girls?' Jessica turned sideways and eyed her reflection. 'These clothes are disgusting. Let's go and get some lunch,' she said peeling off the layers.

In the wine bar they both chose salads, drank wine and got giggly.

'Have you ever done anything truly awful?' Jessica said, 'that you just couldn't tell anyone?'

How did she know, Miranda thought.

'Well yes, have you?'

'Well not really, but I think I might be going to. Let's have another drink first.'

Miranda got the drinks and quietly flipped a coin from the change. Heads tell Jess, tails don't. Heads.

'Go on then,' said Miranda, 'tell me.'

'Well it concerns Andrew's party in a way. I happen to know that he didn't intend to have one. He rang me up and invited me round to the house for the evening and I invited everyone else.'

'Did he really mean only you to come? Didn't you realize?'

'Not till I'd asked everyone, and seen how surprised he looked about the whole thing. I mean it never occurred to me that he'd want to see me alone. Milo says he's lusting after me.'

Miranda giggled and choked over her wine. 'Wow lucky you, just think what you missed.'

'I'm so horrible, that party was all my fault and I sent Milo round to clear up the mess.'

'I shouldn't worry about that,' Miranda said, 'I don't suppose Andrew will want to see you for a while anyway.'

They were both giggling and the barman watched, thinking that they looked quite seriously under-age. They were too pretty to throw out, and besides the other conversations were between rather boring business people, his more usual lunch-time trade.

'Oh poor Andrew. You'll have to make it up to him you know.'

'I know, that's what Milo said. He had a rather terrible idea last night after we got home. I hardly dare tell you though, promise you won't be shocked?'

'No of course I won't be.'

'Well Milo thinks I should go into one of those passport photo booths and take my clothes off and then send the photos to Andrew. I'd have to do it so he couldn't see my face, and it would have to be all anonymous. A sort of strip photo of a strip-tease.'

'God Jess, would you really dare?'

The barman couldn't resist a request for more drinks.

'Milo did a dreadful thing once,' Jessica was saying as the barman brought wine on a tray.

'There was this boy who'd asked me out to dinner at a really smart fish restaurant, promised me lobster and champagne and all that. Anyway I got all dressed up and I waited and waited and he never turned up, didn't phone or anything. The next day Milo bought an ungutted mackerel and a jiffy bag and posted it to the boy, second class. You can imagine what it smelt like when he got it. Milo sent this disgusting note with it that said, "There are only two things that smell of fish: This is a fish, you are the other thing."'

'What?' Miranda said, not catching on.

'He meant "cunt"!' Jessica whispered loudly.

Time for them to leave, the barman thought.

'What have you done that's terrible?' Jessica asked. 'It's your turn.'

Miranda was still laughing, but just managed to get the words out, 'I think that what I've done is gone and got pregnant.'

The barman went back to washing glasses.

Ten

That afternoon, with nothing to do till the sheets were ready for collection in Helston, Clare sat in her garden, thinking that with Jack and all the children out the cottage felt just the right size for her. Tempting fate, she imagined herself widowed, divorced, the children away at school or college. Imagining, she arranged for herself just the necessities for a single life (with the addition of new bathroom, kitchen, central heating, just those things that the cottage needed right now, never mind waiting for the payout of life insurance policies). But deep down, she knew she wouldn't make a cosy village widow. There was a goldfish bowl feeling about living alongside the creek, everyone knowing what everyone else was doing. She felt brave, that afternoon to be out at all – everyone seemed to know that she was the one who should have been in charge of Andrew and his social life the night before. She hadn't dared, alone, go to the village shop for the newspaper, but had cravenly sent Harriet instead. Harriet had reported back that the man in the shop had said, 'I bet your Mum's in for a busy day.'

If it was this bad in summer, when the village population was so diluted by trippers, imagine, she thought, what it must be like in winter, nothing but gossip. Strange how much more private one could be, living in over-populated suburbia. If Jack really didn't go back to the Poly and they sold the Cornish house, the only thing she'd miss about summers would be Eliot and the opportunity for a good deal of lustful fantasy. Guiltily, she abandoned the idea of being

125

alone with the cottage, and offered up a quick prayer for the safe return of Jack and Miranda from Truro.

Clare sat under the pear tree, with her back to the creek and the rest of the village so she couldn't see if she was being stared at. Virtuously, she knitted multi-coloured bobbles to sew on a sweater, trying to keep her fingers in the shade as she worked, so they wouldn't get sticky and hot and ruin the silk. She felt she ought to give some serious thought to Jack and his work problems, rather than to thinking how good an opportunity it would be for Eliot to be making an inpromptu visit. Today she didn't want him, her hands still reeked of disinfectant (as did Celia's entire house), and she didn't feel that Eau de Domestos was at all a seductive scent.

Clare knew quite well that Jack also knew quite well that selling the cottage would not generate anywhere near enough money for them to live on. She would have to get a job, though what as she couldn't imagine. Expanding the knitwear business would take invest-ment and a college course, neither of which they would now be able to afford. It rather looked as if, in order for Jack to give up working at a job that no longer interested him, Clare would have to start work-ing at one which did not particularly interest her. She thought about all the job ads that she read so casually over late breakfasts after the school runs. She felt she was too old now to go out as a perky temporary typist. She would no longer be able to understand the jargon. Clare had learned, at evening classes, secretarial skills in the days when an IBM Golfball was the last word in typewriter technology, and when a man would come round to the office to show the secretaries how to do photo-copier maintenance. Now the ads were all about WordPerfect and Windows and spreadsheets and databases. If Clare had to absorb a mass of unfamiliar technology (and why not? She could programme the washing machine), she would rather it was connected with the problems of wool tension and machine intarsia.

In truth, the working-world out there frightened Clare. She was terrified of hyper-efficient women in expensive suits and no-nonsense shoes. She didn't want to be something in 'recruitment', which she always associated with joining the Brownies, running the world's industries in lycra tights and high heels. She didn't see there could possibly be anything more desirable in business travel and expense account lunches than in driving her own children and their friends to the park for a sandwich, a can of coke and an afternoon of playing on the swings.

Clare knew she was an anachronism. She enjoyed and valued the job she had, a home-maker, a mother. She didn't really care whether it was fashionable or not, what she wanted most of all was not to have to give it up. If Jack was at home painting all day, he would soon get to the point of saying, 'I'll be able to do all those boring domestic things in the house, then you'll be free to go out to work', as if it was what she had been waiting for all those years.

Running alongside her other middle-aged, middle-class problem of fancying someone else's husband and wishing she was up to what she imagined her daughter was up to was a problem that Clare had thought only affected other people. She'd had friends with School Gate Syndrome. She'd seen that look of sorrowful loss on the day the last small child in a family runs for the first time through the gate of the local primary school. She'd seen redundant mothers, devastated by the newly-silent and empty house, immediately planning another accidental pregnancy. Clare now knew how they felt.

Jack had said firmly that mothers like that were lazy sods who just didn't want to rejoin the workforce, thereby at a stroke cancelling out all his dinner-party lip-service to feminism, where he supported the view that bringing up a family was as hard work as being a nurse on a double shift. Clare thought such opinions in the company of pretty women were Jack's version of flirtation. She took his private opinion to mean that definitely he didn't want her to have another baby, and just now sitting knitting in the sun Clare thought that the odds against her getting away with pretending her coil had dropped out unnoticed were pretty bad. Perhaps if Miranda had a child, she thought, as if such a thing could not really happen, how else could she contemplate the idea, she could look after it for her. She put the appalling notion firmly out of her mind and touched wood quickly for Miranda. What a thing to wish on anyone, especially her own daughter, on the verge of A-levels and UCCA forms.

Down in the creek below the garden, Amy and Harriet were grubbing about among the pebbles and rock pools, showing off to the current collection of visiting children. They'd need a good hosing down when they got back, Clare thought, to hell with any hose pipe ban, surely it doesn't apply to the cleaning of children, any more than it had that morning applied to the essential cleaning of the Osbourne's garden.

Amy had said that morning that the river smelt of poo, and Clare hoped that what they were so covered in was really all mud. If it wasn't, that would be another reason for selling the cottage. One way or another, it looked rather as if this was going to be their last summer in the village.

There were about ten children playing together. Clare's two bossed the others around, glorying in their superior status as residents, the fastest and most skillful catchers of the crabs and prawns. Hers were also the scruffiest, their hair bleached fair by the sun and overlaid with a greeny-blonde colouring from the chemicals in the Lynchs' pool. What must it be doing to their insides, Clare thought, perhaps they were all greeny-yellow and pickled too. All the local children, according to Jeannie, had gone off to Greece or Spain with their families. Anywhere, presumably to get away from this influx of tourists in the village. Those who weren't making money out of trippers did all they could to avoid them, leaving children like Amy and Harriet lording it over the village. They could now run around barefoot like the real locals, without wincing over the stones. Every week brought a new set of children in pastel-coloured jelly shoes to be sneered at.

Eliot, in his smoke-filled study, sat in front of his word processor with nothing but good intentions inside his head. When he was younger and keener he had got up at 5.30 every morning and written a thousand words before breakfast. Now he was lucky to write ten. He challenged the complex equipment in front of him: if you're so clever why can't you write the damned book for me? He had to think harder about using the technology than he had ever before had to think about writing his books. If he hadn't spent all that money on the thing, he'd happily have gone back to the old Olivetti portable he had used before fame and fortune had complicated his life. He didn't trust the glow from the machine either. He kept wondering if it was sending out a malevolent dose of cancerous radiation to him as he tried to work. Perhaps the faster he wrote the book, the less radiation he would get. He'd live longer. His main problem, right now though, was lack of inspiration, lack of interest and worst of all, lack of time.

Eliot was getting too old to write about these fast fit young people. He had to invent such daring and unlikely things for them to do. They were so glamorous, powerful, slim and athletic. They were confident, capable. They were not like him. It was harder and harder even to pretend to identify with the heroes he created. Younger authors now wrote more knowledgeably about intrigue and espionage than he ever had. If he had trouble with a simple word processor, how could he be expected to keep up with the technology of the undercover spy world? And who was there to spy against any more with the cold war over? Eliot always got stomach trouble in the Middle East. And the punters weren't slow to tell you if you'd got things wrong. His plots were getting as tired as he was. He'd lost the spark, and was exhausted by the competition. Every time he heard a book programme on the radio, or switched on a TV chat show there was some clever-clever little sod saying 'Oh the book was easy, it just wrote itself. I sat down and finished it in less than a fortnight.' Didn't they have the same rewriting to do, the lunchtime battles with editors, the printing prob-lems? Eliot's only advantage was his track record. His fame guaranteed that his books went straight from publication to massive displays on every airport bookstall, every station, every newsagent with even the smallest bookrack, never mind the critics. And not many got sent back unsold. They'd take anything, Eliot thought with ungrateful disgust. He could have written his name 90,000 times on a length of lavatory paper and there would still be a queue for the film rights.

But Eliot still had a nagging artistic pride that had not yet burned itself out. That was why he agonized over the word processor rather than triumphed over his royalty cheques. He considered changing his pseudonym, just to see if he was still really publish-able, but he remembered acutely the pain of his first ten rejection slips and didn't dare.

Eliot pressed all the right buttons to save the few words he had written and then turned off the machine. One day he would probably lose the lot in the depths of a floppy disc or two, so he stopped work while he was still sober enough to remember what to do.

He felt like some fresh air and decided it was a good moment perhaps to go and call on Clare. She was a warm, sympathetic type, the sort that people trusted with their pets and children and problems. He knew she was alone because Jessica had gone to Truro with Jack and Miranda and somehow, in Eliot's mind, he kept seeing a tempting picture of Clare, mud-covered from rescuing Amy the other night, all rumpled frock and mud-splashed hair. There had been a furious passion in her eyes too, a hint of hidden depths which it might be fun to plumb. Eliot whistled an Irish tune as he wandered into the kitchen and took a bottle of champagne from the fridge. Liz, coming into the kitchen, caught Eliot, bottle in hand, practising what he thought was a seductive smile and which she interpreted as a lecherous leer, and fled, slamming the door and stalking off down the path to the village.

Eliot, humming 'Froggy went a-courting', set off down the same path, cheerfully waving the champagne bottle to a state of undrinkable fizz.

Clare did not see either Liz or Eliot walking down the hill. The effort of keeping the silk from getting sticky in the heat was proving too much, so Clare went back into the cool of the kitchen to make a cup of tea. While she was filling the kettle it occurred to her that with the house empty she had the perfect opportunity to do something that she thought she would never stoop to doing. Back in Barnes, a friend who had been worried about her own daughter's behaviour had once told Clare that she intended to read the girl's diary. Clare, at the time, had been shocked. What an unforgiveable invasion of privacy, she had thought, how completely despicable. It was something she would never, herself, consider doing.

But that was then, when if she wanted to find out what Miranda was up to she only had to ask, and Miranda would hang around the kitchen telling her who fancied whom, who had got drunk, who had been caught smoking on the school bus and what they all got up to at weekends on Richmond Green. Now Miranda hardly spoke at all, rowed round the harbour by herself for hours on end and generally seemed to have something untellable on her mind.

Clare tip-toed up the stairs towards Miranda's room, avoiding the steps that creaked as if there was someone in the house to catch her out. She stopped at the top of the stairs, nervously picking flaking paint off the newel post, hovering outside Miranda's door. It was all very well to read Miranda's diary, but then she would be stuck with whatever awfulness she managed to discover. Suppose Miranda was using drugs? Suppose she was sleeping with six different boys in rotation? How could she say anything to Miranda without betraying how she had found out the truth?

She pushed the door open and breathed in the soft perfume of Miranda's belongings, the mixture of Body Shop potions, roses from the garden. Clothes and books were scattered around and Miranda hadn't made her bed. The diary was sticking out from under the pillow, and Clare hardly dared touch it. Suppose Miranda had left it at a particular angle and would know if anyone touched it? The diary, a girlish, too-young Flower Fairy one, was tied up with pink ribbon. Clare looked behind her and then quickly untied it. She didn't want to read anything irrelevant to what was making Miranda so moody, but didn't know where to start. Her hands shook as she flicked through the pages, which were covered with Miranda's bold handwriting. Clare didn't read, exactly, but absorbed an impression of lots of capital letters and exclamation marks. She found out nothing because she couldn't bring herself to stop and concentrate on any one of the pages, until the end of June – here the pages for the last week of June were missing, and nothing had been written in since. She's torn the pages out, Clare thought, she doesn't trust me!

'Anyone home?' Clare, fingers fumbling, retied the diary and shoved it back at the remembered angle under Miranda's pillow. Liz was down by the back door, her voice trilling up the stairs. 'Are you there, Clare? I've come to see you!' she called, as if she had brought herself as a gift.

Clare almost fell down the stairs in her haste to get away from the scene of her guilt.

'Your kettle's boiling,' Liz said, 'So I knew you must be here. Eliot is in a peculiar mood so I thought I'd escape for a while. The twins are down in the creek playing with your two.'

'What's wrong with Eliot?' Clare asked, trying not to show an undue interest.

'Well this morning he complained about writer's block, or whatever it is. Anyway he said he couldn't write, it was too hot. But when I went and asked him if he wanted to come out for a walk, take that disgusting dog somewhere, he told me to sod off and not interrupt. Just now I saw him getting a bottle of plonk out of the fridge so I decided to get out of his way.'

Through the kitchen doorway, behind Liz, Clare could just see Eliot, leaning on the wooden footbridge. He and his dog were looking down into the shallow water as the tide started to make its slow way up the channel. Just then he looked up and saw her, and started waving the bottle of 'plonk' (which was actually Bollinger), at her. Clare bit her lip to stop herself from giggling, as Eliot danced up and down and made faces at the back of Liz. He pointed to the bottle, made a disappointed face at Clare and shrugged, then whistled to his dog and strolled back the way he had come. Another time, make it another time, Clare wanted to shout after him. Liz went and sat on the grass under the pear tree and irritatedly pulled at the daisies.

'He's always complaining that just because he works from home no-one takes him seriously and we want him to keep joining in with things,' Liz grumbled. 'It's supposed to be his idea of a holiday, coming here. It certainly isn't mine.'

Liz was looking sulky and very young. Her immaculate white linen shorts were about to be covered in grass stains and her silk blouse was going to get snagged on the pear tree bark. Clare felt rather sorry for her, she was as out of place in a country village as a camellia in a corn field.

'I remember when Jack used to work from home,' Clare said. 'It was difficult for any of us to treat it as work, especially, and I don't mean to be disloyal, as he wasn't selling very much of it. Everyone used to visit and stay for coffee or assume that if he was at home he could go out and play tennis, or golf or look after everyone else's children. He had friends who'd want him to go out and get drunk at lunch time and he'd be unable to pick up a brush for the rest of the day.'

Clare was only depressing herself. Was this what she had to come again, second time round, with bigger, more expensive children to support? Was this what he would be doing while she was out temping with twenty-year-olds?

'It's horrid here,' Liz said, in a little-girl voice. 'There's nowhere to get my hair done. I like to have it cut and all that at least once a fortnight.'

Clare watched Liz run her fingers through her shoulder-length streaked hair. The roots were showing through a rather dull mouse-brown, and Clare guessed Liz would never allow herself to be seen like that in public in London.

'You could always find somewhere in Truro,' Clare suggested.

'Heavens no, I couldn't. I have to have Alphonse,' Liz said, shocked. 'I miss so many things here. I miss the club, it's got proper toning tables. For the thighs, you know,' she said, stretching out a slender limb for Clare to admire. 'I go there every day and have lunch with my friends. Or Harvey Nichols. I saw Celia there once.'

Clare imagined Liz in an Armani suit and velvet

headband, squealing over bagfuls of Sloane Street booty with a gaggle of girlfriends.

'And though the garden here is much better than London, I haven't got Conchita to do the flowers.' Liz was almost whining now.

'Isn't that the sort of thing you were taught at finishing school?' Clare asked Liz briskly.

'Oh no, we did Art Appreciation. Lots of time in the Louvre. Oh and cooking.'

Liz trailed dejectedly after Clare back to the kitchen when Clare took the cups back inside. Clare left them in the sink and watched Liz staring round the room. I know what she's thinking, Clare thought. She's wondering how a family of five exist with such a small space. Clare followed Liz's gaze round the room – everything was hanging on the wall: pans; plate rack; children's drawings; notice board covered with years of holiday photos; dried herbs; even the cutlery hung from hooks. The entire ground floor of this cottage would fit into Liz and Eliot's kitchen. Clare's kitchen was about the size of the Lynch laundry room. Clare felt a sudden longing for the space and freedom of the Barnes house. Just a couple more weeks, she thought.

'That party of Andrew's,' Clare said, breaking into Liz's thoughts. 'He's going to get hell from Archie and Celia when they get back from the Scillies. I wouldn't mind being a fly on their wall. I'm sure they'll blame me as much as him, I said I'd keep an eye on him. But you don't expect a boy of that age to need a babysitter do you? I wouldn't have imagined Andrew could get up to anything like that.'

Liz grinned, 'I don't think Andrew quite imagined it either according to Jessica.'

'No,' Clare said, rinsing the cups and peering round to the Aga for a tea towel. Liz obviously wasn't intending to dry anything. 'Andrew seems too innocent for that kind of planning, so old fashioned, and "good".'

Clare felt slightly confused about whether to side with Celia and Archie when they got back, be all grown-up and say 'oh dear, how dreadful' or be ready to make excuses for Andrew.

'I hope he gets away with it,' she said, 'I don't suppose he gets much fun. Anyway, let's just go next door and see if he's feeling any better, he looked dreadful this morning.'

Clare wanted Liz to go home. She thought that by moving her on, away from her own premises she would be helping Liz on her way. Perhaps Liz for once would like to take all the younger children to the beach, so she could be left in peace to think about the missing pages from Miranda's diary.

'Are you feeling any better?' she asked Andrew as she and Liz walked through his garden gate.

'A bit,' Andrew mumbled, shielding his pained eyes from the sun as he tried to look at the two women.

'Do you think the parents will have to know?' he added hopefully.

'I'm not going to tell them,' Clare said, 'But half the village will so you'd better get in first. Just say you had a few people round and it got out of hand. They can hardly blame you then.'

They'll blame me though, she thought.

Liz couldn't help wrinkling her little nose. The aroma of unwashed boy was too apparent. She wanted to be kind, offer him a swim in her pool, a sort of restorative taking of the waters, but she'd rather he took a shower first.

'Would you like to come and swim later?' she asked, 'After tea perhaps?'

'Er, no thanks, I'll just take the Laser out for a while when the tide gets a bit higher. Clear my head,' Andrew said. It wouldn't do to face Jessica for quite a while. He'd have to do his swimming in the cold river.

'I've got an awful feeling that Celia and Archie aren't

going to be speaking to me for some time,' Clare said to Liz as they left Andrew's garden.

'You can't take all the blame, you couldn't have known.'

'Well you and I know that, but they're older. I think of everyone over fifty as properly grown-up, a hangover from school I expect. I imagine I'll be told off.'

Liz thought of everyone over thirty as grown-up, however often they proved not to be.

'I know,' Clare said. 'We'll have a tea party for them, the real old-fashioned out-in-the-garden sort that Celia would appreciate. They won't refuse to come, there are too few of us here to bear grudges for long. End of next week, give them a chance to get back, inspect the damage and get all their grumbling over and done with.'

Clare led Liz firmly towards the wooden bridge and the path home and smiled sweetly at her: 'You can cook, you can make a lovely big cake. It will give you something to do.'

Eleven

By now, mid-August, the village was at its most
crowded. Every rentable bed, bunk and cot was
occupied, the tiny cottages overstuffed with families,
dogs, babies, prams, surfboards and beachmats.
Swimsuits and towels hung dripping from the little
balconies every evening, flying over the main street
like bright celebration flags.

Those locals who had returned from their Mediterranean fortnights ('That's it for this year then' was
frequently heard in the post office), continued to
service and clean the amenities, fighting a losing battle
with sand trodden into carpets, their very survival
depending on the goodwill of the up-country trippers.

Those who owned their cottages basked in the heat
and felt smug about their investments, the crippling
second mortgages, sadly devoid of tax relief. Each
good British summer brought back from abroad those
who'd suffered last-minute surcharges, airport delays
and lager louts and swore they'd never go through all
that ever again. There were, in spite of the recession,
plenty willing to buy into the second home market,
prices eventually could only go up. And although no-
one would have dared say it, not even at a happy-hour
drinks party, when people were usually in a mood
relaxed enough to chance their most reactionary
opinions on people of their own sort, the high prices
that so pleased them also ensured the exclusivity of the
village. In fact, so exclusive was it that there was no
longer any chance that the local Cornish people could
hope to afford the cottages their ancestors had built,

not without a pools win anyway. There was a nagging worry that soon there would be barely enough local characters left to keep the village picturesque. In another ten years, as Jack pointed out to Eliot, it would have all the rustic charm of Putney.

There was an understanding, though not mentioned outside one's own family, that owning a holiday cottage was actually a ploy to keep one's wayward teenage children off the dangerous urban streets. Back at home, in the long school holidays, bored kids drifted around looking for entertainment, getting into trouble. They were too old to be supervised, too young to be responsible. In shopping centres, parks and all along the banks of the Thames, teenagers congregated on warm summer nights, just to hang around in large intimidating groups. They mooched at night in shop doorways, drinking cider, smoking and filling their bodies with junk food, littering the street with cans and wrappers. Youth-orientated entertainment had long ago been closed down by local councils, in deference to the votes of those who counted. So parents feared for the health of their children, their safety and their accents. It was almost impossible to persuade one's child that they might enjoy seeing *A Midsummer Night's Dream* yet again in Regents Park when they had just discovered a talent for racing abandoned supermarket trolleys through empty shopping precincts at night. Parents feared the influence of peer groups, of good old sex, drugs and rock n' roll, just as their own parents had.

So along with their second homes, they bought a period of extended childhood for their sons and daughters. They bribed them with picnics and barbecues and boats and riding and sleeping-bags all over the house for all their visiting friends. Each summer they knew they just had to get them into the car, drive over the Tamar and it would all be all right. They had bought them a better class of street life. One day they would refuse to come, just please God, let it be when the child had got to the age of reason, or at least to a good university. The biggest disadvantage to having teenagers spending the summer in Cornwall, was that there had to be an adult willing, in an evening, to stay sober enough to collect them from the far outposts of local social life. There was no public transport, a reason why the lanes of Cornwall, in summer, are congested with London seventeen-year-olds trying to do three-point turns into farm gateways.

Jack always felt he was one of the luckier ones. The cottage inherited from his grandparents did not carry with it the burden of a mortgage, so although he could only just afford what minimal maintenance that was done, money worries had never been a barrier to his appreciation of his surroundings. With the money from the London house, he thought perhaps they could extend the attic and make another bedroom, maybe build a conservatory out into the side of the garden. He loved the peace of the place, he only had to walk away from the village, through the woods beyond reach of the tired and lazy legs of the trippers, to wind down from the irritations of his work which built up, term by term during each academic year. Working in education, he noticed how many of his colleagues had gone straight from school, to college and then straight back into teaching. They seemed to speak only in the jargon of the profession, quite unaware of the real world out there. The petty squabblings of the staff, most of whom were on shaky contracts that could be quickly terminated, increased as each year progressed, until by July the teaching members of the college seemed, to Jack to be marginally less mature than the students.

Now that Jack had no intention of returning, he waited to feel the exquisite relief of freedom. It hadn't arrived yet, partly because he'd managed to tell Clare only half of the plan. He wanted to give her time to absorb and accept that he wasn't going back to the college before suggesting that they all come to live permanently in Cornwall. He was also finding Clare's concern with Miranda stifling in the small cottage. She was constantly watching the girl, wondering where she was going, what she was doing and too carefully not asking the questions she obviously wanted to know the answers to. The moment that the vague and dreamy Miranda noticed, there'd be an almighty confrontation, he could feel it coming. And Jack hated confrontation, which was why he phoned London estate agents to find out about the current housing market while Clare was safely at the beach.

Jack had taken to going out early in the mornings, walking up on to the headland behind the village just to sit in the peace and stillness of the early morning mists, watching the sky clear to pale cerulean blue. He took with him his sketch book and had started to make a series of drawings of the village from different points on the cliff behind it. He thought perhaps he would use his new water colours for this too, as well as for the elusive hydrangeas, and put together a fairly speedy collection for the craft centre.

He would have been outraged at this idea a few years ago: fast art for holiday sales, seaside tourist painters. The sophistication of his art school training had kept him well out of range of that kind of commercialism. It was only one step away from greetings cards. Now he was older and less naive he realized how restful it was going to be simply to paint what he liked because he liked it, even if it was only scenes of boats, or flowers or whatever, without having to express anything controversial. It was hard enough these days to think about having strong opinions on anything, without having to paint them as well. He could leave behind the heavy-handed abstracts of his youth, his former floppy attempts to convey some deep sentiment that he hadn't really felt. He just liked handling paint, liked the mechanics of using brushes made from the finest sable, liked new fresh tubes of colour, the smell and the texture. He decided he was probably a landscape man and there was nothing wrong with that, it was good enough for Van Gogh. It was development, not defeat. If he'd had any students to go back to, he would have quoted from Henry Miller, 'Paint as you like and die happy'.

As he strolled up the cliff path, he planned life without teaching at all. Clare could find something more lucrative to do, they could share both child care and making a living. They could sell the London house and live down here in the village, interest rates being as they were they wouldn't have much trouble surviving. Miranda could go to the local sixth-form college. It wouldn't be any less secure than being on a contract which could be terminated by a policy-decision whim of a government minister or a hostile head of department.

Down below the cliff the river glimmered in the rising mist. It was going to be hot yet again. In the creeks the water would be still and steamy, the tide rising imperceptibly across the mud and creeping up on the feeding gulls. A few early morning boats were heading out to sea, gently rocking the hippy raft which still loitered by the harbour, occasionally shifting from one creek to another. The residents barely bothered to comment any more, bored with watching gleefully for signs of it sinking. Jack felt a small pang of regret that he now saw no romance in that way of life and wondered when he had become so much more concerned with sensible practicalities like constant water supplies, lavatories in working order, warmth at night and something always waiting in the fridge. There could hardly, he thought, looking out at the raft, be a less convenient site on which to pitch camp.

Jack sat down on a log to sketch, enjoying the aloneness of the time of day. There were no eager hikers, no gawky boys with ghetto blasters, no blustery dog-walking women with headscarves and green wellingtons, no-one jogging with that Sony Walkman blankness and the tinny invasive thump thump of Dire Straits. Clare called the wearing of a Walkman the grown-up equivalent of sucking a dummy, though she had been less dismissive since she discovered that the dustman in Barnes was using his to teach himself Russian as he worked.

Jack could smell the ferns but no traffic fumes, pine resin but no aircraft fuel.

Just as he was starting to draw, Jack heard something crashing around in the woods behind him. The unexpectedness of it alarmed him briefly, then more logically he reasoned that it must be a deer, expecting the same degree of privacy that he hoped for himself. He peered carefully through the branches thinking he could tell Harriet and Amy later and maybe the next day they'd come out together to see. But then he realized it was a man, muttering and stumbling through the bracken. Jack moved to a tree so that he would not be seen. He didn't want to have to make polite good-morning conversation and anyway the person seemed to be talking to himself. Who was it, a loon? a drunk?, someone chatting to their dog? or a murderer staggering along with a stone-dead corpse? Used to nothing more sinister than sedate dog-walkers on Barnes Common Jack's imagination grew lurid, and he shrank back against the tree, away from the shambling man and his mutterings. 'Put him in Bombay' Jack heard, 'Make him large, blond and a bit older than the usual ones. Might be better to have an anti-hero . . . drinks . . . not too much or brain won't work. IRA connection . . .' It was Eliot. Jack knew it was too late to come out and show that he'd been there listening to the poor man who seemed to have flipped at last and should at least be allowed to do so in private. But as Eliot got nearer Jack could see he was talking to a small tape recorder, not to himself. So after all they had something in common, a need to get out there in the trees and the solitude to work. Jack hadn't thought of Eliot as a man who needed to get closer to nature in order to pursue his art, especially as, just to be polite, he had actually read one of his lurid books. Just shows, Jack thought, you never can tell.

Jack was feeling rather cramped and foolish lurking behind his tree, but waited till the preoccupied Eliot had gone past. He'd thought of Eliot as the type to be working all night, an inspired alcoholic, typing and smoking into the early hours, with piles of disorganized papers and a rusting Anglepoise lamp. He didn't draw too well that morning, the lumbering muttering man, brain quite obviously in overdrive, had alarmed him. When we live down here, he thought, we'll get a large dog.

Clare hated making plans about food for the afternoon when she hadn't even had breakfast. It was Jeannie's day for washing floors and Clare would have to make cakes round her. Once last year she had suggested that Jeannie leave it for another time, but Jeannie had looked so astonished and said 'but it's my day for it', that Clare had felt she had insulted her and kept apologetically out of the way. In a village this size you had to behave impeccably towards the cleaning lady, she was God. If you didn't treat her as such you'd never get another. Word would get round. As Clare drank her early coffee on the terrace, she wandered round deadheading the pinks, clearing up dead fish and peanut shells. The problem with using the terrace as an outdoor room was that there was outdoor housework too. It would help if they'd all treat it with the respect a room would get, and not throw crisp packets and bread crusts all over the place. What she really needed, when it came down to it, was litter bins, but then it would look like a pub garden. She was angry too, with the children for leaving collections of little fish and molluscs to die in the sun, gasping to death in the hot plastic buckets. The children were all for save the whale and conservation, but only in the abstract, not when it came to the little creatures they fished out of the creek.

Clare swilled down the terrace with greasy washing-up water, wishing she could still use the hose pipe. For a few brief moments before the sun dried them again, she could savour the fresh dampness of her flowers. She wished she could hose down the house too, just swoosh away all the summer dust and grime with an illegal jet from the hose. England, she thought, just isn't equipped for the heat. There isn't the cool marble and stone of the Mediterranean, the carpets seem to sweat in the clogging heat.

Clare had invited Archie and Celia to tea. They had been arriving at the sailing club for lunch the day before just as Clare was leaving. Still feeling twinges of guilt about Andrew and wondering whether they were justified, she made her invitation. Celia had accepted with grace like royalty, and although she was not the sort of person who would ever have the bad manners to say so, Clare was somehow left with the impression that she was considered almost as naughty a child as Andrew. Jack said it was entirely Celia's fault, she shouldn't have relied so heavily on the theory of grown-up conspiracy, and remembered that she was almost a generation away from Clare, let alone Andrew.

Liz and Eliot were coming too for which Clare felt duly grateful, on the rather dubious premise that if Celia thought Clare wasn't up to standard as an adult, she should really take a closer look at Eliot.

While the scones were defrosting and the cakes were in the oven, Jeannie told Clare she was going upstairs to give Miranda's room a good going-over. Why couldn't she have done that while I was busy cooking round her in the kitchen Clare thought. Clare found it very embarrassing that Jeannie was cleaning her house while her son was possibly doing goodness knows what with Miranda. She was uncomfortably conscious that if Jeannie was a friend and not an employee they could have had a bit of a giggle about it. As it was, if Jeannie knew anything was going on she was keeping it to herself. Clare had too much middle-class angst about employing people to be any good at it. She pretended to herself that she had a thing about exploitation, but in truth she was just not used to it. Jeannie much preferred working for Liz, who had clearly been brought up with servants and didn't dither about what to call her, or what she could ask her to do. She didn't keep apologizing about the state of the sitting room. You knew where you were with people like that. Mrs Lynch wouldn't waste valuable blockbuster reading time trailing around after a cleaning lady plumping up cushions on the sofa. Jeannie knew Clare had wanted her out of the kitchen, but she wasn't going to let her off that easily. There was peace and quiet in Miranda's room, and not that much cleaning to be done either, she was quite a neat girl really. Steve could have done a lot worse if things had worked out. There were no dirty tissues under the bed, no make-up smeared on the dressing table and she did at least seem to have aimed her laundry at the basket, nothing worse than other people's grubby knickers left lying around. Miranda and Steve should by now have been at the holding-hands-in-the-village stage, he should be teaching her to play euchre in the pub so she'd have something to do in winter. It was a pity that Miranda had after all run true to type and abandoned Steve as soon as her own sort arrived.

Jeannie picked up the silky soft clothes from the bed and hung them in the wardrobe, dusted the chest of drawers and tipped the dying posy of roses into the bin. A scarf in the bottom of the bin had to be rescued,

Miranda couldn't be intending to throw that out, it was silk, by the feel of it, and too pretty. Underneath the scarf was a small cardboard box and it didn't seem prying to read what it was, you don't put really private things into a waste paper basket, surely, Jeannie reasoned.

Jeannie read the box and had to sit on the bed. If she's got Steve into trouble, the little tart ... she thought angrily. She put the box on top of the rubbish and carried it down to the dustbin outside the house, where she left it exposed at the top of the bin so Jack or Clare could get the same heart-spearing shock that she had just had.

If Miranda had so thoughtlessly left the pregnancy test kit box lying around her bedroom, Jeannie thought furiously, why couldn't she also have had the decency to leave the result?

Twelve

Well he didn't have to go with them, but he knew what they'd say if he didn't: 'Oh Andrew they'll think it's so odd' or worse, 'Aren't you well?' His mother would put an enquiring hand to his forehead, checking for fever. He didn't want to be touched, not by her, not by anyone now. They'd want a good reason for his absence, and Celia could smell out an untruth like a labrador after a dead pheasant. He was pretty sure that the photos were of Jessica, even though he couldn't see her face behind the scarf. She must have known he'd know too, he didn't actually know that many girls after all, and certainly not with tits like that. And that scarf looked like the kind of silky paisley type of thing that Miranda sometimes wore, which made it worse, they were in it together, mocking him. He could imagine them by the photo booth, giggling, saying 'He's going to love this!', and Jessica posing quickly, half-naked, while the lights flashed, then struggling back into her tee shirt while Miranda kept terrified look-out the other side of the curtain. It had to be them, the envelope had a Truro postmark. It certainly wasn't Beryl from the pub. She had much bigger, darker nipples, he'd seen them outlined against her thin blouse as she reached up to change the gin bottle on the row of optics. He'd thought the nipples rather frightening, but fascinating. She'd seen him looking and winked, shamelessly. It had been yet another of those times when he'd wished he didn't blush.

He would have to go to Clare's, and he'd have to act as if nothing had happened. Then with any luck they'd think the dreadful package had got lost in the post, or been re-routed to Surrey along with the telephone bill and the council tax stuff. Andrew felt he had quite enough to cope with already, what with Celia's tight-lipped hurt silences, and Archie's bluff commiseration, 'Bad luck getting caught old boy!' as if by having the party Andrew had turned into a man at last and now they could be chums. It even seemed he didn't mind about the Chivas Regal. Chip off the old block, that kind of thing. This was not what Andrew wanted at all. All he had wanted was to get his leg over, as the rugby players at school put it. Funny thing to say, he thought, surely they don't just mean one leg?

Andrew also thought that he and Milo had cleared up rather well, but every time Celia moved furniture she managed to find just one more cigarette end. There had been a used and dusty condom under her bed, and the dustmen had refused to take all the sacks of empty bottles and cans at one go, so the garbage sat there outside the cottage reproaching Andrew for his misdemeanours for a whole extra week. The wages of sin had been a good telling-off and a hangover. Andrew therefore resolved to forget about sex and concentrate on his sailing, perhaps getting seriously fit, with a physique worth showing off. Then next time it would be Jessica damn well propositioning him. In the meantime Andrew couldn't quite bring himself to tear up the little strip of photographs and hide them at the bottom of the rubbish bin, as he had with the Marks and Spencer knickers. He thought he should really, but destroying them would have felt like mutilating Jessica herself, and she looked so vulnerable, so 'offered'. So he took them upstairs and opened the shameful box of secrets in his wardrobe, intending to incarcerate them for ever beneath the collection of erotica. All this lot too, he thought, was part of the sin for which he was being punished, and he decided he'd have no more of it. But just unlocking the box, just

149

handling the photos of Jessica, was having the usual effect. No-one was home. Andrew rifled through the box and its rather obscene contents. He giggled quietly at his own small joke, the idea of handling himself with kid gloves, a pair of which he had bought from a junk shop near the school. They were so thin and delicate and did not detract from the sensation like heavier ones did. They felt like skin, someone else's, not his own sweaty impatient hand. Well maybe just this once, he thought, after all Jessica had sent him a gift.

Clare was in the kitchen. She hated icing cakes and did not need Miranda hanging around and picking at the sandwiches.

'Leave them alone Miranda, they're for later.'

'Sorry. Who's coming?'

'Just the usual, Eliot and Liz, Celia and Archie, and all the kids probably, unless you're all off to the beach?'

'No, well I'll be here anyway.'

Miranda was slouching against the doorway, looking bored and moody. She was kicking rhythmically at the chipped skirting board, driving Clare mad.

'Miranda if you can't be useful, please go away.'

'Sorry,' said Miranda, not moving. Clare bustled across to the oven and got out the scones. Please, she thought, don't let this be the moment that she wants to talk, I'm too busy.

'Do you want anyone else to come too?' Clare asked, aware that her subtlety was rather heavy-handed. (As, she thought, were also her scones). She rinsed the icing funnel under the tap so she wouldn't have to be looking at Miranda. No wonder Roman Catholics like those confession boxes, she thought, so much easier not to see each other.

'No. Why should I?' Miranda said, and then flounced out of the kitchen. Clare wasn't sure whether to be annoyed with herself for alienating Miranda yet again by her clumsiness or be glad to have her out of the way. Like Scarlett O'Hara she decided to think about it tomorrow. She still had to butter the scones.

'We should take flowers,' Jessica had said to Milo. They were collecting ox-eye daisies from the hedgerow along the lane, dawdling on their way to Clare's.

'I'm so proud of you,' Milo said, 'I honestly never thought you'd do it.'

'I had to, after you'd dared me,' Jessica said. 'The worst bit was hanging around outside the booth waiting for the photos to come out of the little slot. There was a man there who'd gone in just after us and he was watching for his own pictures to come out. In the end Miranda got so frantic to distract him that she started asking him all sorts of stupid questions about his horrid little dog. He had one of those tiny beige terriers with a hair-ribbon, the sort people carry. Miranda had to keep stroking it and saying isn't it sweet, and asking what it liked to eat and such.'

'I'd love to have seen Andrew's face when he opened the envelope,' Milo said. 'I hope Celia and Archie weren't around.'

'Suppose they open his mail?' said Jessica, suddenly horrified.

'Surely not, and anyway they wouldn't know it was you.'

'Neither will Andrew, I hope. I do feel extremely stupid. Can't we go home?'

'No of course not, you'll have to face him some time. If he does think it's you, we'll know by the bulge growing in his trousers.' Milo and Jessica started giggling.

'I won't be able to look,' Jessica said, 'Too dreadful to think of. Let's go home.' She set off, back up the lane, flowers trailing.

'Not a chance,' Milo said, catching her and hauling

her back again. 'I'll look after you, and anyway let's just be nice to him, the poor sod.'

So they arrived at Clare's, arm in arm, carrying huge bunches of daisies, smiling radiantly at the group assembled on the lawn. How lovely they look, everyone thought, what a picture of filial affection.

Archie and Celia arrived rather late, as if they were regally aware that the tea-party was in their honour. Even in the heat, Celia had a cardigan draped round her shoulders, which she pulled protectively a little tighter as she caught sight of Eliot, grinning at her across a champagne bottle. He noticed the reflex gesture of defence, which set up thoughts of a challenge idly flicking across his mind. Nice legs on Celia, he thought, but hips a bit spiky, could do damage. Only Liz, idly picking buttercups from the dry grass, knew that this was the second bottle he was pouring, the other one had mostly gone into himself and the empty bottle was in her kitchen bin. She'd abandoned the idea of collecting bottles for the bottle bank in Helston, so as to protect Milo and Jessica from the appalling truth about how much their father was capable of drinking. The family could, she thought, probably qualify for the installation of a council bottle bank of their own, right outside the back door.

Clare had noticed Celia's expression of disapproval at Eliot and immediately took her off to admire the penstemons, asking her advice about blackfly on the nasturtiums. Jack overheard her and wondered if she had remembered to hide the can of (ozone and bee friendly) pesticide in the shed. Clare knew perfectly well what to do about bugs in the garden. Obviously, he realized, they were to spend the afternoon talking about anything but the awfulness of teenagers and their destructive social lives.

Archie, benign and cheerful, said that he was not averse to champagne at any time of the day and settled comfortably into a deckchair next to Liz, at the same time sneaking an admiring glance at her tanned legs as he sat down.

Liz noticed and hoped Eliot had too, it was time he realized, she thought, that other people found her extremely attractive. Wouldn't do him any harm. She hitched her silk skirt up a little higher and recrossed her legs to make a more flattering arrangement and then offered her best smile to Archie.

'So how was your trip to Tresco? I love travelling by helicopter, don't you?'

'Well actually we didn't, we went by boat. We're not very adventurous I'm afraid,' Archie said.

So he won't be flashing anything more than a smile at you my dear Liz, Eliot thought, watching.

'The gardens were wonderful,' Celia said, coming to sit next to Archie and overcoming her reluctance to drink Eliot's champagne. 'And in spite of the water shortage too, I don't know how they manage to keep the plants so well.'

'I hope this drought doesn't go on much longer,' Clare said. 'I remember a couple of years ago, syphoning the bath water out of the window, and feeling guilty because I knew we shouldn't really even be having baths.'

'I couldn't exist without a bath,' Liz said languorously, 'That would be just too uncivilized.' She couldn't believe anyone would go to all that trouble with bits of piping for a few plants. One could always buy new ones the following spring.

Jack, smiling to himself at the thought of Liz in a flowered bath cap and nothing else said 'Showers use a lot less water, you know, far more ecologically sound.'

'You're teasing me,' Liz giggled. 'Showers are too much like after games at school. There's always bits of you that don't get wet enough and warm enough and it's so unrelaxing.'

'Yes that's true,' Celia said. 'A shower doesn't do a lot for the old bones after gardening.'

153

'But I don't have old bones,' Liz pointed out, rather cattily.

Clare started handing round scones rather frantically.

'Does anyone remember that thing about putting a brick in the loo cistern so it flushed less water?'

'It usually meant that it didn't quite flush enough,' Archie recalled. 'Then you had to flush twice. Pointless I thought at the time, defeats the object.'

Jack said, 'I remember a man, after it rained for three months that autumn, writing to *The Times* and asking if he was allowed to take his brick out now.'

Clare thought the conversation was getting a bit lavatorial for a Sunday tea-time. She had a look towards the smaller children playing by the swing. They'd go into hysterical giggles if they heard the grown-ups talking like that, they were at that stage.

'When we had baths at school,' Celia was saying, 'we had to wear these cotton smocks so we wouldn't be able to see our bodies and be corrupted. Nuns, you see. So much was unmentionable then.' She looked rather wistful.

'Different things are unmentionable now, even if we can talk about our bodies,' Eliot said. 'Americans, they're always asking how much you earn, soon as you meet them. We British wouldn't even tell our best friends.'

'Like asking how you vote,' Archie said. 'It's very bad form.'

'You can always lie,' Eliot said. 'But no-one would even have to speculate how you vote, Archie. It would be beyond the imagination to take you for other than a true blue Tory.'

'You'd be surprised,' Archie said, smiling.

'I'd be absolutely bloody amazed,' Eliot said, opening another bottle.

The popping of the cork made tourists on the opposite bank of the creek look across to the garden.

How decadent we must look, Jack thought.

It was turning into yet another long boozy afternoon. The humidity, and the slowly looming clouds made everyone languid and rather tetchy. Clare noticed that even the older children were being unusually quiet. She could just make out Milo and Andrew talking about cricket, in that test-match commentator drone that men have when they talk about the game. No-one looked very relaxed, just exhausted, perhaps it was the effort of not mentioning Andrew's party, presumably another unmentionable. Amy and Harriet were not, for once, squabbling, but waiting with unnatural grace for their turn on the swing. Miranda was pushing one of the Lynch twins, while Jessica sat alone on the grass making daisy chains. A few villagers could be seen gardening on the hillside. The locals knew better than to go out for walks in such solid heat. No-one was mowing, the grass was no longer growing enough to need it, so the village was silent in the sunshine.

Clare was getting pleasantly drunk and soon she decided would be in no state to care about anything, not about Miranda's moodiness, or Jack's lack of a job, or the appalling feeling she was getting that she was at a cocktail party in Wimbledon when here she was supposed to be getting back to nature, away from it all. That was the minus side to drinking champagne in the afternoon. It made you not care about the important things, and then it made you depressed and weepy later about the things that didn't matter at all.

Deep grey storm clouds were starting to gather over the hills and the light had that intensity that made the greens of the fields and trees so much more vivid, sharp-edged and brilliant against the sky. Across the creek in another cottage garden a tired man was slowly clearing weeds from his terrace, shoving them firmly into a black plastic sack.

From the idleness of their deckchairs, Clare and the others watched him.

155

'He's wasting his time. The bin men won't take any of that,' Jack said.

'Perhaps he's going to take it all to his compost heap,' Celia said.

'Don't know why he bothers anyway, I'm sure he's only renting the place.' Clare added, 'At least I haven't seen him around before this week.'

As they watched, the man picked up the full bag and strolled down to the creek.

'Jeez, he's not going to put it in the river is he?'

'Well wouldn't you?' said Clare. She put a few weeds in almost every day. Added up over a week they'd probably come to almost a bagful. 'I do sometimes,' she confessed. 'Not many of course,' she added cravenly.

'Yes but you live here,' Celia said.

'Does that matter?' Jack asked. 'It's the same foliage whether we're here or elsewhere.'

'We pay our council tax,' Archie said.

Jack got up and started clearing plates. The argument was ridiculous, they all sounded like smug children. The heat was getting to them. He went into the kitchen. The whole afternoon was ridiculous. Tea, Eliot's case of champagne, sticky cakes, all unnecessary, just so Clare could soothe her conscience over an issue no-one was ever going to mention, ever again. Wouldn't it have been simpler to say to Celia: 'Sorry your house got messed up but that's what happens when you leave kids of that age on their own.' So they'd all had to play tea-parties while he could have been painting.

By the time Jack came back from the house the others were watching Eliot confront the poor gardening man across the creek. All the kids were lined up by the wall gleefully encouraging Eliot while Clare, Celia and Archie were still trying to pretend nothing was happening. Liz had her eyes shut, looking as if it was only what was to be expected.

As Jack approached he could hear what Eliot was shouting: 'What the fuck do you think you're doing, putting all that garbage into the pissing creek. Don't you realize all that shit floats round blocking up the channel, getting round propellors?'

'It's biodegradable,' shouted the gardener smugly.

'Don't care if it's best bullshit,' Eliot roared, playing now to a larger audience, a party of hikers gathering on the bridge halfway across the creek, reluctant to cross over and look as if they were taking sides. They were joined by a couple of families returning from the beach.

'You fat-arsed evil little bugger!' Eliot was yelling, waving his arms.

'Oh God,' groaned Liz, 'This really is the end.'

All the children were shrieking with laughter, the little ones delighting in the fact that Eliot was too big to have a mummy to tell him off but knowing quite well that that was what he needed.

Clare started to giggle quietly, turning away to hide from the children. Archie poured another drink and appeared to be enjoying himself hugely, as did even Celia, Jack noted, so much for being a goody-goody.

'You're disgusting, you're a disgrace to the planet. You people come here renting our property and think you can do any damn fucking thing you like . . .' Eliot was ranting.

The man stared back, amazed. 'It's my cottage. I bought it last week,' he said. So these were the neighbours, Jack could almost hear him thinking.

'Doesn't make any difference. You're still a podgy ignorant bastard cretin. And you ought to know better,' Eliot slurred. Then he picked up the nearest empty champagne bottle and hurled it across the creek. It fell far short of its target and floated down towards the pub.

'This is appalling,' Celia murmured to Jack. 'Now that we know he's a neighbour, how will we ever live it down?'

'Didn't you think it mattered then, if he was just a renter?' Jack asked her, gathering up empty glasses.

'Oh well I suppose so,' she said unconvincingly, 'but we don't have to live with them.'

'And you can all fuck off too, it isn't a circus.' Eliot gestured rudely to the group on the bridge. Some of them gestured back, laughing, but most of them turned away, embarrassed and continued their walk.

'If this was Barnes, the police would be here by now,' Miranda said to Andrew.

'That's just it,' Milo said. 'As we're all on holiday Eliot thinks it doesn't count. He thinks he can do what he likes. And of course he can, you see.'

'Well it certainly brought everyone together,' Clare was saying later as they washed up in the kitchen. 'At least Celia and I are friends again. It only takes someone else to behave badly and they've all got something else to talk about.'

'That's a terrible way of looking at it,' Miranda said. 'What about that poor man? It was quite funny at the time, but really Eliot humiliated him. I think it's awful.'

'No-one would have cared if he'd been a renter,' Jack said. 'And if he'd been a real local you'd all have asked him how his garden was doing and said the weeds were good for encouraging fish. Double standards. Worse, triple standards.'

He was a summer visitor like themselves, that man, Jack thought. He'd have to be socialized with. He would, on the other hand, once he'd become part of the tea and drinks and barbecue circuit in the village, be able to dine out on Eliot's appalling behaviour for weeks to come, Eliot being famous and having been on Wogan. There wasn't that much that was available to form topics of imaginative conversation in the summer, so perhaps they should all be grateful.

It was a quiet evening up at the Lynchs' house. Eliot took Liz straight to bed, leaving Jessica to take care of the twins. Liz was feeling quite excited, Eliot had been so wonderfully dreadful, just as he had been when she had first met him, hitting a journalist who was trying to conduct an interview. She'd thought him powerful and wild, a primitive man who could say and do exactly as he wanted, whereas she had been brought up to do almost exactly the opposite. She only hoped, that evening, that his sexual stamina would survive all the champagne.

The storm started round about ten. The evening light had turned a murky yellowy-grey, the trees silhouetted and blowing black and stark against the billowing sky. The rain and the lightning began together and Jessica, terrified, crept out of bed, along to Milo's room.

'It isn't just the thunder,' she said, climbing into bed with him, 'I've got a secret and I want you to have it too. It's too big for me.'

Milo put his arm round her, the only girl he could tolerate the idea of being in bed with.

'It's Miranda,' Jessica said. 'She's told me she's pregnant. And she doesn't seem to be doing anything about it.'

Oh these women and their unpredictable bodies, Milo thought.

'Well we can't do anything,' he said. 'Can't you persuade her to tell Clare? Perhaps she could have an abortion.'

'She doesn't believe in it.'

'She'll feel differently when she gets back home, things aren't the same down here, it's all happy-ever-after time in the summer isn't it? Why don't you just snuggle down and go to sleep?'

Jessica put her thumb in her mouth and Milo stroked her naked back, thinking vaguely of Oliver, until they both slept, curled together like kittens. In the morning Liz, cheered by a night of passion, came to wake Milo and wondered if this little scene was something sent by the gods to replace all the worrying she did about Eliot.

Thirteen

People said the next day that the weather had broken, as if, in England a spell of sunshine was a fragile, delicate thing. Rain poured persistently all over the village, drenching the lines of swimsuits and the cushions of the sunloungers that people had been overconfident enough to leave out at night. The post office sold out of plastic macs. They were bought with great reluctance, the purchasers feeling disgruntled that they had so foolishly taken a chance on British weather and not brought anything suitable with them, just in case. Eliot was quite happy in his study, aware that there weren't people out there having a better time than he was, and determinedly hurtling through his four thousand word quota so that he could go out to play later. He could see from his window the dreary plastic shapes of the people wandering in the rain, wondering what they should be doing with themselves, and he thought there was no sight more drab than a floral Laura Ashley sundress vanquished by a shapeless plastic mac. He remembered his first wife, once, caught in a rainstorm in a thin flowered frock and espadrilles with soles like blotting paper. She had looked like a kitten someone had tried to drown.

The residents had their own uniform for the wet weather and could be seen taking soggy walks through the woods in camouflage Barbours and obligatory green wellies. Some wore old skiing anoraks or their oilskins, either way items too bulky for the average two-weeker to have room for in the car. Some, such as Celia and Archie, continued to go out sailing as usual, blinking the rain from their eyelashes and relishing the solitude. Up at the bungalows as the walkers strode past, the retired couples could be seen cosily reading their *Telegraphs* by the light from their picture windows, glancing appreciatively at the rain falling softly on their gardens and saving them a job. In the post office, among the mac-buyers and the postcard-browsers, Harriet, Amy and an assortment of small untidy children were gathered around the souvenir and gift section.

'And I'd like a cat made of shells, and one of those lavender bags, and a box of those little mats, and some flowery cards and sweets . . .'

Amy was putting in her order for birthday presents. With no choice of shops, Amy took her party guests solemnly to the post office and instructed them what to bring her. It was a practical if shameless way to go about having a birthday list, but if they wanted a free tea, Harriet had told them all, they'd have to bring the right stuff. They didn't have to do the buying then, just the choosing. Amy and Harriet would go away with the list, and allocate exactly who was to bring what later. They were very organized children.

Miranda wished she hadn't told Jessica. While no-one had known it had been conveniently unreal. Even the word 'pregnant' didn't convey any meaning to her, but when Miranda looked into her mirror and said to herself 'I'm going to have a baby,' she could make herself scared. The more people who knew about it, the longer she left it, the nearer would be the time when she would have to do something about it. Even if it had been a romance, she couldn't imagine staying on in the village, an old-fashioned shotgun wedding and living in Jeannie's cottage with Steve. Yuck. She longed to be back home again, for things that were normal, even for school, the security of the daily bus journey, homework, babysitting. She stayed in out of the rain, glad of the excuse, and lay on her bed reading Jilly Cooper. Real-life sex now rather revolted her. All those hormones that had told her it was the right time the right place, were now keeping her celibate, too late. She felt sick, not sexy. She no longer wanted to spend any time outside communing with nature, even the fruit on the trees, the flowers fattening their seed pods reminded her of fertility. She now preferred to stay close to home, playing Trivial Pursuit with the family, doing jigsaws with Amy, holding the ends of skipping-ropes for Harriet. She'd tried being a grown-up, gone through the glass and wanted to come back again. She couldn't tell Clare, all that compassion and under-standing that she knew Clare had been storing up for just this moment. And what would she advise her to do? Have an abortion? Clare herself could have got rid of the inconvenient Miranda, but had chosen not to. Would she expect Miranda to do the same?

Clare knew it wasn't a good day to be going into Truro. Everyone rushed to the nearest town when the rain came, trying to minimize the depressing effect of all that damp and dripping. No-one could go to the beach, walking the cliff path was likely to be too muddy for the average holidaymaker in sandals, so Penzance and Falmouth would be full of families drifting from shop to shop with children pleading for money for slot machines and amusement arcades. Bemused fathers would be trailing their wives round cosmetic counters, wishing they'd had the nerve to insist on staying behind to watch the highlights of yesterday's cricket on TV. Truro would be full of shoppers looking for crafts and gifts to take home, and there'd be nowhere to park. People like Clare shopped once a week just like at home, regardless of the weather, and today was, like Jeannie with her floors, her day for it.

In spite of the traffic, it was still with a feeling of escape that Clare drove with Jack into Truro. She felt that following Eliot's performance from her garden the day before it might be wise to get away from the village. She wondered what on earth had happened to that feeling of getting away from it all, as the saying goes. She seemed to be bogged down in curiously suburban pursuits and concerns. She decided to treat herself to a trip round the estate agents while Jack was at the framers and see if they had cottages in the middle of nowhere, with land for growing vegetables, and no neighbours whatsoever. Dream on, she thought. She was tired of tourists photographing her house and hearing them say 'Oh how sweet, it looks just like a tea-cosy'. They didn't have to think about the price of thatch, or the wind-rotted window frames. If only Miranda was not so moody, if Jack wasn't so uncommunicative, if Jeannie didn't keep following her round looking as if she was trying to say something that was obviously proving too difficult to express (like she's leaving, or wants a pay rise, Clare thought). If only, let's be honest, she thought as she negotiated a difficult double roundabout, Eliot showed some sign that he'd at least had a passing fancy for her, even if he'd thought better of it since.

Clare was driving badly. Every time they went round a corner Jack glanced back to see if any of his paintings were falling off the seat. He could stretch an arm back and hold on to them, just to keep them in place, but that would draw attention to the fact that he not only thought Clare was driving too fast, but also that he hadn't the guts to say so. She looked so intent, obviously miles away in thought, he'd only get snapped at. What he really needed was a new portfolio to keep them safe, but Clare would only point out that he already had about six at home in perfectly good condition, why not get a friend to mail one down to them. She didn't understand the lure of art shops though.

He smiled at her and thought about cheering her up.

'Isn't it nice to be on our own for a change?'

'Well it's not dinner at the Ritz, we're only going shopping,' she snapped back, her thoughts disturbed. Then she added, 'Couldn't we go away somewhere, to a hotel maybe, just for a couple of nights?'

'I suppose so,' he said hesitating, 'But what about the children, and surely it's a holiday being at the cottage?'

'I feel I could do with being waited on a little sometimes. Here I still have to cook and clean and all that, it's just like home. I need to be somewhere where someone else changes the beds.'

'You've never complained before,' Jack said.

'I'm not complaining now. I just feel sort of stuck, unrested. And there're always so many people around, there's no peace.'

Aha, Jack thought, so it's sex.

'It's not sex,' Clare said, guessing his thoughts.

'We used to do it all the time in summer,' he said. 'You couldn't wait to get to the country. Now you read feminist novels in bed and wear old tee-shirts. You've gone off it.'

'I've got other things to think about,' Clare said, 'And so have you it seems, you say nothing to me, hardly a word from one end of the day to the next, you go out drawing, visiting that old hippy on the raft, then you eat dinner in almost total silence, climb into bed and expect me to feel romantic. I don't have an "On" switch, I need warming up, like an old radio.'

'Well perhaps we could go to Paris or Venice at half-term. Would you like that?'

'I'd love it,' she said, turning to him with the first smile he'd seen from her that day. 'But it doesn't make me feel any better now. Miranda and you hardly say a word, and living with her at the moment is like treading on eggs. One wrong word and she storms off to her room and stays there for hours.'

'Why be so careful with her?' Jack asked. 'Why not

just ask her straight out what's bugging her and point out that she's upsetting you.'

'If I start asking her then she'll never tell me, she never has told me what's been wrong with her before, I've always had to guess even when she's had things like tonsillitis.'

'Well perhaps nothing much does go wrong for her. You can't expect people to produce problems just so you can have the satisfaction of sorting them out.'

'She's sixteen Jack, she must have some insecurities. I always thought we'd made it so easy for her to talk to us about anything at all, providing just the right atmosphere, not like our parents' generation.'

'We've been too careful, that's the problem,' Jack murmured.

The traffic was slowing to a crawl, there'd be a queue for the Tesco's car park.

'Perhaps she's unhappy about someone,' Clare mused.

'Or maybe it's her exam results, they're due soon,' Jack countered.

'Perhaps she's on the pill and it's making her feel ill.'

'More likely she's just bored in the village.'

'It's bound to be sex, it's her age.'

'God, Clare, for someone who's gone off sex, you sure do sound obsessive. She's not telling you anything because there's nothing to tell. She doesn't need you, she's growing up. I'm sorry if it sounds cruel.'

Clare stopped the car in the traffic queue.

'Suppose she's pregnant?' she persisted.

'And now you're being ridiculous.'

Go on, say it, she thought, 'They're not all like you were'.

An old lady backed her car very carefully out of a parking space and Clare pulled into it briskly. Jack wrapped his paintings in polythene and cradled them protectively against the drizzle. As he stalked off to the framers Clare reflected that once again she was left with the domestic side of things to organize while he went off to play. She was being deliberately unfair, she knew, to make herself feel aggrieved. This was after all now his job. But when he did it on holiday too, it was hard not to think of the painting as a hobby. You had to make as much money as Eliot did, she thought, for something that most people do as a hobby to count as a proper job.

Clare put Jack completely out of her mind as she entered the fray at Tesco's. There was too much to think about buying. Shopping for Amy's birthday party, Clare was overtaken by a comfortable, doing-the right-thing sort of feeling. She started to feel quite good-motherish as she ignored the ready-made icing and instant cake mixes, choosing instead wholemeal flour, molasses, jelly to make into animal shapes, additive-free sausages to put on sticks. Her children didn't often get the chance to experience what she thought of as real children's parties, she thought. They were all too sophisticated, too young. Clare was going to give Amy a real party, with musical chairs, pass the parcel, hats and crackers. They could whine all they liked for a puppet show or a magic man, they could get all that at other peoples' parties back at home. Parents had started renting discos for eight-year-olds. Bit much, Clare thought, if you can't entertain a few children for a couple of hours in your own home without resorting to outside help and an entertainment agency. To hell with the mess on the carpet. Children didn't need all that stuff, just good old-fashioned games and a well-filled going-home bag.

Clare was just reaching for a pack of balloons when she spotted Liz wheeling a trolley down the aisle towards her. Clare didn't like meeting people she knew in supermarkets. She didn't like the leaning on the trolleys, each eyeing what the other had bought, trying hard not to express surprise that someone like that would actually buy frozen oven chips, and in turn suppressing the urge to explain that the children just couldn't exist without tinned tomato soup, comfort food. And then there is the continuation of the trek around the store, you say goodbye and then keep meeting up again with nothing else to say except exchange little inane remarks about the price of cheese, and the awful furtive reaching up for the sliced white bread just as the wholemeal and lentils friend creeps up from behind the cat food.

But Liz had seen Clare, and Clare saw that her trolley was shamelessly stuffed with ready-made chilled food.

'Are you still speaking to me after Eliot's dreadful exhibition?'

'Yes of course. Anyway he was quite fun, livened the village up a bit. I suppose the rain is the reason this place is so crowded today. I'm just getting all the food for Amy's party. Your two are coming aren't they?'

'Yes they're looking forward to it. After I've paid for this lot I'm going off to get her a present. You're so brave having a proper party. You've got tons of food in there,' Liz said, peering into Clare's trolley. 'I hope the weather comes back for you,' she continued. 'When the twins were six we just took a dozen of their friends to see *Cats*, and then the Hard Rock Café afterwards, it saved an awful lot of effort.'

Liz sailed off with her trolley full of expensive delicacies. Clare, quickly calculating the horrendous total cost of the Lynch twins' birthday treat, venomously wished a manky wheel on Liz's trolley, and pulled a can of coke from hers for an instant reviving drink.

Outside in the car park, Clare trundled her goods towards her car and saw a woman trying to hang a bulging carrier bag from the handlebars of an ancient bicycle. The woman looked about Clare's age, in jeans, her hair grown rather too long, making her thin face look longer than it had to. She wore a faded Fair Isle sweater. In her other hand she held a big silver helium-filled balloon which struggled to get away in the wind.

Dealing with the bike and the shopping was all too much and the balloon escaped. The woman stared at it for a moment, the long face drooping like a disappointed child's. How old do you have to be, Clare wondered, as she stacked the slippery bags of shopping into the back of the Volvo, before you were grown-up enough not to mind losing your balloon? She watched the woman to see what she would do. She was too old, perhaps too busy, to go back into the store and ask for another one. Clare wanted to go and get one for her, to lie and say 'it's for my daughter', but it was too late. Clare had finished loading the car and others were queueing for her space. The woman, who perhaps hadn't minded that much at all, climbed on to her bike and peddled slowly away into the traffic.

Fourteen

Miranda stood in front of the mirror, a full-length one on the inside of her wardrobe door. She zipped herself into her jodhpurs and tried to work out whether they felt tight because she was a year older and bigger than the last time she had worn them or if she was already starting to expand with pregnancy. Beyond the mirror inside the wardrobe she could see all the clothes that she wouldn't be able to wear soon if 'the situation' as she now called it in her head, continued. All those little thirties dresses with their neat waists, the skirts whose buttons she had had to move to stop them sliding down her narrow hips. She'd have to move them all back again. The riding boots still fitted, did that mean that her feet, and presumably the rest of her, had now stopped growing? Could God let you start growing another person inside you before you'd stopped growing yourself? It didn't happen with plants, it didn't seem natural. Miranda took off her riding gear and inspected her flat stomach. She was still so thin she could almost see right through to her insides. What was going on in there? She looked inside the wardrobe and chose a pale pink cotton dress, one of the smallest she had. Might as well wear it while she could.

'Ought to be doing some physical jerks,' Archie said to Andrew. 'Should have joined the CCF at school, no need for all this equipment, that's for poncey body-builders and the like.'

Over the top of his *Telegraph*, from his comfortable

seat under the rowan tree Archie watched Andrew work out with his weights.

'It's not poncey, Dad, boxers use them, and weight-lifters and such.'

'Perhaps so,' said Archie, 'But if you want real sport, it should be related to survival, that's how it all came about, being out there in the wild. Pentathlon stuff. Now there's an event, run after your quarry, over the obstacles, throw your spear at it, that sort of thing. Sense of purpose. What's the point of lifting all those weights if you can't do all the running and jumping as well.'

Andrew lifted the twin weights rhythmically up and down. 'I'm doing my pectorals,' he said, 'Then when I've speared my wild boar I'll be able to pick it up won't I?'

'I suppose it's useful for sailing,' Archie conceded, folding *The Telegraph* for the crossword. Andrew did after all have rather a puny body still. He'd look a lot more manly with a bit of muscle. At least flabbiness didn't run in the family. There was nothing worse: flabby body, flabby mind.

'Not going out on the water today?' Archie asked.

Andrew straightened up, put down his weights and consulted his instruction book.

'Milo's gone into Truro and the others are going to help supervise Amy's birthday party over at Clare's. I could ask you the same thing.'

Archie filled in twenty-three across with his fountain pen.

'Your mother's making buns or something for Clare,' he said. 'You and I could take the Laser round the point later, look for a mackerel or two if you like.'

He could hardly read what he'd written, the ink spread over the newspaper, however carefully and lightly he wrote. He couldn't bring himself to use a Biro, a gentleman used a proper pen. Inheriting his father's old pen had made him hope for the sharp cryptic brain that had gone along with it, to help with the more difficult crossword clues. Andrew's lips moved as he read the weightlifting instructions, Archie noticed. That brilliant brain of his father's must have got well-diluted by the time it got to Andrew, he thought. Funny too how little actual writing one did these days, he wasn't going to wear out the old Parker just signing his name occasionally and filling in half the clues in *The Daily Telegraph.*

'Be careful with that icing Miranda,' Clare said. 'It would be a shame to spoil that dress, it's bound to need dry-cleaning.'

'It's only cotton Mum,' said Miranda. 'I've washed it before by hand. And I'm being careful. Did you remember the Smarties?'

'Two big boxes,' Clare said. 'And some of those little boxes to put in their going-home bags. They'll be sick to death of them by tomorrow. And there're blue ones, I don't know about those, they look the wrong colour for food.'

Miranda spread the pink icing carefully over the cake, and then licked the spoon.

'Don't lick it!' Clare shouted.

'Didn't think you were looking,' grinned Miranda. 'Anyway who's to know? I'm not infectious.'

'You know quite well it's unhygienic, and anyway you might have a cold coming.'

'We should have got some of those cake tins that are letter shaped,' Miranda said. 'It's only three letters after all and I bet we could have hired them in Truro.'

'It's quite enough making one cake, let alone three,' Clare said. They moved around the tiny kitchen, organizing their different party contributions. Clare cut pretty circular sandwiches, marmite and apple, cheese and celery, tuna and tomato. They'd probably rather have jam, she thought, but she had to try.

171

Miranda ran her finger round the bottom of the cake where some of the icing was beginning to trickle on to the plate.

'Do I put the smarties on now or wait till it sets?' she asked.

'Wait till it's half set, when it's decided to stop sliding down the cake, otherwise if you make a pattern with them it will be all over the place.' Clare looked at the piles of sandwiches. 'I wish I knew exactly how many were coming,' she said, 'They just go round the village dredging up everyone who looks the right age.'

Miranda laughed. 'I think that's what Milo did with Andrew's party, that Celia said should Never Have Happened.'

Clare laughed too, rinsing knives under the tap.

'Now I won't hear a word against Celia, she's making buns for the party. Blast there's the phone.'

Miranda turned back to the cake and started opening Smartie packets.

'If it's anyone for me,' she said, 'please will you tell them I'm not here.'

Anyone must mean Steve, Clare thought, she couldn't possibly not want to speak to Milo or Jess or friends from London. So whatever it is is over, that must be what Jeannie wanted to talk about. But there was obviously nothing to discuss. Good.

Eliot had got to the part in his story where the hero had got to do something erotic with the beautiful spy. He faced the word processor and the screen stared back at him, daring him to make its controls smoulder with some highly original sexual athletics. Eliot was floundering at this point. This was the bit where he always got stuck, for although he was a man much given to sexual infidelities, and considered himself highly experienced, his tastes were fairly traditional. On a good day, a straightforward bonk was quite adequate, he had found. He rather liked, if he thought about it, red French knickers. Liz had some and he'd always thought them pretty rude. Women who thought about their underwear, not just flinging on the nearest, most practical Marks and Spencer stuff, they must give those underneath bits of their bodies a lot of thought too. Though he wasn't sure if this was true in Liz's case. She thought about her body the whole time, it seemed to him. It was all very highly polished, like a table you were scared to put anything hot on to in case you made rings.

Of course what he really needed to do, Eliot decided, was to go out and look for some inspiration. It was no good looking at Liz, lying out there by the pool with sunblock on her nose and her nipples. He needed to look at more ordinary women, overheated young mothers on beaches, with swimsuit straps falling down, showing those endearing white bits of flesh where the sun couldn't reach. He switched off the word processor.

'I'm going out for a walk with the dog,' he called out to Liz, 'Don't want to come do you?'

'No thanks Eliot. Don't forget you said you'd collect the twins from Clare's, it's Amy's party. About sixish, don't be late.'

'I won't, in fact I'll be early and then she'll have to give me a drink,' he called cheerfully. He put cigarettes in his pocket and collected a cold beer from the fridge. Might as well have some refreshment down on the beach, it was a long time till 6 p.m. Now Clare, he thought, there was an erotic lady, so constantly anxious, all her feelings up there at the top. Quite a thought, and good for the novel.

'Where did all these kids come from?' Jack asked, looking around at the gathering in his garden. 'Who on earth do they all belong to?'

'Renters' kids of course,' Clare said. 'Our two go fishing with them, you've seen them. They'll all be gone in a week or two. They all brought presents, isn't that sweet of them?'

They had too, a funny little assortment from the village, which had corresponded most satisfyingly with the list Harriet and Amy had drawn up in the post office. All were unwrapped, just handed over like an entrance fee from grubby little fingers. The only wrapped gift had come from the Lynch twins, a lavishly packaged painting set wrapped in Pooh Bear paper, inside a Pooh Bear carrier bag, with a Pooh Bear tag and about twelve feet of yellow ribbon (Pooh Bear coloured, presumably, thought Clare), done up in bows.

'Liz doesn't worry too much about packaging being a waste of trees then,' Miranda had observed.

'Never mind,' said Jack, taking her too seriously. 'We'll make sure it goes in the paper bank.'

The children were all out on the cottage lawn, fighting over the swing. 'We'll have to start playing games with them soon,' Clare said to Miranda.

Jessica came in from the garden, 'By the way Clare, there are fourteen of them, in case any go wandering off, I thought you might need to know.'

'Thanks Jess, but to be honest I don't think it makes much difference seeing I don't even know their names. The tide's out and they can't even fall into the creek. Still it's only for a couple of hours, what can'happen.'

Clare went into the sitting room to collect cushions for musical chairs. Miranda drifted around looking elegant but useful, carrying trays of lemonade, bowls of jelly and paper plates to the sheet spread out picnic-style under the cherry tree. Little children dashed about shrieking, and Clare came out to look at them anxiously, aware that there was usually one who was shy, couldn't join in, and might even need to be returned to its parents, wherever and whoever they were. This was not like the parties back home, she thought.

'Do you think they'll eat this stuff?' Jack asked, coming out of the kitchen with a bowl of mixed nuts and dried fruit.

'All that dried fruit? They'll love it!' Clare said. 'Ours do, and besides it's much better for them than crisps.'

Miranda and Jessica supervised the games, with such skill and tact that nobody had to fight for prizes, and the children sat down under the tree for tea.

'See, they are eating it,' Clare said to Jack, watching the children tackle the dried fruits and the wholemeal sandwiches.

'True, but if you listen carefully,' Jack said as he pulled the cork from a bottle of wine, 'you can hear the words "Monster Munch" and "bat-crisps".'

'Amy's so lucky,' Miranda said to Jessica as they lazed on the wall by the creek. 'She gets to have her birthday down here. Mine's November and I always have to share it with the street firework party.'

Jessica rolled over on the wall to brown her back.

'Well think of poor Milo, his is at Christmas, so he only gets half the annual presents, but they are usually rather good to make up for it. Usually better than mine anyway,' Jessica added.

Miranda sucked the sweetness from a stem of clover, 'You two never seem to be short of anything, if you don't mind me saying,' she said, smiling at Jessica and wondering if she had maybe gone too far.

'All that sports equipment do you mean?' Jessica laughed and Miranda nodded. 'Dad's got a thing about it. He says you can't do sports the way they're supposed to be done unless you've got state of the art equipment, best tennis raquet, newest Nikes, etc. But what he really means is that he can't do them, not us. Having all the right gear is to psych the opposition. And besides he likes shopping. It gets him away from that word processor he's so scared of. He'll do anything not to work.'

*　　*　　*

Eliot, away from his word processor, was researching on the beach. All the women he looked at seemed to be too shrill, too harrassed for him to get a calm erotic feeling about. The only one he considered vaguely fanciable had seen him sitting on his rock swigging beer from the bottle and noticed his constant staring at her. Startled by his obvious interest, by his lime green linen jacket and old straw hat, she had a quiet word with her husband and they had silently packed up their child, their windbreak, towels and radio and moved to the other end of the beach. Lucky not to have been clobbered by her old man, Eliot thought. Nice tits, shame about the attitude. A truly erotic lady would have noticed his interest, flaunted her bikinied bottom at him. Still, it was nearly 5 p.m. and probably not too early to call on Clare and Jack. As he strolled back from the beach, Eliot could hear the children's shrieks of excited laughter from Clare's garden, and over the creek a couple of balloons were flying away. Further along he could see Celia weeding her rose bed and she looked up and waved cheerfully at him. Angular woman, he reminded himself, angular family in fact. Probably not much given to naughtiness, but it could be fun risking a casual grope at a beach barbecue just to see which way the land lay, so to speak.

Clare was carrying plates back to the kitchen when Eliot arrived. Her hair hung in wind-blown wisps around her face and she wore a stained apron over her sundress. Embarrassed by the ancient apron she blushed and grinned at Eliot who said, 'Here let me carry those for you' and took the plates from her.

'Thanks,' she said, pushing her hair back out of her eyes. 'All of it goes in the bin liner in the kitchen, I'm afraid it's a pit in there.'

'It's a kids' party, of course there's a mess,' Eliot replied.

Clare caught up with him in the kitchen on her next trip into the house, hands full of chicken bones and plastic spoons. God what a mess, she thought, but he didn't seem to be noticing, casually opening one of Jack's bottles of Rioja and pouring them each a conspiratorial glass.

'Ah but you're lookin' lovely, missus,' Eliot said, in the accent of his ancestors.

'That must be the most untrue thing you've ever said,' Clare laughed, tipping leftover mixed nuts into the bin (they didn't like them that much, after all).

'Ah well tis solace you'll be needing,' he said, putting his arms round her and pushing her against the dresser.

'Eliot, you're so wicked!' Clare giggled, squirming for a more comfortable position. Eliot took that as an encouraging sign, but she was being pushed against the wet tea towels and she'd get a grubby damp patch on the back of her dress. She wished things like that didn't go through her mind on such occasions.

'Bejesus then give an old man a kiss,' demanded Eliot and didn't wait for an answer, but started kissing Clare, pushing her more firmly against the wood.

I'm in my filthy kitchen, with Jack only a wall away, with fourteen children and two teenagers in my garden and I'm having the most erotic experience I've had in years, Clare thought. She closed her eyes and gave in to the bliss of it. Eliot's tongue was in her mouth, his hand was moving expertly up her skirt. Clare opened one eye to remind herself that this was real. In the kitchen window, fetchingly framed by the hanging dried flowers, the knife rack and the shelf of storage jars was Celia, mouth open like a codfish, staring in at Clare. Clare pulled away from Eliot abruptly and reluctantly. Oh God, she thought, now what. Over Eliot's shoulder a dark shadow was filling the doorway. Clare couldn't see who it was but thought, please God don't let it be Jack. It wasn't, but this was no relief as the figure was that of a large uniformed policeman.

Clare disentangled herself from Eliot and straightened her dress. The wet tea towels had made her dress damp and clingy at the back, it was hard to collect her dignity.

'Yes, Officer, can I help you?' she asked, in her best south west London voice.

'I think you can Madam,' the policeman said, getting the inevitable notebook from his pocket. 'We've had a report from the postmistress. There's been a large amount of pilfering from the village shop.'

'I don't think Clare is likely to go shoplifting, Sergeant,' Eliot said. 'Fancy a drink?' he offered.

'No thank you Sir. No it's not you, Madam. I'm afraid the culprits are children. Some of these are yours aren't they? Perhaps we could have a word.'

Outside was another policeman, and a woman police officer (they have to bring one if it's children, Clare thought), and there was a panda car, blue light still going round, quite unnecessarily drawing the attention of the entire village. Trippers were collecting on the bridge to get a good look. Anxious parents of the party guests, seeing the light from their gardens and balconies, arrived to retrieve their children. Clare sat on the grass, her head whirling from the afternoon's events. She looked at Celia and noted a sly little grin on her face. The police were talking to Jack, in that low monotone that police have when they're going about their duty. She caught the words 'prosecution' and 'taking this further' and 'serious'.

'I think it's time to open another bottle,' said Eliot.

'It'll be all round the village by closing time,' Jack said to Clare as the police, the children and their tight-lipped parents dispersed. 'They've forgotten their going-home bags,' said Clare, feeling forlorn. Some of these families weren't going home for another ten days and would have to be faced in the pub and post office. Except of course, Clare thought, we can't really go in the post office any more. She'd have to get in the car every morning and drive for papers and milk in the next village. Ought to make Amy and Harriet cycle for them, that would teach them.

'What are we going to do about the children?' Clare asked Jack as she collected burst balloons from the garden.

'Well ours didn't actually do the stealing,' Jack said. 'They only organized it, really.'

'What do you mean "only organized" it. The Mafia only organize crimes too, it doesn't make them any less guilty. They dared those kids, they made it a condition of coming to the party.'

'I suppose so. I suppose we'll have to think of some punishment for them. Seems a shame on holiday,' Jack said reluctantly.

'You suppose right,' Clare said. 'Honestly Jack, don't be so wet-liberal. They've behaved appallingly and they should damn well know that we both think so, holiday or not.'

Eliot was still there, lounging now on a deckchair, glass in hand.

'Come on now Clare, every kid nicks stuff from Woollies at some stage, it's traditional, a rite of passage.'

'No they don't, I never did. They haven't been brought up to be criminals, "organizers" or otherwise. Why is it only me that takes it seriously?'

'Are you sure you're not just slightly over-reacting?' Jack said tentatively. The two men were now both sitting in deckchairs, looking up at her. They looked like a pair of school-boys, she thought. The grin on Eliot's face reminded her that small children don't have the monopoly on naughty behaviour.

'Don't be too hard on them Clare,' Eliot put in his plea for clemency.

'They wouldn't behave like this normally,' Jack added. Harriet and Amy could be heard at the window above them, sniggering at the adults' indecision.

'No excuse,' Clare said. 'This is "normally", we live

here a lot of the time. They'll grow up into a pair of lager louts or something. Why did those kids steal anyway, why didn't they just buy the presents, not that they needed to bring anything at all.'

'I must take my kids home,' Eliot said. 'Liz will be wondering what's happened. If it's any help, I shall not be treating your family as the village outcasts. You and your delinquent children are welcome to come and play with me and my children any time at all.' Eliot bowed, and winked at Clare. The children weren't the only ones to misbehave that afternoon. Celia, Clare remembered, where had she gone off to?

Celia was sipping a gin and tonic on her terrace and telling Archie: 'I don't know how she could, Eliot is so unkempt, and that was when the police arrived.'

'Gosh,' said Archie, boyishly. 'Clare and Eliot. I wonder how long that's been going on.'

'Years probably. I can't imagine what Clare thinks she's up to. Of course one expects that sort of thing with Eliot, he's the Type,' Celia said firmly.

'Better not let Andrew know anything about it,' Archie said. 'He's very friendly with Milo and Jessica and Miranda too of course. Wouldn't do for them to know.'

'Perhaps we shouldn't see so much of them from now on,' Celia said, sipping her drink.

'Oh of course we must. It will be much more fun, knowing what we know. Just like watching a play!'

Fifteen

Clare faced the collective wrath of the village by painting the kitchen doors out in her garden. She unscrewed the louvre doors from the unit frames and carried them outside, leaning them against the bench and the pear tree, trying to keep them in the shade as much as possible to stop the sun drying the paint too fast.

Her pleasure in the dirty-rose pink colours she had chosen was marred by a sense that she was out there doing penance for the collective sins of herself and her children. Amy and Harriet were allowed to go to the beach with Miranda or Jack, but had to be kept away from other children, as if they were covered with chicken pox scabs. It wasn't difficult, for most of the villagers were just as intent on keeping their children away from Amy and Harriet.

Clare's guilt also extended to cover the knowledge that, unforgiveably, she had snooped on Miranda, trying to find out what was in her diary. Perhaps it was time to let go a little, to realize that she should be happy that Miranda could feel capable of dealing with life's inevitable problems by herself. Wasn't that what being grown up was supposed to be about?

Clare smoothed the paint on to the knotty chipped old wood as gently as she could. The one thing she didn't feel bad about was Eliot. The thought of him squashing her none too gently against the dresser and rummaging under her dress made her face crease into an involuntary gleeful smile and her hand trembled so the paint dripped. Aware that her solitary grin must make her, from the other side of the creek, look like she was deranged, she leapt up at the first ring of the phone, glad of an excuse to get her elated expression safely into the cool of the house.

'I was so sorry to hear about your little bit of trouble at Amy's party,' Liz purred down the phone to Clare. 'Eliot says it was ghastly for you, all those police. He says we should take you and Jack out for dinner at the Parrot, just to keep the communal flag flying. What do you think?'

She certainly managed to make it clear it wasn't her idea of fun, Clare thought, but what she said was: 'Yes we'd love to, thank you, a super idea.'

'Oh and we've asked Archie and Celia too,' Liz said. 'Just to keep our numbers up.'

'We've got to show our faces in the village then,' Jack said, when Clare told him.

'We can show our faces any time,' Clare said. 'We've done nothing wrong. It's the children who need to keep out of the way.'

'And we're not responsible for what they do?' Jack said filling in the last clue in *The Times* with a casual skill that Archie would have envied.

'Not to the extent that we can't go anywhere and be seen. I shall have to wear that black linen dress again.'

Of course the villagers weren't talking about the family at all, even though everyone knew. The summer visitors always caused some trouble or other, and this would be stored up for the winter months when boredom set in and you could hear yourself think in the bar at the Mariners. Then the apocryphal tales of the summer could be got out, exaggerated, pulled apart, reputations shredded and innocent personalities damned, ready for the next year when the poor victims would return for a fresh start, in cheerful innocence. It was the wrath of the renters from which Jack was hiding, all their children led astray by his. These no-good middle-class second-home types with no morals, ruining the only holiday some people get in the year, and no come-back from the police either. Jack was guiltily collecting his newspaper from the next village, shopping at Safeway in Carn Brea instead of Tesco's in Truro as if the notoriety of his brood could possibly extend that far. His paintings were hanging in the craft centre, but he was too cowardly to go and find out if they were selling, scared that when he got there he would find they had all been removed in disgrace from the walls and be out piled up in the back storage room with all the other rejects. He'd have to get over that one, there was a living to be earned, and he still hadn't told Clare he wanted to leave London and settle down here.

The dustmen had been that morning. Just as careless as binmen anywhere else, the village had slightly the air of an upended litter bin. Tissues blew about, cats sat in doorways crunching discarded chicken bones, and bits of torn plastic were caught at the bottom of the hedges. Clare conscientiously tidying up around her own front door, picked up the cardboard box she had found crushed beneath her own upended bin lid, and wondered who in the village was testing for pregnancy. The unhappy-looking tenant up the road perhaps, or that pale peaky waitress at the Parrot. She put the carton in the bin and forgot about it.

'Isn't it a bit hot for wetsuits?' Andrew asked Milo on the beach the next morning.

'You'll need it,' Milo said. 'You'll spend far more time in the water than on the board at first and it gets surprisingly cold and tiring. I know you're an ace sailor but this is as much to do with balance as anything else. It's a knack, it takes time.'

Andrew and Milo carried the board down to the water's edge.

'You're not going in the water yet,' Milo said, 'I'll give you your first lesson here on the beach.'

Andrew looked around to see if there was anyone he knew. How embarrassing, he felt, he hated learning things in front of others. It reminded him of when Archie had taught him to swim. Andrew must have been about six, and his daddy was the one with the loudest voice at the local pool, yelling 'one two three breathe, one two three breathe!' Andrew had wanted to join the other children with their Wednesday afternoon Penguin Club lessons but Archie had been going through a phase of Involvement in his son's development and took on the teaching of swimming to Andrew much as a proud new owner takes on the training of a puppy.

After that, Andrew had become wary about the learning of new skills and wherever possible did it in the company of his peers where there was less chance of being singled out as the new boy. He made sure his name was one of the first on the list for the school ski trips, the sailing weeks in Norfolk, the extra tennis lessons.

Andrew wandered self-consciously back to the clubhouse to get the windsurfer's rig. Milo even had to tell him how to carry it.

'Wishbone over your shoulder Andrew,' he yelled up the beach, while Andrew changed its ungainly position and tried to look as if he was sauntering casually down to the water. There weren't many people on the beach this early, but the water was packed with eager sailors. The windsurfers whizzed among the dinghies, like go-faster road hogs on a motorway. Andrew wanted to look that flash, but the wetsuit he had rented from the club wasn't something he particularly wanted to be seen in. It was a good brisk day for windsurfing, so most of the boards and wetsuits had been rented out to eager holiday-makers. All that was left that came close to Andrew's size was an old black one that was rather too large in the body and perished in places. Andrew had to roll up the sleeves and legs a bit and he felt like a toddler who has been bought an outfit to grow into. He wondered if it would be easier to get his father to fork out for a state-of-the-art wetsuit than it would be to get his mother to buy the towelling robe he had not yet dared ask for.

Andrew stood on the board clutching the boom, leaning back as instructed by Milo. 'The further you lean back, the faster you'll go.' Andrew let a brief vision of himself flash across his mind, himself in a luminous blue shortie wetsuit, good and tight around his new muscles, tanned legs braced on the board, leaping across the swell as Jessica watched admiringly from the sailing club balcony. He saw himself redeemed, her interest and lust at last awakened. He had once heard Clare say to Liz about some actor or other 'one feels ones thighs part involuntarily every time he's on TV'. Andrew wanted Jessica, or anyone female in fact, to feel exactly like that about him.

But when they put the board in the water it was quite different.

'Try to keep the wind behind you,' Milo said. 'Lean the mast forward if you want to turn to the right, and if you feel you're overbalancing, just drop the sail.'

Andrew overbalanced and fell in the water.

'And concentrate!' yelled Milo, as if he could read thoughts.

'Richmond Park it isn't,' Miranda whispered to Jessica as they picked their riding-booted way across the field to where several sleepy-looking ponies were tethered to a gate. The churned-up mud on the paddock had dried into uneven brick-hard clumps and Miranda pitied the little holiday children taking their first ever riding lesson in this field – ponies losing their footing and stumbling, speeding up whenever they got near the water trough, and snatching greedy

185

bites at the hedge. She, like most of her London friends, had learnt in a smart indoor sand ring where the sharp-voiced instructress had by her manner made the learning of leg-commands to the horse almost superfluous. One change of tone and they all knew what to do. Suburban children don't go for a casual ride like country children, they go for riding lessons. Here at this riding establishment Miranda had heard that Mrs Smith didn't use a voice of authority to bully her horses, she would just chase behind the lazy ones with a plastic bin liner and frighten them into a fast trot whenever they were being idle. Not a happy thought for a beginner, but Miranda was experienced, and Harriet and Amy didn't seem to mind, they enjoyed the opportunity to play cowboys and indians and hang around the tack room.

Mrs Smith had a quick look at her clients for the morning ride. 'You two big girls are on these larger ones,' she indicated vaguely to Jessica and Miranda. 'You've both done a fair bit of riding, I remember from Easter, so you'll be OK.' Miranda and Jessica were not the tallest people in the group, so Miranda assumed the ponies were probably the two most difficult to handle.

'Do you really think you should,' Jessica whispered, giving Miranda a leg-up on to the grey mare. 'You know, in your condition?'

'Yes of course I should. Don't fuss. I don't suppose we'll be doing more than a slow trot anyway.'

'Yes I know, but you won't, you know, you wouldn't, sort of do anything on purpose . . .'

'Like jump off and break my neck do you mean?' Miranda said. 'No of course I won't. It would have been cheaper to fall down the stairs at the cottage. Give me a break, Jess. Let me pretend there's nothing happening, while I still can.'

The assortment of ponies set off towards the woods. In the distance was the sea, little sailing boats skudding across the harbour entrance using the hippy raft as a marker buoy. Ahead of Miranda and Jessica, little girls chatted about Ponies they had Ridden, outdoing each other with tales of pony club camps and gymkhana triumphs.

Listening in to their conversation, Jessica turned to Miranda and said, 'Just shows, you never can tell can you?'

'You'd think, wouldn't you, that if they do that much riding, they'd bring all their gear with them.'

'Don't know, depends on the size of the car, and of course the mother. Not the size of her, but you know they say things like "well it's either your riding boots darling",' Jessica mocked a home-counties yowl, ' "or it's Daddy's case of Chablis." '

'Yes and guess which wins.'

Eliot was sitting quietly on a log in the woods when he heard the ponies. His tape recorder was abandoned on the ground, his dog was snuffling for rabbits, and he sat idly filleting leaves with his fingers, wondering if going round titillating housewives counted as infidelity. It was a bit like when he was young and girls used to warn him against going 'too far'. What constituted 'too far' used to vary from girl to girl, and finding out their individual limits was an exhilaratingly risky mind and body game. One had always to be prepared, condom-wise, for the ones who thought that going too far involved getting pregnant, but were all right with anything short of that. But one also had to be prepared, self-control wise, for those whose 'too far' meant a warm eager hand inside the bra. 'Nothing below the waist' was how one of them had coyly put it. She'd worn, he recalled, a very tightly belted skirt, as if to emphasize the instruction, but also a half-cup black lacy bra. He should have taken that as a sign, and tried a bit harder to find out if all her underwear matched. Oh these lost opportunities. He could have had Clare against her kitchen dresser if it hadn't been for those little local difficulties. (Quite a lot, really, he remembered, fourteen children, her husband, Celia, three police officers). It was the thought that counted. The horses he had heard in the distance were trotting now along the woodland path. He could hear the voices of children and got up to look and see if any of them were his. Jessica had said she was going out that morning with Miranda. As he got up and moved, he saw the front horse, a grey, shy away from something, rear up and he watched as if in slow motion the girl crashed to the ground. She didn't scream, just lay quietly looking stunned. The other horses bunched up behind her, stopping. Eliot came forward, to be helpful, and saw that the fallen rider was Miranda, lying on the ground looking up at him, pale and fragile, her riding hat askew but apparently having done its job, for her eyes focused clearly on his and she smiled.

'Hello Eliot, what are you doing here?' she said.

'Miranda! Are you all right? What did you do that for, you said you wouldn't,' Jessica came up, shouting to her.

'I didn't do anything. The horse shied, it saw something.'

Later Jack said 'It was probably Eliot, the sight of him in the woods is enough to frighten anything half out of its wits' remembering his own early morning moment of terror when Eliot had come shambling like a bear through the bracken.

But Miranda wasn't hurt. She lay there looking up at Mrs Smith and Jessica and Eliot, and the strange upside-down faces of the curious horses. Her pony had wandered away nonchalantly to graze under the trees, as if it was nothing to do with her. Miranda moved her limbs in turn to give each of them a chance to hurt individually, but the only sensation she was aware of was a pleasing dampness inside her jodhpurs. If she hadn't known she was pregnant, she'd have sworn it was a period starting, and she'd have begun to worry about blood beginning to show through. When did you get over that nervousness? Did one ever become confident enough to wear a white skirt at any old time of the month, even when you were due? Miranda's mind wandered as she lay there, in a rather happy and vague way. Is this concussion she thought?

'Well we can't stay here all day can we,' Mrs Smith said briskly. 'If you're not hurt, then up you get. Back on the horse immediately, it's the only way to keep your confidence.'

Miranda got back on the pony, helped by Eliot.

'I'll lead you back,' he said quietly to her, taking hold of the bridle. 'I don't go for this confidence nonsense. You don't get right back into a car after a smash.'

'I'm all right really, Eliot, but thanks, it's kind of you,' Miranda said, smiling. She kept smiling in the same secret way, looking disconcertingly happy and serene for someone who would feel the bruises tomorrow. But that's youth for you, Eliot thought. If he'd fallen like that, he'd be in bed for a week, not to mention spending a good afternoon queuing in X-ray.

But it wasn't just youth. Miranda was smiling about the increasing damp feeling, which had just started to be accompanied by an old familiar low dragging pain in her stomach. She simply wanted to get back home as quickly as possible and take a look in her knickers.

That afternoon Jack tore up a painting. He didn't like doing that, it was such a waste of time, such an admission that it had got the better of him. When he had worked in oils, all those years ago, he had been able to rework a painting till it felt right, in fact the problem had been recognizing when it was finished. Watercolour was less forgiving, let you get away with nothing. A mark on the paper was your finished mark. Overworking the paint meant dull mud-like colour, and Jack was still working on getting the delicate balance right. It was the view across the river towards the raft, he'd had several goes at it, some very successful. This time the trees all merged into a splodge of viridian and olive. The colours were changing, autumn was on its way and Jack was finding the technique difficult. Like life, he thought. How was one ever supposed to be ready for that great autumn when it came? Would he just keep plodding on pretending he was still in his salad days, till the very end? It would be typical of his generation. Meanwhile, the painting was torn to shreds. There was always another piece of paper to have a go at. He took the reject down to the dustbin, not wanting to leave it in the kitchen bin for the family to comment on. In the bottom of the bin he found the little blue and white package, just where Clare had left it, and his heart sank to the bottom of the bin with it. Why hadn't Clare said anything? How many more years was he going to have to go on being Supportive. Just when he thought his hunter-gatherer days were coming neatly to an end. There went freedom.

Sixteen

Miranda had expected more blood. She associated miscarriage with haemorrhage and had wondered if she might have to be taken off to Truro in the air ambulance. That was rather a thrilling thought, but then of course if that happened they'd all know, and there'd be all the family complications associated with that. As it was, the blood had gone through and stained her jodhpurs, but not more than unexpected blood usually did. She took them off, screwed them up and buried them in the laundry basket, hoping Clare's environmentally-friendly washing powder was up to the challenge. The pain was still there, but no worse than she had had with her first few periods only a couple of years ago, when she had tried to get off hockey and been made to play in goal instead, sweating from the cramps in her stomach and letting in goals obliviously, caring only that her insides felt they were draining away.

Miranda turned on the bath taps and undressed. Clare had once told her that her own mother hadn't let her have baths when she was bleeding, in case the blood went to her head. What strange mental maps of their insides some people must have, Miranda thought, and fancy telling your mother whenever you had a period anyway. One thing left to do, she thought, before getting in the bath. She took the tweezers from the basket on the window ledge and firmly quashing both scruples and distaste, collected clotted bits of blood from her knickers. If anyone saw me doing this, she thought, they'd be appalled, but disgusting as it was, it was also fascinating. This stuff might have been my child, she thought, trying out the possibility of feeling some emotion. But she felt nothing but curiosity and relief. Disinterestedly, she wondered how she could get to borrow Andrew's microscope to see if this brownish blob was human shaped, or just a brownish blob.

I'm assuming the worst is over, Miranda thought as she got in the bath, or was the water about to turn scarlet, and the pain get so much worse they'd have to break down the door and find her lying soaking in the gore as if her wrists were slashed.

Too embarrassing. She washed quickly and dressed in clean fresh clothes. She washed her hair under the shower hose, rinsing away the last of her sins, like Lady Macbeth, leaving only the stains on her underwear and on her conscience.

'Miranda are you in there?' Clare was knocking impatiently. 'Hurry up, I need to wash my hair, we're going out tonight don't forget.'

'OK Mum, just give me a minute.'

Miranda looked round the bathroom, picked up the soap box in which she had hidden the blood clots and hiding it under a heap of her clothes, carried it out to her bedroom.

'About time,' said Clare. 'What do you find to do in there?' she said as Miranda wafted a cloud of Clare's Bluebell perfume out of the bathroom with her.

'Don't forget you're babysitting.'

'I know, I know, but I might go out for half an hour or so, can I take Amy and Harriet with me?'

'Well you certainly can't leave them on their own, and please try to make sure they're in bed by nine. Oh and please don't let them near anyone else's children.'

Miranda went downstairs to the phone, from upstairs she could still hear Clare complaining about the lack of hot water. Miranda phoned Jessica.

'Meet me at about 8 p.m. here, there's something I

want to do on our beach. I'll tell you when I see you.'

'Sounds exciting!' Jessica said. 'A mystery, like we used to play when we were little.'

'It's absolutely not like when we were little,' Miranda told her. 'I wish it was.'

Liz was one of those people who always have the right clothes. She never agonized over what she was going to wear. She would have been appalled at the heap of rejected clothes on Clare's bed, the last-minute ironing, and the bathroom scrubbing of the only possible (but uncomfortable) pair of shoes with a J-cloth soaked in Flash. Liz left enough time for her nail varnish, hair and deodorant to dry. She did not shave her legs in the bath and then have to put up with the feeling of wanting to scratch her ankles all evening. Liz's twins had eaten a neat Marks and Spencer's supper at 6.30 p.m. and Jessica would put them to bed. The evening was well-organized, except for Eliot who lay on the bed in socks and purple boxer shorts, the newspaper propped up on his paunch.

'We'll be late Eliot, do hurry,' Liz said, now at the final point of decoration, the putting-on of the earrings.

'No rush,' he mumbled, 'It's only down the lane.'

Eliot didn't like eating out. That was something he associated with his work. He was taken out to lunch to be told off by his publisher about deadlines, to talk of sales figures, book launches and public appearances. Lunch was never free, as they say, someone always wanted something in return for the filet mignon. Smooth journalists interviewed him over dinner in fashionable places, noting what he ate, checking over his consumption of alcohol, eyeing his waistline and ignoring what he said, judging by the rubbish they made up back in their offices. Eliot's heart sank whenever he read a rave review of a new restaurant, a sure sign that that was where the next greedy expense-account hack would be suggesting they meet. 'Haven't you been there yet?' 'Heard it's terribly good' they always said. Some pithy comment about his paunch usually followed the meal, in one colour-supplement or another. Sometimes he was recognized by other customers, people who had seen him on chat shows they would never admit to watching, discreetly craning their heads past their companions and whispering.

The Parrot was in the Good Food Guide. The villagers waitressed and cooked in it but didn't eat there. When they wanted a meal out they got in their cars and drove to Penzance or Truro. It couldn't be called a night out if you just walked up the road, no matter how good the food, and you could get a three course Indian for a tenner at the Ganges in Penzance.

The visitors from London were more used to those traumatic evenings in which they had first allowed an extra half-hour for parking, and then spent much of their time worrying about their cars, which option would it be, clamped, broken into, vandalized or towed away? No wonder in London they all got indigestion and never listened to anything that was said to them. For Eliot, however, the advantage of the Parrot's proximity was nothing to do with cars and parking: it was simply that he could get as drunk as a skunk and it was only fifty yards to bed.

Clare and Jack arrived at the Parrot at the same time as Liz and Eliot. Clare looked sleek, clean and slightly uncomfortable in her high-heeled shoes. She looked rather self-conscious, as if she had made a tremendous effort, which depressed Eliot: the whole point of her attraction for him was her rather unkempt look. He preferred her with a bra-strap showing, with her hair falling over her eyes, and with her feet slightly grubby in old flip-flops. He'd never seen her with a handbag before either, she didn't look as if she quite knew what to do with it. All that gloss and polish he could get at home.

It was a pretty restaurant, decorated in a pastel

version of country house chintz. The curtains had frills and fringes but not swags and bows, rosettes or ribbons. Someone had been careful not to overdo it. There were flowers on the tables, but not so many that there wasn't enough room for the glasses, and the chairs were comfortably padded, no stocking-snagging cane. Eliot noted the air of careful restraint and hoped he'd get enough to eat.

Archie and Celia had already arrived, and everyone kissed everyone else with dinner-party politeness. Celia looked a little excited and gleeful with that 'I know a secret' smirk that small children have. Clare hoped she wouldn't drink too much and make sly remarks. She'd never seen Celia drink more than one glass of anything and wasn't therefore sure how it would affect her if she did.

'Shall we go straight in?' Archie said, already leading the way.

'Who was it said that that was the most depressing phrase in the English language?' Jack said quietly to Eliot as they both looked longingly towards the bar.

'I'm fairly sure it was John Mortimer,' Eliot replied. 'And I'm absolutely certain that he was right.'

Andrew was lying on the sofa looking through his dinghy brochures. They all featured glowing, tanned, weekending young executive types in wetsuits and heavy-duty diving watches, leaning confidently out from their boats, grinning inanely through the sea-spray. Their women wore pale lip-gloss and their hair was blonde and flowing, though in reality Andrew knew that no serious woman sailor would let her hair flap around like that, they all tied it into neat French plaits on the Surrey reservoirs he frequented, so it wouldn't whip out their contact lenses or prevent them seeing the boom. Andrew was feeling happier. His weight had gone up, and he was sure it was all muscle.

He felt bulkier and stronger and could lift the weights for longer now. Sometimes in the village he had to stop himself swaggering like John Wayne, conscious as he was of his increasing power. He thought he'd grown too, either that or his jeans had shrunk. He no longer had to roll the bottoms of the legs up, and there was an indelible line where the fold used to be and a darker piece of denim below it to testify to an extra inch or so. He had tried to measure the width of his shoulders when he had started with the weights, but found it impossible. It meant holding down one side of the tape measure with his chin, which gave him a distorted shape, and then he had tried holding the tape with his fingers and looking in the mirror to try and read the results. He had been so appalled at how camp he looked with his fingers perched like that on his shoulders that he had given up. He thought of asking his mother, but she'd have only thought he was hinting to have something knitted.

One of the girls in the brochure looked rather like Jessica. Andrew hadn't seen her for several days. She had, he heard, been spending most of her time up at the stables. He still wished she would ride him instead of the horses, and at that thought he closed his eyes and groaned quietly. What chance did he have now? Soon it would be the end of summer and back he would go to his chaste little boarding school. He still had the precious little strip of photos, now absolutely convinced they were of Jessica. They had, in spite of his good resolutions, given him many a moment of lonely pleasure. Thinking of this reminded Andrew that his parents were out and here was an opportunity to get the more exotic items out of his experiment box. Ever since he had heard Oliver Reed on Desert Island Discs requesting an inflatable woman to take with him as his luxury, Andrew had wished he had the nerve to send away for one. But there wasn't anywhere he could even get one delivered to. Both home and school were out of the question. And suppose he didn't get caught having it delivered, but worse, got caught in possession of it. It wasn't, he imagined, something that would deflate in a hurry. And all the boys at school would want to have a go. He wouldn't fancy her after that.

Andrew started wandering up the stairs, starting to feel the familiar rising pleasure, but nearing the top, from the landing window he noticed Jessica and Miranda walking together along the street towards the cottage. He wasn't sure he wanted to be seen, and glanced down to see if the bulge in his trousers was likely to be visible to them. It was not, which was half a disappointment, but at least meant that he could talk to the girls. He opened the window and waved to them. Jessica's tee-shirt had an off-the-shoulder neckline and there was no white strap mark. Topless sunbathing in her garden, Andrew thought, as the trouser-bulge lurched up a notch. Lucky gardener.

'Where are you going?' he asked them, trying to sound casual and as if he didn't mind whether they told him or not.

'Nowhere special, just to the beach,' Jessica said.

'Wait for me,' Andrew said, 'I'll come with you.'

'We're not doing anything particular, just walking the children,' Miranda said, rather off-puttingly.

'That's OK, I don't mind,' said Andrew. 'Wait for me.' He refused to take her hint, after all how much longer could summer last? He ran down the stairs, grabbing a long erection-covering sweater from the bannister rail as he did.

Outside the cottage Jessica was contrite.

'I'm sorry Miranda, it's just that when I'm put on the spot I automatically tell the truth. That's why I never get away with anything at school.'

'Well I suppose it's all right. He won't know what we're doing, it's already sealed in the shell. We can tell him it's a baby bird or something.'

'I'm glad it's in the shell, I'd have had to look otherwise. Is it gruesome?'

'No, just a clot, hardly even that really. Nothing to see. And I've stuck the shell down with glue. Don't want seagulls.'

Andrew joined them, slamming the cottage door and running up the path.

'Getting dark earlier now isn't it?' Andrew remarked feebly. Miranda thought that was exactly the sort of thing his father would have said.

'We're going to have a funeral on the beach,' she said to him abruptly, and deliberately for shock effect.

'Oh. Whose?' Andrew asked.

'A baby bird,' Jessica said quickly. Miranda was looking sulky. 'Found it in the garden.' Miranda was relieved to hear Jessica had had time to think about what lie to tell.

'Little children like that sort of thing,' Andrew said comfortably. 'Where are they by the way?' for the small ones were noticeably absent.

'We've let them walk through the creek, the tide's just low enough for them. They'll be at the beach before us I should think.'

I'm talking to Jessica, Andrew thought. I'm walking through the village at dusk and she is next to me. We're only talking about a dead bird and the little children but she is with me. If Miranda wasn't here, we'd be walking all alone. We would look like a couple. It would be so easy to get hold of her hand. Not that she looks like the hand-holding type. She was wearing jeans so torn that Andrew wondered why she hadn't thrown them away. His mother would have done long ago if they'd been his. It couldn't be lack of money, Eliot was one of the all-time best-selling authors. If he married Jessica, Andrew thought, Celia would be telling all her friends he had Done Well. Even better than passing exams.

Miranda walked a little ahead, comfortable now that

the dragging pain was being numbed by the strong pain killers she had found lying around in the kitchen drawer. If she'd had this baby, she allowed herself to think, she would never have allowed dangerous drugs like that to lie around. She had put them away in the bathroom cabinet, just in case, even though Amy and Harriet were both past the age of popping pills into their mouths mistaking them for sweeties.

Across the creek, as she neared the beach, Miranda could see the fishermen on the pontoon unloading crabs. Steve was probably with them, and she stopped looking across in case he was, and she would have to wave to him. She'd wanted this to be a woman's thing, like Tess of the D'Urbervilles baptizing her dying child, and she minded very much the presence of Andrew, tagging along.

The tourists had all gone from the beach for that day. They were all by now watching TV, putting children to bed or sitting in the pub garden admiring the view and battling with the sleepy wasps. There was a line of litter left by the tide, plastic mineral water bottles, middle-class debris, Eliot called it. Clare always bought water in glass bottles and was careful to visit the bottle banks with them.

'What do we do now?' Jessica said to Miranda.

'Send it out to sea I suppose,' Miranda said, feeling rather self-conscious. What exactly were they supposed to do, now she came to think of it. She was too old to play uninhibitedly at funerals like small children can, and she'd only been to one, her grandmother's cremation, a sterile affair that had seemed.

'We should ask the little ones,' Andrew said, 'Isn't it supposed to be their game?'

'Oh I think they've forgotten about it. They're looking for jellyfish,' Jessica said quickly, tactfully.

'We should say a prayer,' said Miranda. 'Does anyone know a suitable one?'

'Well there's the Lord's Prayer, but it's a bit long,' said Andrew, 'especially for a baby bird.'

'The peace of God, which passeth all understanding . . .' Jessica started declaiming, the twins looked up from their jellyfish, startled.

'Ssh!' said Miranda, starting to giggle. 'There might be people on the footpath, they'll think we're crazy!'

Not far wrong, thought Andrew.

Miranda put the clamshell on a piece of broken polystyrene and they all walked down to the water's edge. She sailed it out into the waves but the sea kept bringing it back.

'Go away, damn you,' she shouted at it angrily. She waded out into the water, past her knees, past the hem of her dress so it stuck to her legs and flowed out at the edge like seaweed on the water's surface as she walked. Jessica and Andrew watched her from the sand.

'May the Lord bless and keep you, and bring you peace now and ever more,' Miranda murmured, recalling the words from school assemblies, as she let go of the makeshift raft. The shell floated away on the ebbing tide. Miranda watched for a moment and then turned quickly back to the beach, not wanting to be looking when it sank.

'Not terribly appropriate for something dead, but not bad,' Andrew commented. 'Could've just said "Rest In Peace", that would have done for a baby bird. Was it a cat do you think . . .' but he stopped, his sentence trailing away. There were tears on Miranda's face.

'Come on Miranda,' Jessica said kindly, putting an arm around her. 'Let's go to the pub.'

'I can't. I promised Mum because of the children. I'll just take them home to bed,' Miranda said weepily.

Lot of fuss over a bird, Andrew thought. He hadn't realized Miranda was that wet. He'd seen her catch and gut many a mackerel in the five summers he'd known her, never a hint of a tear then.

Jessica rounded up the little ones.

'Why was there a piece of God in that shell?' Amy asked.

'For that you deserve a coke,' Miranda said, laughing. 'OK, we'll all go to the pub, if you promise not to tell.'

Nobody minded Miranda's wet dress in the pub. The male customers thought it clung to her slim legs in a most alluring way, and they watched interestedly as the filmy fabric started to dry and fall back into gentle translucent folds. Beryl served Andrew three illegal vodkas and gave him a come-hither wink with his change. Andrew smiled back uncertainly, but speculated whether Beryl might do to practise on; it was getting rather monotonous on his own.

Andrew took the drinks into the garden and saw Milo sitting at a table by the swing.

'Aren't we going to sit with Milo?' Andrew said to the girls, who were heading for another table.

'Er, I don't think so,' Jessica said, 'He's got a hot date. I don't think he'd like to be disturbed.'

Well they must have had a row at home or something, Andrew thought, and not be speaking to each other. Milo was leaning across a small table, his elegant hands wafting gracefully as he talked intently to a young and very blond boy, who was laughing back at him, admiringly. Well anyone would admire Milo, Andrew thought, his life seemed so effortless. He was one of those people that others tried to emulate, not one of those gauche boys who always felt out of place. Poor old Andrew, Miranda thought, watching him. What an awful lot he doesn't know.

Back at the cottage Miranda sent Amy and Harriet to bed and felt the need for an early night. She brushed her hair and cleaned her teeth, wanting to be asleep well before her parents came crashing in from the restaurant.

It's really a mess in here, she thought, looking round the little bathroom. They were a terribly untidy family, Jeannie's cleaning couldn't keep up with them. No-one had even noticed the little glass phial from the pregnancy test kit still sitting on the window ledge. Miranda rinsed it out and put it back on the ledge while she put moisturiser on her face. Poor Mum, Miranda thought, even when I leave clues like that sitting under her nose she doesn't manage to work out what's going on. Now she had neither a problem nor an embryo to carry around, Miranda rather looked forward to being nice to Clare again.

Seventeen

In the Parrot, while her daughter conducted the burial at sea, Clare was happily eating things she couldn't organize at home, like a mushroom souffle for which she'd never have got everyone to sit at the table before it sank flat to irretrievable sogginess. Then she had rabbit, which would have had all the children saying, 'ugh, yuck' and 'How could you, the poor little bunny' and Amy would have been in tears. She munched away delightedly, hoping Jack would not mention the recent outbreak of myxamatosis in Richmond Park, and wishing she hadn't thought of it herself. Later, she planned to choose a raspberry concoction which would have taken her all day to assemble. This, she thought, was the entire point of going out to eat. How sad it must be to be so accustomed to waitress service that you could, like Liz, pick away at a warm duck salad like an anorexic eating under protest.

Liz was concentrating hard on her plate, trying to avoid having to watch all three of the men eating lobsters. She couldn't think why they were supposed to be an aphrodisiac when any potential partner watching could only be repelled by the messiness of the process, especially the way Eliot ate. The butter was floating down through his beard on to the napkin tucked into his neck. Liz found it most unerotic to watch him eat like a toddler and thought perhaps she should have had oysters so that their moods at bedtime had some small chance of coinciding.

Clare thought Eliot looked magnificent. Jack handled the unfamiliar creature with fastidious and irritating care, as if there was still a chance the claws might nip him, whereas Eliot attacked his with uninhibited and noisy enthusiasm, finally sucking at the claws greedily to lick out the last of the juice.

I could do with some of that kind of attention, Clare thought lasciviously.

Conversation was standard dinner party, covering such familiar items as builders and the difficulties therewith, bits of houses that cleaning ladies won't touch (Clare pink with embarrassment of knowing that Jeannie was just through the swing doors, washing up in the kitchen), the cost of pool heating, power steering versus manual.

Jack realized he hadn't read a newspaper for anything but the crossword for several weeks, and as they hadn't a TV at the cottage either, he could not for once complain that no-one discussed current affairs. He'd never talked about politics in Cornwall, not with anyone, for everyone was too polite to get into that sort of discussion. There were too few people to be friends with to risk expressing radical views. You might find, in the pub or sailing club, that there were only half the usual number of people to talk to if you started claiming sympathy with the Monday Club, or asked people to concede that Tony Benn often had a point.

By the time the cheese arrived they were all inevitably on to education, that mainstay of suburban conversation. Liz had said, 'It's beginning to feel like the end of the holidays. I've already sent a case full of clothes back to London with Eliot's secretary. I shan't be needing them again this year.'

Or next, probably, thought Clare, imagining Liz's one-season cast-offs being passed on to a poor relation, if she had any, and a new lot being bought by next May.

'I'm quite looking forward to going back, seeing the garden again,' Celia said. 'The exam results are due out about now, aren't they and I feel that will mark the end of our summer. If Andrew hasn't done well we shall have to think about our arrangements for the autumn.'

'Why not just let him leave school?' asked Jack, provocatively.

'And do what?' Archie asked. 'He won't be qualified for anything, he'll need A-levels at least.'

'I'm afraid that if he hasn't done well at GCSE level he probably won't do well at A-level either,' said Jack in his authoritarian teacher voice. 'The level of work is much more intense, and needs a high degree of motivation.'

'Oh well, it's a good school,' Celia said, sensing conflict on the way, 'They'll be able to sort it out.'

Jack felt cross, these complacent people expecting schools to babysit their children till they were eighteen and not even consider the vocational courses on offer at more enlightened tertiary colleges.

'Perhaps he could go to college and do a B. Tech,' suggested Clare gently.

'Oh Clare, I don't think so,' Liz chipped in brightly. 'He's surely too young to be taking a degree . . .'

'It's not a degree . . .' Clare attempted to explain and then gave up, infuriated that Liz had charmed all three men into easy laughter by being so utterly thick. She looked at Jack's bewitched smile. If I'd said anything as dopey as that I'd be getting an earful of sarcasm, she thought. Clare wondered if Jack had had a lot to drink, there was no way of knowing for the waitresses had efficiently and discreetly removed the bottles from the table as soon as they became empty.

The educationally-deprived villagers in the kitchen were fully aware how much drink had been consumed and had no trouble at all, without so much as an O-level in maths between them, in calculating how much must get spent per week on booze if these people from up-country drank like that all the time. The likely tips from that night were also calculated quite accurately to be roughly equivalent to a good fish supper for each of them in Truro.

Eliot, whose children had always been so clever that their education had never needed discussion, was falling asleep quite rudely.

Liz prodded him, not very gently.

'You never get chairs this comfortable in London restaurants,' she said, making an excuse for him. Eliot's head drooped forward and a teddy-bear rumble sounded suspiciously like a snore.

'They always want you out in time for the after-theatre rush,' Liz went on, as if the others wouldn't know this. Celia turned away disapprovingly from Eliot, and found herself having to talk to Clare, of whom she was beginning to disapprove even more.

'What are you going to do this autumn, Clare?' she asked politely, 'Do you have any plans for Miranda after the exam results?'

'Well, actually Miranda's already made her own plans,' Clare said carefully, 'She's going to do A-levels staying at the same school.'

Jack saw the great moment for his plan, now, safely while he and Clare were not terrifying alone.

'Of course, there's no real need for us to go back to London at all,' he said rather loudly, laughing a bit as if he'd only just thought of it. Clare stared at him, her Bath Oliver and Stilton crumbling on to her plate. Eliot woke up and paid attention as Jack went on, giving his precious plans a tentative airing in the safety of company.

'What I thought was, maybe we could sell the London house, live here while I paint. Invest the money while interest rates are so good.'

'What about the children?' asked Liz.

'Well they do have schools down here you know,' Jack said rather sharply, as if, Clare thought, he had anticipated that question from her and not from Liz. 'Miranda could go to the sixth-form college or be a weekly boarder at Truro if she wanted.'

'Actually,' Jack said, grinning and looking modestly

down at his plate, 'I've been doing rather well this summer. Up at the craft centre, I've sold a whopping great wall full of paintings.'

'Would you live here all the time?' Liz said, incredulous, and insultingly ignoring his proud achievement.

'You can't do that, nobody does!' Celia joined in.

'Well of course they do,' Clare said, exasperated by their snobbery, though furious with Jack. 'But I'm not sure I want to,' she said, firmly.

She made it sound non-negotiable, infuriating Jack: 'Well what do you do in London that you'd be so sorry to miss? Aerobics in the church hall? Getting ripped off in those chic little food shops? Grumbling with the neighbours about number thirteen's attic conversion?' Jack banged his glass impatiently on the table and leaned closer to Clare, looking menacingly across at her. He'd kept all this inside for far too long; 'You're always saying we never do anything spontaneously any more. Here's your chance!' He waved his arm around dramatically, spilling wine.

'You can do whatever you damned well like here! Be creative! Write something! Knit something! Make another bloody baby!'

'Baby? What makes you think I want another baby?' Clare asked loudly. The others sat back, listening intently. The swing doors to the kitchen opened just a little further, as the staff sensed an interesting row.

'Just a small suspicion, just the odd hint,' Jack said. 'When we live down here you can have as many as you like, a whole tribe of them. But I can't face any more in London, that's the deal.'

He sat back in his chair and folded his arms defiantly. If he'd made his point, Clare wasn't quite sure what it was. Could he not face any more children in London, or simply life in London?

'We'll talk about this at home,' she hissed. 'You've obviously given a lot more thought to being "spontaneous" than I have.'

'Could we have the bill please?' Archie's crisp voice cut through the silence. 'I think it's time to go, don't you agree?'

In the kitchen the waitress told the rest of the staff that some of those dreadful people from up-country might be descending on the village to live there full-time. No-one was exactly thrilled, even by the prospect of one less empty cottage in winter. The village shop would be full of organic milk and mineral water. Full or part-time, these people changed everything they touched. They all wanted free-range eggs, as long as they didn't have bits of feather (or worse) stuck to them, and organic veg. But who had ever seen them buy any of the local apples in the shop that had even the tiniest bruise? Or mushrooms with real earth on them?

'Do you think they really will come and live here?' Liz and Eliot later in their bedroom as she peeled off her stockings. Eliot looked at her and wondered when it was that she'd stopped leaving the taking-off of the stockings till last, as she had done when he had first met her and he had been committing delicious lunch-time adultery with her. Liz's mother had told her that tights were common and would give her nasty infections. It wasn't her fault that men always thought stockings were just for erotic impact.

'I don't suppose so, people rarely do,' Eliot said, 'But they'd fit in better than the rest of us, with all the other old hippies in the area. And Cornwall is full of artists, always has been.'

Liz said, 'I think Clare would go completely crazy down here. She'd still have to do all those things that she's always done with the children, dancing lessons, parties, concerts, school visits, all that, but everything would take twice as long to get to. You have to drive miles to anything round here. Though I suppose they could go to boarding school.'

'Don't be silly,' said Eliot, who remembered harder

times. 'Think of the money. Anyway those children are Clare's career, if she sent them away what would she do?'

'Well she can always have another.' Liz said, as if it was as easy as buying a kitten. 'Like Jack said.' Liz and Eliot were circling each other, preparing for bed. How awfully clean she is, he thought. She'd put moisturiser on her face and neck, gel on her eyes, cream on her hands. It seemed to be a night when sex would be allowed, he noted with depression, for she'd sprayed the perfume that used to be his favourite down the front of her silk nightdress. Oh for the days when he had rolled in the back of a Ford Anglia with Brenda-the-bike from Dungannon, a woman who smelled of sweat and cigarettes and lust, not the entire sterile perfume counter at Harrods.

'Well we could couldn't we?' Jack was saying, trying hard to revive the discussion of his precious plans for their future in the face of Clare's bewildered silence. 'I mean it doesn't matter where we live, I can paint anywhere and you can have babies anywhere. Except in London.'

'I'm not having a baby, Jack, I don't know where you got that idea from. And how could you, springing all this on me in public. You're such a coward.'

They were outside the cottage now, both drunk enough not to care that their rising voices were causing windows to open (such a warm night) and curtains to twitch all over the village.

'You are pregnant aren't you?' Jack shouted. 'Why didn't you tell me? That's what I call cowardly, not to mention sneaky, I found that pregnancy test kit in the bin, don't tell me you didn't put it there.'

'Yes I put it there. I found it in the road. God knows whose it is, could be anyone in the village. Good grief, Jack do you really think I need a chemical kit to tell me if I'm pregnant?'

Miranda, upstairs and listening, cowered under her duvet. If a non-existent baby could cause so much argument, how much more trouble would hers have caused?

Eighteen

In the morning Clare and Jack were woken from their disgruntled sleep by a man from the village who wanted to attach one end of the regatta flags to their big cherry tree and string them across the creek. While Jack was dropping noisy Alka Selzer into two glasses of orange juice there was another head-shattering knock at the door and Miranda's exam results were delivered by the woman from the post office, all hostility to the family overcome shamelessly by curiosity. She hung around on the doorstep, commenting on the weather, hoping that Miranda would open the envelope there and then and make her visit worthwhile. But Miranda rushed off to her bedroom, only emerging when she knew that she was to be congratulated, not cross-examined. She had passed all nine, with grades A or B.

'Not that anyone fails anything, not any more, not like O-levels,' Jack complained grumpily. Miranda didn't care, she'd got good results, and everyone knew that they used your GCSE results as a basis for university offers. She'd done well, she wasn't pregnant. It must be karma for all that worry. She felt that being rather spiritual might suit her.

Miranda allowed her family to congratulate her and hoped she would be rewarded, perhaps financially for her hard work.

'We knew you could do it,' Clare said, thrilled. 'You worked so hard.'

'Well you gave me a lot of help, you did almost as much revision as me,' Miranda said laughing.

'I got a bike for passing my 11-plus,' Jack said, hugging her. 'Perhaps we ought to get you something, for doing so well. What do you need?'

'Well actually, I need a bike! I'd really love a mountain bike.'

'Is that wise, in London?' Clare asked, 'You hardly need one for pottering about in Richmond Park, and bikes are always being stolen.'

But Miranda had heard what she had heard from her window the night before, and said,

'Yes but in the country there is further to cycle, and things don't get stolen so much do they?'

One vote for Jack, Clare thought, as Miranda tactfully went back upstairs to get dressed, smiling slyly back at her mother.

Jessica's results, all grade A, were faxed from Eliot's secretary in London and Jessica was making a list over breakfast of expensive well-done presents she wanted Eliot to buy her.

'I want to go back to London,' she told Milo. 'I need to go shopping.'

'No-one needs to go shopping,' Milo said. 'But I know what you mean. Still there's not much time to go now and you know you always cry when it actually comes to leaving.'

'Not this time,' Jessica said decisively. 'I think I might have outgrown it. You know, been there, done that. One can only do so much water-skiing.'

Andrew had been telephoned by both Miranda and Jessica and had done his bit with the congratulations. He had then rushed to the post office, but there was nothing there for him and he had to resort to telephoning the school and asking the secretary who was clearly sick and tired of having to give the good and bad news to pupils with unreliable postmen.

Andrew thought he'd done rather better than

expected, but Archie of course thought he'd done rather worse. Somehow the secretly-cherished plan of Andrew following him into the legal profession was beginning to make less than good sense.

'Perhaps he could be an estate agent,' Celia suggested. 'That's what thick boys of good family do these days isn't it?'

'He's not thick,' Archie protested, over coffee in the garden. 'Just doesn't apply himself.'

'You used to say he was a late developer,' she reminded him. 'But then he didn't develop. Now you're saying he's lazy. I think the time has come to admit that intellectually he's willing but mediocre, and stop pushing him into something he can't do. Perhaps he could do something with his hands,' she concluded, a little desperately.

'He hasn't done anything with his hands since he made those balsa wood aeroplanes when he was twelve,' Archie said. 'We should let him take a couple of A-levels and decide after that.'

'He won't pass those either,' Celia said. 'They're much harder than GCSEs and you heard what Jack said last night. If he was a girl it would have to be a secretarial course.'

'Well what's the equivalent, for a boy?' Archie asked. 'Language courses, the city, selling upmarket cars in Kensington. I don't know. I'm at a loss. Perhaps he could have just one more year at school and then we'll see. I don't know if they let them retake things they've retaken already.'

Andrew, who had been in the bathroom, was now listening to his parents from the window above them. He didn't feel ready yet to take a place in the grown-up working world, and decided it was now as important to impress his parents as it was to impress Jessica. He went into his bedroom to take another look at the regatta programme.

*   *   *

The regatta traditionally marked the end of the tourist season in the village. Flags went up all over the village in a determined revival of the holiday spirit. After the August Bank Holiday, the little roads were less crowded, all the Dutch and French, who didn't understand that you could only drive one car at a time down the hill, had gone home. You could drive as far as the shop without there being a line of cars backed into the creek out of the way. Most visitors with school-age children had gone home to re-equip them with winter shoes and new school uniforms. The second-homers rushed into Truro for shoes and phoned friends at home for new school blazers and sports kit, crossing their fingers that they would fit.

In the village the hanging baskets were well past their best, bright blue lobelia still putting on a brave face but at the end of brown and shrivelled stems. Little heaps of dying flower heads dropped on to customers' heads at the Mariners and into drinks along with the sleepy wasps. No-one was bothering any more to dead-head the geraniums. At the sailing club they had stopped serving lunches on the balcony, because the wind had gone round, and they were allowing the fishermen to drink in the bar again.

The parched lawns of the bungalows on the hill showed the sad effects of the hose pipe ban. Just one lawn, a pristine billiard table green, invited accusations of cheating.

'No-one could have carried that much bathwater, not at their age,' Celia said. 'They must have Watered in the Night.'

Jack argued charitably that they'd probably siphoned it out of the window and wondered what odds anyone would give on the possibility of his being in the village in winter to hear the truth, for this was the real stuff of village feuds, especially if the owner of the perfect lawn also happened to have the best onions in the produce show.

Eliot who had actually been sneaking out after dark to keep his swimming pool illicitly topped up, had now allowed the water to drop almost to the level of the filter, beyond which no more swimming would be allowed anyway. But as Liz pointed out, there was beginning to be a chill little wind in the late afternoon, just enough to stop you wanting to get in the pool in the first place, because when you came out again you'd shiver. How sultry it would be just now in the Caribbean, she hinted heavily.

On the way to the regatta, Jack, emboldened by Miranda's obvious 'yes' vote for leaving London, made Clare go with him for a triumphant viewing at the craft centre.

'I just want you to see how much stuff I've sold,' he said. 'More than I ever did when I was doing that abstract stuff. Just come and look.'

Clare went into the gallery, noticing first that the beige knitted bikini was still hanging where she had last seen it.

Ahead of her was an entire wall of Jack's water colours, his version of summer produce. He had painted fast and with a skillful flourish she had never seen in his work before. For water colours they looked strong, none of that insubstantial dithery wash that most painters of rural scenes seem to manage.

'These are good, Jack,' she said, admiring both the paintings and the 'sold' stickers. 'I didn't really get a good look at them when you were actually painting them.'

'No, well, I wanted to get them hung and sold as fast as possible, I thought it would be the only way to impress you that I was really serious about moving out of town. I needed to show you I could do this.'

'I never believed you couldn't do it,' Clare said, sighing. 'What I can't believe is that I can live here, permanently, full-time in this village. We just don't fit.'

Jack's face looked sad, almost defeated, but he wanted one last shot.

'Well keep thinking about it Clare, I'm sure we could extend the cottage a bit, think hard and try to meet me at least halfway on this.'

It always drizzled on the day of the regatta, as if to make sure that the participants got wet all over, not just feet and bottoms, from sitting in damp boats. Clare and Jack, in a state of pensive truce walked together from the Craft Centre down through the village, early enough to get seats outside the Mariners and also to be able to get to the bar for a drink. In the pecking order at the bar, second-home-owners like Jack and Archie were served last of all and their women hardly ever.

Clare wanted to be in time to watch the children's fancy dress because Amy and Harriet were in it. This year Jessica and Miranda had dressed them as Antony and Cleopatra, hastily cobbling together costumes from old sheets, cardboard and bin liners. They had spent the morning putting it all together in Miranda's bedroom and Clare had heard them all shrieking with giggles at each other – a sound from Miranda that she'd been missing all summer, a sound that told her Miranda had nothing more sinister on her mind than where to find enough safety pins for Amy's headdress.

The two little girls looked, Clare thought, rather magnificent, considering the scarcity of good raw materials, although Harriet's laurel wreath should perhaps not have been made with variegated leaves – she looked as a result, more Romford than Roman. There was a good turnout on the shore, perhaps fifteen children, mostly a drizzle-sodden mess of damp crepe paper as the fairies and pirates disintegrated in the drizzle. Clare had primed her children not to expect to win, not this year, or possibly any other year, memories being rather long in the village. Beryl from the pub was one of the judges and had been inclined to give them a prize, but she was overruled by the Commodore of the sailing club who felt that lack of virtue and moral fibre did not deserve reward and gave the prize to a smug little holiday-maker dressed rather disgustingly as Mae West.

On the terrace outside the pub, Celia came to sit with Clare and Jack.

'Your two looked lovely. I think they should have won.'

'Not much chance this year,' Jack said. 'They are convicted thieves, or as good as, they might as well be branded.'

'Letting them win would have been a sign they had been forgiven,' Clare said. 'And that won't be for some time yet I fear.'

'Anyway,' Jack pointed out, 'the little Mae West was a splendid effort.'

'Rubbish,' Celia retorted. 'The child looked like a tart. I do hope she won't be allowed to walk around the village like that all afternoon. Goodness knows what could happen to her. Men in Cars, you know.'

Archie came up with a couple of bottles of wine.

'I got these from the pub, they had to search the cellars but it's quite drinkable stuff. Didn't want to have to keep popping back to the bar, never get served in that crush.'

'Aren't you racing?' Clare asked him. 'Don't you need to conserve your strength or stay sober or something?'

'It's not like being a racing driver,' Archie said. 'A bit of lubrication might loosen the right muscles. Just a little something to keep warm out there.'

Celia leaned across to Clare and whispered loudly, 'He spent all last night polishing his cups. He has to hand them back to the regatta committee you know.'

'Yes I know,' Clare said, 'but he'll win them all back to take home again tonight. He always does.'

'I don't know about that,' Archie said, flattered at her confidence. 'One isn't getting any younger you know.'

No he wasn't, Clare thought. He could give Eliot twenty years but look at the difference in condition. Archie was still trim and firm-muscled, as well maintained as his house and garden. By all that was natural he should be the one Clare partnered in her fantasies, not Eliot. Liz arrived while Clare was thinking this.

'Eliot is in the bar buying champagne, but I see we're already well stocked up. Can I sit here?' she asked Jack, wiping ineffectually at the damp bench with a paper tissue. She looked pink and windswept, but cosy in a cream cashmere sweater that must have arrived, Clare thought, via the same secretary who had conveniently taken away the case full of summer clothes.

'Let me do that for you,' Jack said, dabbing at the bench with the edge of Harriet's discarded costume.

'Oh thank you Jack darling, you're so kind.' Clare looked away as Liz sat down, queen-like, next to Jack and patted his leg in appreciation, much as one might pat a spaniel who had retrieved a ball.

The children's races were first, which Clare thought rather a mistake because it meant they spent the rest of the afternoon whining, demanding sweets and crisps and getting in the way in their little dinghies when the serious rowing and sailing took place. It was too long a gap with nothing for them to do but get into trouble and fall in the river. Someone always did and had to be hauled out like a puppy. Swimming races had been abandoned, through reasons which involved blue algae, pollution, jellyfish, or a shark once seen off the point, it depended who you spoke to. So children spent the afternoon rowing each other round the creek in hire boats and yacht tenders, straying on to the course and being shouted at by the Commodore on the committee boat.

Eliot arrived with his champagne in time to see

Harriet winning the under-tens rowing. He cheered loudly and shouted 'That's right, you show the bastards Harry!'

'What have you won Harriet?' Jack asked her as she scrambled on to the terrace next to them a brown envelope clutched between her teeth. She opened it and said 'It's a £2 coin.'

'What will you do with it,' Clare asked, 'put it in your piggy or spend it?'

'I shall spend it,' Harriet told her, then added loudly, 'But not at the post office.'

Andrew was getting nervous. If Jessica wasn't there it was going to be a waste of a whole new wetsuit (black and turquoise, all smart zips and pockets, from the Surf Shack). Not to mention all those hours spent alone sweating with the weights and putting the Laser through its paces out in the estuary while he could have lazed around watching women tanning on the beach. He had already won two of his three races, without her being there to see it. There was only the big one to go, the all-comers menagerie class, up against every kind of boat and some excellent sailors.

He paced around the pub terrace watching the adults getting drunker, watching his father win only one less cup than the year before in the rowing. (Later Celia would call that the Beginning of the End, Anno Domini creeping up, as if Steve, who had caught up and overtaken Archie at the finishing line, had been the grim reaper himself).

Andrew went and sat on the edge of the terrace, some distance from his parents. He didn't want to listen to Liz and Clare oohing and aahing over the fishermen racing in Cornish gigs. The fast sleek boats sped through the water, at speeds which put the panting tourists to shame. They looked, he thought, like those Hawaiian boats that cut so powerfully through the surf. One of the few races that distracted the villagers, they abandoned the shop and the bar and the ferry to line up in front of the drinking visitors on the terrace and cheer.

Then it was the turn of the men to ogle the fishermen's wives, strong and tanned from working year round in the open, first in the bulb fields, then harvesting and potato picking. The girls raced in tee-shirts and jeans, not the clutter of oilskins, guernseys and life jackets that the tourists seemed to need. They manouevred their skiffs with the same single-minded aggression with which they drove their battered Cortinas along the narrow lanes, frightening elderly trippers half to death.

'You never seem to get the holiday-makers and the locals in the same race do you?' Jack commented to Archie.

'Our sort of rowing, the prams and dinghies stuff, must seem rather tame to them, being out there on the water all year round,' Clare said. 'And hardly any of them seem to sail.'

She glanced at Eliot. He was watching the girls who were now climbing up the terrace. The winner of the skiff race was still smoking the cigarette that had been in the corner of her mouth throughout the race. He really was shameless, Clare thought, watching Eliot raise his glass to the girl in appreciation, though not of her rowing. It was like window-shopping to him. Coming down through the pub garden Clare saw Miranda with Jessica and Milo.

'Come and join us,' she shouted, 'have a drink, there's plenty here.'

The three regarded their parents with slight disgust. There among the neat holiday-makers and villagers was the carnage of their parents' table. Four bottles of wine stood open and nearly finished, glasses and crisp packets, remains of pasties, puddles of beer, Archie's trophies, all mingled like the strewn-out contents of a bin liner. Around them, small parties of villagers eyed them warily, clutching half pints and the hands of their small children, just in case.

'I'm going down to the beach to get a better look at the races,' Miranda said.

'Have you seen Andrew?' Milo asked. 'Jess and I are going to enter one of the races that he's in.'

Andrew heard them. He had been watching for Jessica and seen her from a distance walking with her brother and Miranda through the village. He had had time to compose his mind and his body (the wetsuit was reliably flattening, he was glad to find, as well as rather flattering).

'How can you be in the same race,' Liz said, 'He's racing a Laser and you've got the Fireball.'

'It's a mixed class, we'll all be in it together, won't we Andrew,' Milo said with a sly challenging grin.

'Shall we put money on them?' Eliot said. '£1 on Jess and Milo, any offers?'

Sulkily, Andrew pushed the Laser out from the shore and clambered aboard. It wasn't enough that he had won two races, he wanted Jessica there on the shore to watch and cheer. She wasn't to know, and he couldn't point it out, that the two largest trophies on the table in front of his proud father belonged to him and not Archie. He had seen himself as a medieval knight, claiming her as his prize. It had been all he could do not to go to her house that morning and ask to wear her favour, a scarf, or her life jacket, or whatever twentieth-century equivalent to a lace handkerchief or kid glove she would bestow on him. Even with two of them on board the Fireball could easily beat the Laser.

The start-gun went, and all the boats became entangled in the usual scramble. Fathers shouting frantically at their children, shrieks for water, giggling boys out of control in their ancient Mirrors, Toppers capsizing, and the rescue boat buzzing about like a wasp, not knowing who to help first. Gradually the mess sorted itself out. Ahead of him Andrew could see

Jessica leaning out on the trapeze, competent and concentrating, eyes firmly fixed on the buoy ahead and not at all on him.

Gradually, Andrew pulled away from the struggling armada and headed out, catching some good gusts of wind. He and a few of the experienced sailors took off towards the buoy, Andrew's Laser light and strong enough to be catching up with the Fireball. I could still do it, Andrew thought, though maybe I should let her win. But a combination of social codes, from his father and from school, wouldn't let him do this, playing the game meant playing to win, so he let the Laser skim the waves and speed towards the estuary. Milo and Jessica had hit a calm spot.

'Andrew's catching up!' Jessica shouted to Milo. 'He's in a much better position, he'll be at the buoy before us!'

Andrew relaxed, watching her watching him. Confident of his skill, he swung the Laser out past the other boats and headed in to the buoy, meeting it at the same time as Milo. Behind him, but not too close, he could hear shouts of 'water!' as boats fought to avoid collision. He tried to take it on the inside of the Fireball and lost, Milo had gone about and was safely round the buoy heading for home. In panic, Andrew turned too fast and the Laser clipped the edge of the buoy. He felt hot. No-one had seen.

Jessica was tired now, she lost concentration a few times and Milo had started to shout at her. Her feet were sore from the toe straps and her back was aching. She didn't particularly care whether she won or not, though she'd done her best for Milo. Winning things, she thought, seemed to be something that boys minded about most terribly. It was probably hormones, or sex or something. Not watching properly, she headed the boat straight into a mooring rope. She was actually yawning when Andrew, his face taut with concentration whizzed past them on the Laser. She heard the gun go as he passed the line, and close after it sounded again as Milo, the boat safely disentangled, cruised past the committee boat. On the shore Archie beamed with pride.

'You see, there are some things he can do,' he said to Celia. 'What you might call a chip off the old block I think.'

'It doesn't earn a living, playing with boats,' Celia said.

'I don't know,' said Jack. 'Someone has to teach people how to sail. Perhaps Andrew could do that.'

'Of course he might not have won,' Archie said. 'It depends on the handicap. The Laser is a fast boat.'

'How do they work it out?' Clare asked.

'It's a peculiar system, a thing called the Portsmouth Yardstick,' Archie explained patiently. Liz choked on her drink.

'I think my filthy-minded wife thinks it's a device for measuring sailors' dicks,' said Eliot.

'No actually,' said Archie, still with his serious face on, 'it's all to do with weight, and length and speed and such. They'll be some time before they announce the actual winner, though I rather think it will still be Andrew.'

Andrew could hear him as he walked up the terrace. All the well dones and congratulations could not make up for the fact that he knew what he knew. He had hit the buoy. Automatic disqualification. Jessica and Milo panted up the steps behind him.

'Well done Andrew,' said Jess and kissed him in a brief and sisterly way on the cheek. 'You beat us by miles,' she said. 'You were brilliant.'

Andrew glowed, and he made his decision. If she admired him as a winner, how much more would she admire him as a man of honour? He smiled at her, thanked her, and went to find the Commodore.

Nineteen

'The trouble with two parties on the same day with the same people is that you've run out of things to say by the time you get to the second one,' Clare was saying that evening as she emerged from the bathroom with her washed hair up in a towel.

'Not to mention having a hangover from the first one before starting all over again,' Jack said, 'and I still want to talk to you about moving. Have you done any thinking about it this afternoon?'

'That's an abrupt change of subject,' Clare said evasively switching on the hair dryer.

'Can't you turn that thing off? This is the rest of our lives we're supposed to be discussing.'

'Sorry,' Clare said. She sat down heavily on the bed and looked around the little room. 'You know, we can't live here, we're used to so much more space.'

There was hardly room for more than the sagging old brass bed. Clare could remember the trouble they'd had trying to put it together. The wardrobe door hadn't opened properly since. She hadn't got round to painting the room yet either.

'We don't need half the stuff we've got in London. I feel it's time to jettison some of our possessions,' Jack said solemnly.

Clare laughed. 'You sound like an old hippy.'

'I AM an old hippy. I want to be free again, like that guy out there on the raft. I'm shackled to all these bits and pieces, and the mortgage.'

'And to me and our children I suppose,' Clare finished for him. 'Most of these possessions you're so keen to get rid of are part of us. You jettison what you like, but leave us some choices too.'

'All right, all right, but will you think about it? We could have just one house, here in the country. A house we don't spend half the year driving away from. I'll be able to work at something I want to do, not something I'm stuck with to pay for a house we don't need.'

In just a few days, Clare thought, as she combed through her tangled wet hair, she would be rejoining the Volvo Valkyries on the school run, back to those repetitive little routines, the lunch boxes, ballet classes, piano lessons, gym clubs. Traffic jams, pushy mothers, Barnes Common that no-one dared walk on because of flashers and rapists. Public transport that wasn't safe after dark. Bomb scares. All those things she celebrated escaping from at the beginning of every summer. I don't want to go back either, thought Clare. But neither do I want to stay here.

Jack was still hovering in the doorway as Clare studied her mouse-and-grey-coloured hair roots in the mirror. She looked at his anxious face and tried to explain how she was feeling.

'It's not that I'm desperate, not any more, to stay in Barnes. You've convinced me that far. But it's here, this village. We're outsiders, even more so after this summer, we'll never fit in. It's all right if you've always lived here; when everyone's gone, all the visitors, that's when it feels normal for them. It wouldn't for us. We'll always be incomers here, I can't face being part of the bungalow-on-the-hill brigade, not for a million years yet. And this house really is too small, you'll need a proper studio.'

There was a gleam of hope in Jack's eyes. Clare could see it in the mirror and smiled at him.

'Don't worry too much. I think I might be able to do what you want, literally to meet you halfway, like you said this afternoon. Go and tell the kids they don't need to bother doing too much packing.'

* * *

In Eliot's house everyone was shouting at everyone else to answer the doorbell. The dog was barking furiously, running first to Liz, who sneakily kicked it away from her newly-laundered trousers, then to Milo who gave it a biscuit and finally to Eliot who grudgingly trailed to the door, glass in hand.

On the step stood the Commodore of the sailing club.

'What can I do for you Admiral?' Eliot asked, waving his brandy glass. 'Come in and have a sundowner.'

'I don't think so, this is rather serious.'

'Nothing is so serious that it doesn't call for a drink,' said Eliot determinedly, waving the man into the kitchen and preparing himself for a speech declining to open the Harvest Fete.

'It's your son,' the Commodore began nervously.

'Which one,' said Eliot. 'Big or little?'

'Big I suppose,' the man hesitated, grabbing one of the glasses of brandy from the kitchen table and taking a large gulp. 'He's been seeing, been seen seeing, my son.'

Eliot was at a loss.

'What do you mean, "seen seeing him"? You can see anyone seeing everyone round here, can't miss them. What's the problem?'

The man gulped more brandy and shifted his feet awkwardly.

'Well I understand he's been seeing rather a lot of him in fact. My wife . . .' he became cowardly now, shifting responsibility, 'she's not exactly happy . . .'

Eliot understood now and was angry, but not with Milo. He baited the commodore.

'But seeing Milo is a wonderful thing. I love it when I see him, everyone does. Your wife should be very happy, your little Kevin or Nigel is it, is very lucky.'

'Simon actually,' said the man, recklessly gulping

the last of the brandy. 'Look I'm sorry,' he said. 'This is rather embarrassing.'

'Tell me,' Eliot said playfully, 'does your son go to boarding school by any chance?'

'Well yes, rather a good one actually.'

'Well if you really want boys like my son, who I'll have you know is an artist and a genius, not a common or garden shirt-lifting sodomist, if you want boys like him to keep away from your pretty son, you should transfer the commonplace little sod to the local comprehensive forthwith and let him get roughed up by the run of the mill riff-raff. That'll make a man of him. Also you'll know where he is nights. As far as I am concerned it is a rare and wonderful privilege for anyone, man, woman or adolescent bumboy to be taken notice of by my son. I shall see you later at the sailing club party. I suggest you keep out of my way. Good night.'

The dog showed the Commodore the way to the door, barking its contribution after him.

So it's going to be boys, Eliot thought sadly, pouring himself another large brandy. Whose fault would Liz say that was, he wondered, and did wife number one know?

Andrew was embarrassed. His parents liked to arrive at parties early 'in case we want to stay just a little while' Celia explained, as if she had to put in exactly two and a half hours and wanted to get them over and done with. Andrew felt like their prize little boy, being shown off at the sailing club for not quite winning the largest trophy of the afternoon, and all because he had been Honest.

'We brought him up to be Honest,' Celia kept saying, as if nobody else did that any more. People kept saying 'never mind' about the race, and Andrew had to pretend that he didn't. He scowled and kicked at the balcony rail and wished he were one of the village

227

boys larking about in the car park throwing lager cans at each other and exploding crisp packets behind startled girls. His father bought him half a pint of lager, in a generously man to man gesture, but the barmaid had absent mindedly put lime in it and Andrew would have poured it into the creek if he could have been sure of getting another one that night. He stood shuffling on the edge of his parents' conversation with the Commodore, forgotten and bored and waiting for Jessica, with a pessimistic feeling that here too he was about to blow his last opportunity.

Miranda waved up to Andrew as she walked through the car park with Clare and Jack. She too noticed the boys in the car park, one of them was Steve. He leaned against his motor bike and smiled gently at her, just a small acknowledgement. So he hadn't told anyone either, she thought. It might all never have happened. She didn't feel anything for him, just perhaps a little natural rancour that he obviously didn't feel anything either. She saw him walk into the bar with a girl not much older than herself, maybe seventeen or eighteen or so, tight short skirt, high heels, sharp laughter. They'd probably be married by the time Miranda next came to the village. While they brought up their children, Miranda would still be a schoolgirl. She'd be a lot more careful next time, that much she'd learned.

In the sailing club Clare offered Miranda some wine, as it was their last night. How they could drink again when they'd been drinking all afternoon was beyond Miranda and she refused, going off outside to the balcony to cheer up Andrew.

At least the drizzle had stopped, people were spreading out, wandering round both inside and outside the clubhouse wondering which social group to join. The regular members swaggered around, shouting loud greetings to their friends, taking up a lot of space. Teenagers who looked as if they would rather be somewhere more fashionable on a Saturday night were misbehaving down on the pontoon, yelling across the creek to friends, kicking aimlessly at moored tenders, jumping in and out of rubber dinghies. The retired couples from the hillside had come down for an evening of sherry and gentle conversation about golf and gardens. They settled themselves into the best chairs on the balcony, from which they had no intention of moving. If they got up to go to the loo, or the bar, they quietly urged the person next to them to 'keep my place' as if well aware that this was really rather unacceptable but excusable on the grounds of age.

Villagers hung around in little family groups, talking and drinking cheerfully, celebrating the end of the season and looking forward to a bit of peace. They talked of the nights drawing in, huddled into pastel cardigans over floral frocks, congratulated each other on the good weather that had made it a profitable year. The fishermen in unaccustomed suits shifted their feet uncomfortably and took refuge from the noisy middle-classes in the rather warm beer and leathery sausage rolls.

The second-homers, who never went out without a pre-party drink inside them arrived in cheerful mood, all except for Eliot. He was fuming quietly about the Commodore and wondering if Milo ought to be spoken to. Milo should perhaps be warned to stay on the right side of what was legal. Eliot did not of course care whether Milo stayed on the right side of the Commodore.

The little children were excited. The Lynch twins pleaded to be allowed to show off, rowing their rubber dinghies in the creek. Liz wavered but Clare said it was getting too dark, they hadn't got their life jackets and sensible things like that. What she really meant was that Amy and Harriet would follow them and she didn't want the hassle of having to go and keep an eye on them.

'I think you should all stay where we can see you,' she said to her daughters. 'Then there's no danger of you getting into any more trouble.'

'I think we're being forgiven,' Clare whispered to Jack as the lady from the post office said a quiet hallo.

'Possibly,' said Jack, 'but I feel it's a slow process.'

'And you're the one who thought we could live here!' Clare teased, laughing at him.

Liz was standing with her hands over her ears, exaggeratedly protecting them from the music which was faltering in bursts from the speakers set up in the trees.

'If it rains again someone will get electrocuted,' she said. 'God it's cold. I wish someone would light the bonfire.'

'That's supposed to be the highlight of the evening,' Jack said. 'There'll be fireworks at 9 p.m., it says on the regatta programme.'

'You get fireworks at any old party these days,' Clare complained. 'I want to go on associating them with treacle toffee and the smell of November.'

'They didn't used to let Christmas start till after bonfire night either,' said Archie, who had extricated himself from the golfers on the balcony in order to stand close to Liz and her intoxicating perfume. 'Now it's in the shops as soon as we get back to Surrey.'

'I always feel sorry for the children in July,' Liz said. 'By the time the school holidays start there're those awful "Back to School" notices in all the shops and we're all supposed to rush out and buy geometry sets and woolly socks for them.'

'They spell "school" wrong as often as not,' Jack complained gloomily. 'How are kids supposed to take learning to spell seriously if it's obvious that grown-ups get away with jokey little numbers like s-k-o-o-l?'

'Where are they by the way?' Liz wondered, refilling her glass from one of the several bottles on their table. 'I haven't seen them for a while.'

'As long as they keep away from the fireworks and the river I don't really mind where they are,' said Eliot, 'But if you're worried I'll go and look.'

He could have casually said, 'Are you coming with me Clare?' and I'd have wandered off with him to look for my own kids in all apparent innocence, Clare thought. The highlight of her holiday this year was destined to be no more than that uncomfortable and absurd grope in her kitchen, watched by hawk-eyed Celia. She was glad now that it hadn't been any more than that, it was enough that it could have been more. There was plenty of thrill in that. She moved closer to Jack and teenager-like, held his hand.

Liz was still peering into the dark for the children.

'I can see them, they're down there by the bonfire,' Liz said. 'Let's just pray they haven't nicked a box of matches between them.'

'No they're fine,' Celia said, 'they're with the village children.'

You could tell which were the local children, Jack thought, they were the ones who had dressed up for the party. The little girls wore neat dresses with sashes, frilled white socks, proper shoes. The boys wore trousers that they had been told to keep clean, and if they wore trainers they were clean ones. Jack could imagine the little boys persuading, cunningly manipulating their mothers: 'you wouldn't want me to muck up my new school shoes would you?'

'Trust the kids to start getting friendly with the local children just as we're about to go home,' Clare said. 'They'll have to start all over again with them next holidays.' Or perhaps they won't she thought, suddenly excited that she didn't know where they'd be next year.

'It's only because there are no more holiday-makers to terrorize,' Liz said, observing her own two in filthy old jeans, tee-shirts that Jeannie would soon be using for dusters, shoes that weren't good enough for the jumble. Only the rich, she knew, could afford to be so badly dressed.

'I hate this kind of party,' Jessica was saying to Milo as they strolled down the lane towards the sailing club. 'No-one knows who the party is aimed at, there's always a disco that no-one will dance to because all their parents are around and watching, and there's all the old grannies looking out for a bit of debauchery to talk about.'

'And all the little kids are a pain because they are up too late and their parents are too drunk to care,' added Milo. 'And when it's really late the disco starts on with a few sixties hits and they all get up and leap around to Honky Tonk Women.'

'And make total fools of themselves,' Jessica laughed.

'We'll just ignore them, we always do,' Milo said, 'Are you going to be specially nice to poor old Andrew tonight?'

'Because of the race, or because of his persistence?'

'Both.'

'How nice do I have to be? I rather thought I might be "nice" to Paul from the boatyard. He's been persistent too.'

'But Paul won't be here next year. Andrew will.'

'Exactly,' Jessica said. 'Perhaps he'll improve with time, like wine.'

Andrew pretended he hadn't been watching Jessica arriving. When she and Milo approached he just grunted hello, as if he hadn't really been gazing at her bare midriff slinking along the road. He clutched his hand tightly into his pocket to stop it sliding involuntarily under her cut-off tee-shirt. There wasn't much skirt either. Perhaps fourteen inches or so of pink lycra, and a lot more inches of warm brown thigh.

'Want a drink?' he offered, thinking a walk to the bar would at least give his body an alternative outlet for its energy. If he could walk. He and Milo crossed the floor of the bar together, Andrew's confusion disguised by the flashing lights of the disco. Jessica had been right, Milo noticed, the dance floor was empty, the DJ playing records for his own amusement and looking quite happy. Round the walls sat the elderly ladies in hand-knitted cardigans, trying to hold conversations against the noise and shouting to each other. Excited children ran across the floor, skidding on spilt beer and sending glasses and walking sticks crashing to the ground.

Andrew bought drinks and Milo disappeared with his through the door out to the car park. Outside on the balcony there was still Jessica. Andrew could see her as he walked across the bar. She was talking to someone, Miranda he thought he could see. But when he got there it was Miranda and that Paul. Paul who never, as far as Andrew could tell, had trouble with finding something to say, or an out-of-control erection. All Andrew could do was be polite. He turned back to the bar and went to get more drinks.

'Nights are drawing in,' Archie was saying, rubbing his hands together in a gesture that reminded Clare of boy scouts starting a fire. She doubted that Archie was hot-blooded enough to burst into flames.

'I'm sure they're about to light the bonfire,' she said.

'I do hope so,' Liz said, 'I'm freezing,' she shivered in her cashmere sweater and turned to Eliot for a warming hug. Clare felt disturbed. She'd never seen Eliot touch Liz with affection before, and rather stupidly assumed that he didn't. He actually loves her, she realized.

'We could always go inside,' Celia suggested.

'Too noisy,' said Archie. 'And besides, we won't have many more nights this year we can enjoy being outside like this, might as well make the most of it.'

The Commodore appeared out of the gloomy twilight next to Eliot.

'Your son, did you speak to him?'

The others looked up with interest.

'No I didn't. Why don't you, if you're so keen on moral lectures?'

'Because he's in the car park with my son, that's why,' fumed the Commodore.

'Well you know where to find him then don't you?' Eliot said, snuggling back into Liz's collar, nuzzling the soft wool.

'Find who? Me?' Milo said, his soft tread unheard as he joined his family.

'This man wants to speak to you about morals,' Eliot said dangerously quiet.

'Oh really?' said Milo, cheerfully. 'Oh well before you do perhaps I can give you this. It's for Simon, he wanted to borrow it, you don't mind taking it for him do you? I'm just going up to have a drink with my sister,' and Milo wandered off leaving the Commodore holding a copy of *The Birds of Britain and Europe*.

Eliot hissed at the Commodore 'You don't mind, of course do you "old chap"?' The man backed away, he wasn't known for his aggression, but Eliot was. As he backed, the Commodore's foot slipped on the wet grass, and the rest of his body followed it, like slow motion in the greying light, down into the mud-filled creek. A few yards away in the twilight the soft knowing laughter of Milo could be heard, back towards the clubhouse. No-one would be able to say Eliot had pushed.

God these people, Celia thought, what on earth was going on. She'd be glad to be back in Surrey where people knew how to behave.

'I think it's time to light the bonfire now,' Archie called in his best rallying voice, taking charge. 'Someone go and tell all those in the clubhouse to grab a sausage roll and come outside or they'll miss the fireworks.'

It was just as Archie lit a match that Clare noticed the

small children standing at a safer than usual distance, giggling and pointing. As Archie bent to light the fire she heard one of the fishermen say 'What happened to that other box of rockets?' But it was too late.

At least they'd placed them carefully, and upright, so they didn't kill or maim anyone. There were many shrieks from old ladies, squeals of delight from all the children and groans of despair from all the parents. As the fire took hold, rocket after rocket whooshed and whizzed with terrifying unpredictability heavenwards, showering sparks and slivers of light all over the river.

'What a wicked waste,' said Celia, tight-lipped.

But no-one was watching the fireworks any more, the flames of the bonfire lit up something much more interesting. Against the dead elm by the car park, just where the serious dark began and the clubhouse lights ended, a pair of humping buttocks, bright white where the sun hadn't tanned, could be seen. It crossed Clare's mind that Andrew, for it was he, looked rather like a woodpecker drilling into a duvet. Oblivious to the audience, to the gathering hilarity and applause, Beryl from the pub was leaning back ecstatically against the tree, a pint of Cornish ale slopping dangerously in one hand and her purple knickers in the other. Celia and Archie watched in a shock of slow recognition as their only son, trousers round his ankles and head smothered in the folds of Beryl's ample and comforting breasts, finished what he had set out to do six weeks ago. He wasn't about to stop now. He couldn't.

Twenty

In the morning the air smelled of left-over bonfire, of smoke and dewy leaf mould. Clare, up early, could see chill clouds of breath when she went out for a last look out along the creek and out into the misted harbour.

The hippy on the raft had gone, off to the Azores to pick up a crewing job on a yacht to the Caribbean for the winter, heading south like a migrating swallow. Clare wondered where he had parked the raft, or if he dismantled it and built a new one each summer, like a new nest. You had to be alone to live life as such an insecure adventure, she thought.

'I can smell autumn,' Miranda said, coming to stand next to Clare by the creek wall, and sniffing at the air like a cat.

Clare put an arm round her thin shoulders. Miranda, at last did not flinch, or flounce off into the house. I've got her back again, however temporarily, thought Clare, glad now that Liz had saved her from a close intrusion into Miranda's diary, glad about the torn-out pages, and knowing that she would never be tempted to pry like that again.

'You'll catch your death in that thin kimono, let's go in,' she said.

The sounds of furious cleaning could be heard very early in Celia and Archie's cottage. The sink was scoured, the fridge emptied and scrubbed, the terrace hosed down. There were soda crystals down the drains, bleach down the loo. Archie kept well out of Celia's way, doing things with the dinghy, the trailer and the car. He had already made one mistake, the night before, of admitting with a smirk that he had found the whole episode rather amusing. He couldn't help grinning to himself, even now, alone in the garage at the thought of Beryl and Andrew. Fancy the boy having that much nerve.

Celia, in a state of profound and unrelenting shock, had said nothing more than 'humiliation'. If she could have scrubbed Andrew's soul that morning, disinfected it along with the kitchen floor, she would surely have done so.

In the car she sat silent throughout the long drive, longing and longing for the safety of Surrey.

Andrew had less luggage to take home than he had brought with him. He wished he could be around to see the dustmen's faces when they emptied the bins at the Parrot. Before the rest of the village was awake he had taken his collection of pornography, gloves, magazines, notebooks and all and dumped them, unwrapped and exposed in one of the restaurant bins. Probably, he thought, the one from which he had taken the empty wine bottles all those weeks ago, before the non-seduction of Jessica. He didn't need any of that stuff any more.

In the back of the Rover he watched contentedly as Devon went by, smiled quietly to himself and slotted a tape of Mozart opera into the Walkman.

Eliot unplugged the word processor, packed the disks ready for use in London and wished his deadline was a couple of months later. It might be an idea to take Liz somewhere hot, so she could keep herself occupied doing nothing in comfort while he finished the book. He thought Jamaica might appeal to her, he'd mention it in the sleeper on the way home. It would put her in an excellent mood, and he liked sex in trains, so very James Bond.

Liz did not need to empty her fridge and clean her

house, that was what Jeannie did. There wasn't much to pack either, the secretary had taken most of it. So with Milo, Jessica and the dog despatched by taxi to the airport, and the twins more than ready for a good night's sleep, Liz boarded the sleeper at Penzance in her best knickers and an accommodating frame of mind. If she was nice to Eliot, he might be persuaded to take her somewhere hot, then she could recover from the summer.

Clare drove up the A38 past Plymouth, thinking about the family's future.

'What we really need is somewhere with a few out-buildings,' she said to Jack.

'A studio each, you mean, so we can work properly?'

'Partly that, though what I really had in mind was something like stables that we could convert into holiday cottages, rent them out,' she smiled broadly. 'There'll always be people like us, wanting a brief taste of country life.'

'Poacher turned gamekeeper!' Jack laughed. 'We could do painting holidays too, where people pay and I teach them and accommodation is included . . . What do you think Miranda? How much do you mind about where you finish your schooling?'

But Miranda wasn't listening. She was playing a noisy fortune-telling card game with Harriet on the back seat, giggling like a tickled child.

A little later when the game finished she looked up and gazed out of the window. A spiritual county, Devon, full of mysteries, it would do very well. She settled back into her seat, making a start on her A-level reading list, with James Joyce. The syllabus would probably be much the same wherever they decided to live.

As Miranda read she thanked whatever gods there might be out on the Devon hills that when she started to feel sick it would be entirely due to the fact that she was reading in the car.

As the car filled up with sweet papers and crisp packets, Dartmoor was looming temptingly ahead and Clare took a turning off the main road.

'Can you find Totnes on the map for me please Jack,' Clare said, smiling. 'I think that's about halfway.'

'Are we going to find somewhere for lunch?' Amy, ever-hungry, asked.

'No, love,' said Jack, grinning at her happily, 'We're going to find somewhere to live.'

Jeannie took a large cardboard box up to Eliot's house. You needed one that big, for the contents of their fridge and larder. It was lunchtime. She rooted round the cupboards and made herself a sandwich and a cup of tea. Then she wandered into the sitting room and went and sat with her feet up on Liz's cream sofa. She didn't bother to take off her shoes. Who was to know? Jeannie picked up the remote control, switched on the vast television and settled back on the silk cushions to watch *Neighbours*.

They've all gone home, she thought. No question, this is always the very best day of the year.

THE END

A SELECTED LIST OF FINE NOVELS
AVAILABLE FROM BLACK SWAN

THE PRICES SHOWN BELOW WERE CORRECT AT THE TIME OF GOING TO
PRESS. HOWEVER TRANSWORLD PUBLISHERS RESERVE THE RIGHT TO SHOW
NEW PRICES ON COVERS WHICH MAY DIFFER FROM THOSE PREVIOUSLY
ADVERTISED IN THE TEXT OR ELSEWHERE.

All Transworld titles are available by post from:

Bookpost, P.O. Box 29, Douglas, Isle of Man IM99 1BQ

Credit cards accepted. Please telephone 01624 836000,
fax 01624 837033, Internet http://www.bookpost.co.uk or
e-mail: bookshop@enterprise.net for details.

Free postage and packing in the UK. Overseas customers allow
£1 per book (paperbacks) and £3 per book (hardbacks).